MW00648174

ALSO BY PAUL B KOHLER

The Humanity's Edge Trilogy
Turn, Book One
Detour, Book Two

The Hunted Assassin

The Borrowed Souls

The Immortality Chronicles
Rememorations (contributed)

Linear Shift, A Novel

Silo Sage: Recoil

An Anthology of Short Stories
Summer 2014
Winter 2016

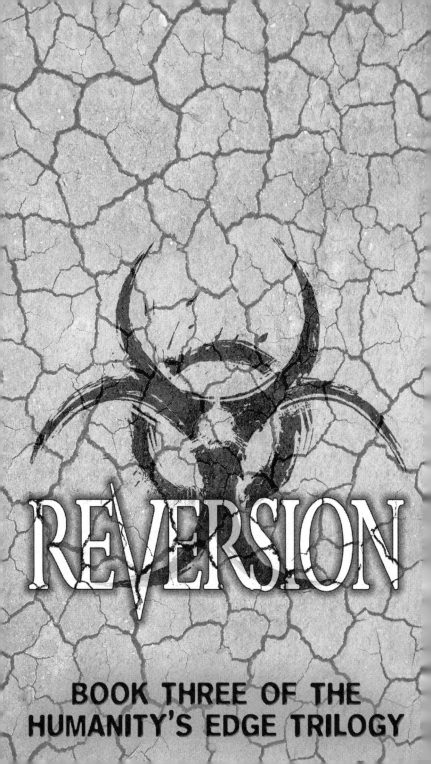

REVERSION

BOOK THREE OF THE
HUMANITY'S EDGE TRILOGY

Edited by Ellen Campbell and Allison Krupp
Cover design by Paul B. Kohler
Interior design and layout by Paul B. Kohler

ISBN-13: 978-1-940740-19-5
ISBN-10: 1-940740-19-3

www.paulkohler.net

Give feedback on the book at:
Amazon: amazon.com/author/paulkohler
info@paul-kohler.net
Twitter: @PaulBKohler
Facebook: facebook.com/Paul.B.Kohler.Author

Printed in the United States of America

First Edition

1.

The converted grain silo at the edge of the lake—somewhere deep in the wilderness of what was once Colorado—gleamed in the strange and penetrating sunlight. Atop it were two people, one sprawling on a lawn chair, with rifles in their hands. They shot casually from their perch, trying to pick off some of the strange, thrashing creatures down below. The crazed: once human but no longer. As each shot blasted through heads, green and amber blood burst from the back, sending the monsters to the ground, where they flailed like fish out of water. They hadn't been human for quite some time. The exterminators above hadn't seen another mortal for even longer.

Rex grunted, pointing at Megan's stance. "You're fucking it up again," he grunted, lurching toward her and fixing her grip. "We been up here how long, and you still can't hold the rifle right. It was a sore day when you were the one I stumbled upon on up here."

Megan pressed her lips together, and gave him an outraged look, but kept her tongue in check. Across the lake, she could still see the dark and shadowed cabin to which she'd hurried when the crazed had taken over the town of Carterville. She'd raced up to the cabin in her little, now-dilapidated car, her anxiety through the roof as she abandoned the only woman she'd ever loved.

Rex followed Megan's gaze. "What's wrong, missy? You thinkin' about your little lesbian friend?" he asked, spitting at the ground. "I don't have time for any of that bullshit, and you know that."

"I should have never fucking told you," Megan spat back, glaring at him. She raised the rifle, took aim, then missed all of the crazed that roamed aimlessly below. She'd told Rex in a moment of weakness, when she'd thought sure they would die anyway. They'd guzzled hooch, saying things like, "What's the point of the end of the world, if you can't drink as much whiskey and shoot as many guns as you wanted to?"

But that mantra was running a little thin.

Megan missed again. She heard Rex sip his drink behind her, then sigh loudly, showing his increased frustration. "I never should have come over here," she murmured, mostly to herself. "Should have stuck it out over at my cabin."

He leaned in close behind her, whispering into her ear, "If you hadn't come to me, you'd be undead now—one of those monsters I'd be shooting at, you idiot." Shivers rippled up and down Megan's spine.

Rex was a prepper. According to him, he'd had a large arsenal of weapons at his house in Carterville, "just in case something like this ever happened." But since he'd been hunting in the mountains when the outbreak happened (and heard the news of it on the radio), he'd hung back, with his weapons and food and water, and watched the world fall around him. Megan was just lucky enough to get to watch it with him.

Megan tried again, blasting at the crazed. But

once again, she missed and dropped the rifle to her side. She felt tears begin behind her eyes, reminding her just how lonely she was. She could have stayed, been with Alayna. She could have held Alayna's hand into the nothingness that was this reality. And now—

"Give me the damn thing," Rex said, yanking the rifle from Megan's grip. "How many times do I have to show you?"

He shouldered the rifle and squeezed the trigger once, twice, and a third time. Each bullet found the skull of a crazed below.

"See? No wasted bullets. I'd like to see your lesbian cop friend do that," Rex boasted.

He tossed the rifle back to Megan and collapsed in his lawn chair, scratching his nails over his large and bulbous belly. Megan shouldered the rifle, bringing it to bear on his head. It was pointed at his skull when he turned around, making him flinch.

Megan huffed.

"Now, if you're done belittling me, I think I'd like to get the hell out of here. Right now," she growled.

Rex grunted a laugh. He nodded at the crazed and drawled, "Do you really think you're ready to get out there, missy?"

A surge of adrenaline burst through her. With a quick motion, she swung back toward the lone, final crazed, staggering toward them through the trees, a good four hundred yards away. For the first time, she felt at one with the rifle—as if it was an extension of herself. She squeezed the trigger.

Bullseye.

She whirled back, her nostrils flared and her eyes burning with rage. Rex gaped at her. Megan held the rifle confidently and leaned toward Rex.

"You were saying?"

2.

There were twelve of them. Maybe thirteen. The crazed spewed from the red painted barn, as Clay and three of Sam's men bumbled past. Clay leaped back, feeling an animalistic survival instinct kick in. Reaching for his gun, he blasted the first of the crazed before the monsters wide, toothy mouth wrapped around Damon's thick and juicy neck. The crazed fell back, his blood and guts spraying everywhere.

"FUCK!" Damon wailed, grabbing his own gun and joining Clay in the massacre. The other two, Al and Sherman, lumbered up beside them. The crazed poured from the barn like spiders. Behind them, the field stretched out far and wide, the mountains blue in the distance. Clay knew that they couldn't escape. In fact, it was foolish to even hope. They just couldn't outrun them. They had to shoot.

Sam's men began to flank the outpouring of crazed, using tactics that kept them alive for the several months they'd been on the road. They held their guns ready to fire, and their eyes were glittering, fierce. Seeing an opening, Clay sprinted through the center of the crowd, sending bullets through the heads of one, two, then a third crazed and finding himself behind the pack. Clay took cover behind the large barn door, taking shots when he could and trying to stay out of the cognizant and searching horde's line of sight. His experience taught him if they couldn't see you, and you weren't making a racket, they'd go after easier targets.

Even as he pushed himself through the battle—yet another in an endless stream—Clay felt a desolation and emptiness. God, they'd been hunting for Malcolm's compound for what seemed like ages at this point. Malcolm felt to Clay like his own white whale.

It didn't help that the only person who claimed to know where the compound was, was a strung-out, pneumonia-stricken kid of about thirteen named Alex. They'd found him locked up in a hotel where Malcolm had been squatting. Malcolm had left the kid for dead, thinking he'd been infected by a crazed himself. What had begun as a cold had devolved to a dreadful illness, and Clay's team had found him—wide-eyed and half out of his mind. They saved his life.

The kid had known his daughter Maia. And Clay hoped that Alex had the secret to finding her and saving her from all the horrors in Clay's own mind. But goddamn. The kid pointed at the map and appeared to make guesses. "I think it's out east," Alex would murmur, his finger white against the grey paper. He would shake, quiver, as he thought about it. "I'm pretty sure it's just out east."

But each time, Alex led them to a dead end, and then another.

Frustration brimmed within Clay as he raised his rifle and blasted another crazed. Al cut through the last of the monsters, doing a strange flourish with his knife and driving it through one of the crazed's heads. Clay rolled his eyes slightly, having grown accustomed to their tactics, if not appreciative. Sometimes, they got a bit too artistic with this murdering they were forced to do. Sometimes, they enjoyed it.

But as Al pushed himself toward the last of the crazed, his knife glittering in the sun, one of the crazed—wearing a V-neck sweater, ragged and torn—reached out and caught Al's shoulder, and whirled him back. The crazed's mouth opened to reveal a green and snakelike tongue, which circled Al's ear before gliding along Al's neck. Clay felt that familiar pang of fear, knowing that this was leading to something none of them could comprehend. That Al was about to face the end.

"NO!" Damon cried. He took several shots at its head, but it was too late. The crazed's teeth had sunk into Al's upper arm, making blood splatter across the ground. Puddles began to form in the dirt. The crazed gnawed at him, holding his arm as you might a hamburger. Damon's screams were staccato, like those of a child, as he blasted the eating crazed a final time. That crazed dropped to the ground, a bleeding Al still across his lap.

Sherman took out the last two. Damon raced to Al's side and wrapped his hands around Al's chin, trying to slow the bleeding. "It's going to be all right, bud . . ." he tried.

But Clay had seen this too many goddamn times. With the certainty and authority of a much more heartless man, he stepped toward Al and Damon and lifted his rifle.

"Damon, if you don't get out of my way, I'll shoot you, too," he said.

Damon glared at him. His cheeks were ruddy,

spattered with crazed blood. "Fuck off, Clay."

"You know what happens if we let this go on one second more. You want to see your pal turn into one of them? Huh?" Clay demanded.

Reluctantly, Damon allowed Al to drop to the ground. After a long, horrible moan bubbled from Al's lips, Clay let the bullet fly. It blasted through Al's brain, sending grey brain matter across the ground.

For a moment, Clay was sure he would vomit. But he bucked up cast his eyes toward the horizon. "That little prick Alex doesn't know what the hell he's doing," he murmured, his mind returning on Maia. "And I'm about tired of it."

3.

When they reached the hotel a few hours later, Clay realized that he and Sam's men hadn't said a word since Al's death. They marched up the steps with the sun setting behind them and dropped their guns on the front foyer table. The faint smell of beans cooking in the kitchen filled Clay's nose. Something about it turned his stomach, and he went into the bathroom, hacking into a toilet. Outside, he heard Sam greeting Damon and Sherman.

"Where the hell is Al?" she asked, her voice gruff—such a contrast to her blonde haired, blue eyed beauty. "Damon, what happened out there?"

Clay stared at himself in the mirror before joining the inevitable conversation. Damon and Sherman stared at the ground, unable to answer Sam. The four of them had been a dominant force on the dystopian plains for the past several months—very nearly robbing Clay and Alayna in the process. Only when they'd discovered they were after the same ego-driven asshole, Malcolm, had she agreed to stay and help destroy him.

"He was fucking better than both of you," Sam said, her shoulders shaking. "He saved both your lives time and time again, and this is how you repay him . . ."

Clay had been through this countless times now. Losing a member of the crew always felt so pointless; it left a part of you empty. Sam turned to him, eyes burning with rage.

"And you. You're supposed to be some kind of leader. And you take my men out, MY crew—"

"Sam, it was an accident," Clay said, knowing just how useless his words were. Nothing had any meaning, not anymore. "You know he was getting a little extravagant out there. It was his own damn fault."

Sam grunted. Clay sensed she was about to unleash hell upon him. But just as she parted her lips to speak, Clay spotted the doctor slipping in through the side door. Clay's own rage flared, and the air around him seemed to turn red. Clay abandoned Sam, bolting to catch the doctor. The doctor's eyes went wide and orb-like, clearly frightened of—and accustomed to—Clay's rage.

"What's going on up there, Doc?" Clay demanded, trying his damnedest not to shake the doctor like a terrier with a rat. "You keep telling me he'll be better soon. That his mind is all lost and chaotic because of the flu, or whatever. But you know what? He sent us on another wild goose chase today, and we lost a man because of it."

The doctor raked his balding hair with his fingers, hiding behind thick glasses. Finally, he said, "No matter how much you yell, Clay, Alex won't get better any faster. He's anemic. Do you, somewhere in that thick skull of yours, know what that means?"

Clay glared at him. Without waiting another second, he bolted toward the room they'd moved Alex to. He knew that Lane would be tending to him, as she so frequently did these days. She'd taken on a kind of mothering quality, saying words like, "Many hands make light work," and ensuring that Alex was well-fed, well-watered, and spoken to frequently, in a loving manner.

And Clay was about sick of it.

Clay smashed his knuckles against the door. He howled her name, "LANE! ALEX! OPEN THIS DOOR!"

The doctor appeared at the top of the steps, with Sam and her goons traipsing up behind him. They observed Clay's minor breakdown, although it was certainly not the first. Lane came out of the bedroom, clearly agitated at the tantrum.

"CLAY! He's sleeping!" she hissed. She carefully closed the door behind her and crossed her arms over her chest. "You absolutely cannot wake him. Doc's orders."

"I don't care," Clay snapped. "The kid is sending us into dangerous situations, and I demand to talk to him. I think he's up to something."

"You think a kid that was left for dead by his absolute nut job of a father is trying to lead us astray?" she asked, giving Clay an almost playful smile. "Because that's the craziest thing I've ever heard."

Then Sam was beside him. Rage made her voice shake. She jabbed her finger, pressing it against Lane's chest. Lane's smile fell. She wasn't as accustomed to Sam and thought she was a loose cannon.

"Let me say this in a way you can understand," Sam snarled, pressing harder against Lane's chest. "If you don't let us in so Clay can talk to this little idiot—who's responsible, as far as I'm concerned, for Al's death, then I will destroy you."

4.

C lay's nose filled with the smell of sickness and medicine when he barged into Alex's room, with Sam and Lane trailing close behind. The doctor remained at the edge of the room, his hands on his hips. Clay knew that the doctor respected Sam more than anyone and that whatever she said, had to be so. But still, his medical duty was probably eating at him. Clay's decision to badger the kid could kill him.

And a part of Clay didn't care.

Alex's eyes blinked open slowly, revealing yellowish eyeballs. His skin was pale and slimy-looking beneath the hospital gown that Lane had crafted from hotel sheets. He attempted to draw himself up against his pillow, but he fell back, his shoulders not strong enough to hold his weight. For a moment, Clay felt some empathy for the boy. What kind of monsters tied up a kid and left him to die?

He pushed it away. Alex was his only hope of finding Maia. Clay had to make him remember. He had to demand more of Alex and his sloppy anemic brain. Alex's eyes closed once more, and his chest seemed to cave inward. Clay recognized the boy was trying to hide from them, however futilely.

"Alex. I know you're awake," Clay said. "But there's a few of us here. We really need to talk to you."

Slowly, Alex opened his baby-bird eyes again. He looked almost angelic, except for the bit of vomit caked in the corner of his mouth. He sought Lane, almost asking permission. Lane nodded her head just once, coaxing him. "I'll kick him out soon," she reassured him. "Don't worry."

Clay glared at Lane outraged by her betrayal, then back at Alex. "Do you realize what you did? You sent us to the wrong location—again! And because of it, we lost Al. He was out there trying to save the freakin' world, Alex, and you're in here just pointing your finger, willy-nilly, and telling us where we should go and die next. It's unacceptable."

Clay leaned down, putting his face just inches from Alex's. The stench of his vomit-laced breath was overwhelming. "You know that with every passing second, Maia could be getting further and further away from us? You know that I don't care if *you* live or die, as long as Maia makes it? Right?"

"I don't think that's helping—" Lane began.

But Clay cut through her words, continuing his tirade. "Where the hell is it, Alex? Where is Malcolm's compound?"

Alex's breath hitched several times but he managed, "I told you. I've only been there a few times. I—I really thought it was east of town . . ."

"Well, you told us it was west of town last time. And now we're out there playing some game of tag with the crazed. So which is it, Alex? Is it west, or east?"

"W—west . . ." Alex whispered, drawing his hands over his chest. The fingers looked shrunken, white and skeletal. "That's what I said. Wasn't it?"

"All right," Lane said, stepping in. "I think it's pretty clear that you're not getting anywhere with this, isn't it, Clay?" She inserted herself between Clay and Alex. She crossed her arms over her chest.

Clay stepped back, assessing Lane. It felt as though he'd known her forever. She'd been a large part of his recent life: someone he could count on, could turn to. Searching her eyes, his anger dissipated, if only for a moment.

"Come back tomorrow," she said, her voice softening. "He'll be better tomorrow. I know it, and you know it. This isn't working."

Clay nodded. He needed to think, to regroup. He marched down the hallway in search of a moment alone. The hotel was filled with empty rooms, with hollow spaces.

5.

B randon felt the engine rev beneath him as his scooter tore down the wide Colorado highway. Even though they'd just ridden into Helen a week or so earlier, it somehow felt more freeing: with the wind whipping through his hair, his eyes on the horizon. The sunlight was almost too penetrating in the bright blue sky.

Despite his sense of abandonment, Brandon still felt the weight of all they'd been through, all the people they'd lost along the way. His entire family, to start, and his sister—the person who'd been his best friend for the better part of his life. And then, when he'd gotten closer to that ratty old man, Ralph, he'd died too. Leaving Brandon staggering along with the rest of the ragtag group, save for Clay and the others who'd left them to hunt for Clay's daughter.

Along with Brandon, there was Leland Jacobs, the wide-eyed and idiotic-appearing scientist, who Brandon couldn't help but distrust, Lieutenant Adam Daniels, who was quick with a rifle, but whose conversation was definitely lacking, and Marcia White, the blonde scientist they'd found in Helen. Together, they motored through the afternoon, heading toward whatever safety they'd hoped to find in Earlton. Brandon wasn't optimistic about the possibility. He'd become accustomed, at this point, to expect death and destruction.

Daniels waved his left hand, signaling he was running low on gas. Brandon slid in behind him as they cut off the highway toward a gas station. The station was crooked-looking, ragged, with only four pumps in front of a kind of shack. Brandon shut off his scooter and the others followed suit, touching their feet to the ground for the first time in what felt like days.

"There's no way this place has fuel," Marcia scoffed. She walked across the pavement, her small shoes scuffing at the cracks where grass grew. "I think this might be a bust, Adam."

"Sometimes these places surprise you," Daniels said. "You just gotta coax the fuel up."

Daniels busied himself, sliding the fuel pump into his scooter and attempting to draw fuel from the underground tank. Brandon headed for the shack, his stomach groaning. The apocalypse had unfortunately led to a diet of salty and sugary snacks, which had left him feeling strung out and nearly always hungry. He now dreamed about fruits and vegetables in a kind of sensual way. One night, he'd dreamed that he'd eaten an apple in the rain, and he'd woken up with tears in his eyes. Was that something he'd never get back?

Brandon leaned into the window of the gas station, listening to the others banter and bicker behind him. Marcia and Daniels didn't get along, although it was clear Daniels yearned to sleep with her. He was constantly trying to speak nicely to her, which only revved her up more.

"See, if you do it like this—" Daniels said, gesturing at the gas pump.

"It's barely coming out at all," Marcia retorted. "Some wiz you are."

Brandon couldn't see into the gas station, despite straining his eyes. It was dusty and grey, without much light in the interior. As he leaned closer, he heard something—a clatter, inside. After a pause, he heard another, and then another. Something was off. Something about this stop was horribly wrong.

And if he knew anything after the past few weeks, he knew that he had to trust his gut.

Brandon eased back toward Daniels, gesturing toward the station. He muttered to him, not wanting to speak too loudly. "There's something in there," Brandon whispered. "I think we should get going, before they come."

Of course, by *they*, he meant the crazed.

But Daniels just huffed, muttering under his breath. "You know, if you just leave it alone, they won't come out. You know that, Brandon."

"But shouldn't we—" Brandon began.

His words were cut short by a guttural cry from behind the station's obscured glass. Daniels reached for his gun and lifted it, his motions automatic.

"Everyone stay back!" Daniels warned. "I'm going to check it out."

"Ha. As if we'll just stay back and get eaten without you," Marcia retorted, her words sassy. "You idiot, you're the only one who can protect us. You're not going anywhere without us."

Brandon felt a stirring of anger. He'd been training with his gun for weeks, and he'd killed countless crazed. But as Daniels inched forward, Leland and Marcia followed him, dutifully, like dogs. And not wanting to be left in the open alone, Brandon chased after, his eyes darting side to side. It seemed that no matter how many chaotic scenarios they fell into, fear always felt fresh.

Fear was always a force he had to reckon with.

Daniels kicked open the door and entered cautiously. The group stepped tentatively through the grey, Brandon sliding his fingers across the various snacks. Somewhere in the back, they heard another clamor. Daniels sprang forward, racing toward it. Brandon followed, with Marcia and Leland holding back, their faces ashen.

Brandon and Daniels bolted into an almost-hidden storage room near the back of the station, chasing the noise. But when they reached the back of the building, they found a door swinging wildly, back and forth. With each swing, light blinked in through the opening, causing shadows to dance across the floor.

"Shit," Daniels said.

As if on cue, they heard the revving of engines from out front. Brandon bolted out the back door, racing around the building and toward the parking lot. There, he saw three of their four scooters buzzing away, heading back toward Helen. Losing his balance, Brandon toppled onto his knees, feeling the pavement dig into his skin.

And in the silence that followed, Brandon recognized that, for the first time, something horrendous had happened that hadn't ended in bloodshed. Somehow, that was comforting. For another day, he was alive.

6.

Sam waited patiently as a pot of coffee finished brewing in the hotel's community room. Her anger had dissipated, leaving room only for silence. Her face was grey, almost mask-like. She passed a mug to Clay, who was leaning back in a lopsided chair.

"Thanks," he said, his first words since the tirade earlier.

Sam blinked at him, sipping her own mug. Clay felt sure she was going to castigate him again. She would blame him for Al's death. But she held back, finding other words. "Is Alayna back yet?"

"Haven't heard," Clay said. He dropped a small spoonful of sugar into his coffee and stirred it, clinking on the sides of the mug. "It's been, what, a few hours?"

"They were going all the way to the next town. But those guys—Hank and Walt—they're good guys, Clay," Sam said. "I wouldn't have let her go with anyone who wasn't, you know. Strong. Safe."

Clay considered her words. Did Sam think there was something between him and Alayna? "What's that to me?" Clay asked, hating how angry, how volatile he sounded.

He couldn't blunt his hard edge.

Sam shrugged, her eyes filled with mystery, with darkness. In the lobby, the door burst open and Hank came in, his voice carrying across the hotel. Clay's heart leaped in his chest. Was Sam's insinuation right? Was there more to him and Alayna? He couldn't say.

Clay and Sam went to the lobby, finding the doors propped wide open. At the base of the steps that led up from the street, a wagon was loaded with supplies scavenged from the nearby homes, whatever had been left behind when people had run for the hills. Whatever had been forgotten when, well, they'd been murdered.

Alayna was leaning over the side of the wagon, scouring through their loot. Clay took in the beauty, her dark cloud of hair, her slight shoulders and her exotic, near-black eyes. For years, she'd worked as his deputy—becoming his best friend, his confidant. And then, when they were faced with the end of the world, they'd slept together. And things hadn't been especially clear between them since.

"Hey!" Alayna called, finally noticing him. She strode up the steps, carrying a box of supplies. Clay peeked in, noting the beef jerky, the nuts. Protein, which made his mouth water. "How did the search go?"

"Not great," Clay said, giving her a look that told her not to ask again. "And with you?"

Hank and Walt appeared. Hank, all gangly arms and legs, with stringy red hair and a thick beard. And Walt, with his dark curly hair, thick glasses, and his pasty, easily sunburned skin. The pair were maybe thirty or so, around Alayna's age, and they flirted with her shamelessly—teasing her like brothers, or like lovers. Clay couldn't decide.

"We got loads of stuff. Medicine. Jars and jars of peanut butter. I mean, you should have seen how much this old lady had in her cabinet," Hank chuckled.

"Great," Clay said, hearing the strain in his voice. "Any trouble?"

"Naw, nothing we couldn't handle," Alayna said, though her face blanched. "We *cleansed* a few more crazed from this beautiful world." She clutched at her stomach with her free hand. "Damn. I just—wow."

"Is it happening again?" Walt asked, taking her supplies.

"Just can't seem to keep anything down," Alayna sighed. "It's ridiculous. I know it's just that I'm eating too much gluten. But what can we do in this reality? It's not like I can just go grab an apple or something."

Hank clapped a hand on her back, guiding her into the foyer. "Our little vommy-Alayna," he said playfully.

They dropped their supplies near the couch. Clay was curious about the nausea. He remembered that Alayna'd had several bouts of sickness the past few weeks, but she'd brushed them off. Clay's own stomach stirred, reminding him that too much stress could manifest this way. He'd just retched himself. Bodies were mysterious things.

"How'd it go?" Sam asked from the foyer couch where she waited. "Did you get . . ."

At this, Alayna hunted through a second box, dropping several prepaid cell phones onto the couch beside Sam. Tilting her head, she said, "I don't know why you need these, though. Like we said, cell towers have been down since we left Carterville."

Sam tore open the packaging and turned the phone over in her hands. "Sure. I know that. But we've got a guy that converts these into walkie-talkies."

"I remember reading about that," Clay said as he picked up one of the boxes. "It was an article in some magazine a year or so back. Something about AD-HOC   . . ." He dropped the phone back on the cushion.

"Hell, I don't know. As long as it works, I don't ask the science-y questions," Sam said, cracking her first smile of the evening.

7.

Finished bringing in the supplies, Alayna leaned in between Sam and Clay, and said, "I really need to talk to the both of you, if you have the time now."

Sam raised an eyebrow. She jerked her chin toward the community room, away from Hank and Walt who'd ripped open a bag of Cheetos and were tossing the orange crinkles at each other's mouths.

"Imbeciles," Sam sighed, giving Alayna a small smile. "But they had your back out there, right?"

"Sure," Alayna said. Still, her face went an off shade of green, and her fingers trembled. She collapsed in a chair, wrapping her arms around her knees and dropping her eyes. Shivering, she said, "They're good guys. A little squirrely at times."

"Glad to hear it," Sam said. Frowning, she reached into a side cabinet and drew out a bottle of water and a small pack of crackers. She handed them wordlessly to Alayna. Alayna took the bottle with trembling fingers, managed to get to her lips and guzzled it.

"You need to stay hydrated," Sam said firmly. "You know that."

"I know," Alayna agreed, staring into Clay's eyes. "Listen, we saw something out there."

Clay alerted.

"There were . . . others out there," she said. "They were scouting houses just like us. It was like they were constantly one step ahead of us."

Clay leaned closer. "Did they see you?" he asked, concern in his voice.

"I don't think so. We hid from them at first. But every time we came across them, I felt like we should have gone after them."

Sam smacked her palm against the table with a report like a gunshot. Alayna nearly leapt from her chair. "We talked about this. You were supposed to be scouting supplies. Nothing more," Sam snapped.

Alayna glared at Sam. "I know. Hank and Walt made quite sure of that. They wouldn't let me follow them no matter how tempting it was."

"That's good. My men know how to follow orders," Sam leaned back and crossed her arms over her chest. "And my orders were clear. Gather supplies, and report anything out of the ordinary."

"Well, that's what I'm doing, isn't it?" Alayna protested. "Reporting as ordered, your heinous."

"Easy there, Alayna," Clay said and placed a hand on her leg. "We don't know what their intentions were. With just the three of you out there, your safety is more important."

"Hey! Not every single damn thing that Sam says is gospel, you know. What if we could have found their compound? What if we'd have gotten eyes on Maia?" Alayna scowled. "We were *right there*. We could have followed them without being seen," Alayna's face lost its meek demeanor and flushed red. "I guess we'll never know now. And besides, we couldn't follow them in the end, because they took off."

"Which direction?" Clay squeezed her knee slightly. His brain felt like it was snapping, as if he was creating a mathematical equation, an understanding of what this meant in the bigger picture of this post-apocalyptic world.

"North, I think," Alayna said, her eyes defeated. "There was no way to be sure, Clay. As far as we know, they could have seen us and turned around once they were out of sight."

Silence fell, the room filled with tension. Clay ticked his tongue against his teeth, assessing her words. When he spoke, he chose his words carefully.

"Maybe this story could trigger something in Alex's mind," he said. "I think we should talk to him. Maybe you could describe their vehicles. What they looked like—"

"I really don't think you're getting back in there tonight, Clay," Sam said, her eyes stony. "That kid's a basket case. He's anemic and can barely remember his name, let alone remember some vehicle, that might—*only might*—lead us to Malcolm's compound."

Clay burst from his chair, furious. Raising his chin, he snapped, "I wouldn't have expected such compassion for Malcolm's son out of you, Sam."

She slammed her mug on the table between them, causing a small crack to form at the base.

"I just think you'd be an idiot to waste your time, Clay. Although let's be real. I think you're an idiot anyway."

8.

It was just past midnight. Clay sat at the edge of his bed, his mind spinning over Alayna's news. After Sam had bolted from the room, Clay had pressed Alayna for more information: the make and model of the vehicles, how many in the group, what their tactics had been, and so on. As Alayna answered, her face had grown progressively greener—eventually sending her from the room to be sick. Clay's thoughts spun obsessively, dismissing Alayna's illness for now. After all, his daughter was the one in real danger. And couldn't Alayna handle herself?

Standing, Clay trudged down the hallway to Alayna's bedroom, knocking softly on the door. It took several seconds for Alayna to appear, though she was still wide awake. She sighed.

"I suppose I knew you wouldn't let this wait till morning," she said. "You wouldn't be you if you did."

"Just a few minutes with him. You can help me explain it," Clay said. "You were the one there, and I don't trust Hank and Walt to have the memory you do. You're—you're still my deputy, in a sense."

Alayna allowed a slight smile. "Well then, we have to play good cop, Clay. We have to make this kid think we trust him. Use the old police tactics.

Don't let your anger get the best of you. Okay?"

Clay felt the truth of her words and tried to restructure his thoughts. He played them over in his head, the ones that had worked in the past—in other interviews—before the end of the world. *Listen, we're on your side. We're just trying to figure out what happened here. We're just trying to find the truth.*

Clay and Alayna arrived at Alex's door. Alayna said, "Lane's supposed to be on duty, outside the door. I heard her mention it to the doctor earlier. But it seems like, well. She's—"

"We don't have much time," Clay said, knowing they'd gotten lucky. He cracked open the door, and a slit of light drew over the edge of the bed. The boy's eyes flicked open almost immediately, as if he'd been waiting for them. As if he'd always known Clay wouldn't allow this to lie.

"Hey there, Alex," Clay said, flipping on the light switch. The brightness was alarming, even for Clay. It seemed to capture the emotion of the moment. The volatility of it. Everything had to happen; everything had to be said. It had to be now. "Don't suppose I can have a bit of your time?"

Alayna followed Clay in, her face pale in the light. She sat at the edge of the bed and comforted Alex, her fingers caressing his. This mothering shook Clay for a moment, but he shrugged it off and started pacing.

"Alayna saw some people out and about town today. A group of them, who took off in several green SUV's. Alayna says they were heading north."

Alayna leaned closer to Alex. "Do you think these people could be from your father's compound?"

Alex pressed his eyes together tightly. He seemed to be analyzing their words. And just as Clay was about to grab his shoulders and shake him like a doll, Alex's eyes popped open again. He smiled happily, almost excited

"Oh, God. I can't believe I didn't think of it before!" Alex said. He pushed himself up, still smiling his grey, anemic smile. "Of course! That's exactly where it is."

Clay was incredulous. He stopped pacing and stared at the boy, unsure if this was a genuine moment between them. He tried to read the wrinkle on his forehead, the tilt of his chin but he couldn't. After a pause, he said, "Are you sure?"

"Absolutely," Alex tittered excitedly. "Oh yes. I had my bearings wrong, because, you see, I oriented everything from where I grew up. You know, when you think places are north that aren't really, just because of where you're driving from? That's probably what happened. Anyway. I think that's it. The compound, it's up that stretch of highway, by the old Wal-Mart."

Clay sat down beside Alayna. He remembered the big-box store. It was dilapidated, with countless holes punched through the sign. He visualized the road, how it twisted up toward the mountain. Could that be where the compound was? Tucked between the peaks?

Alayna smacked her hand over her mouth and jumped from the bed. If it was at all possible, she looked even greener than before. Her eyes said everything that needed to be said. She barreled through the door and dashed down the hallway.

Clay and Alex were alone—a feeble boy and a burly ex-sheriff. Clay was struck by a sudden wave of guilt that he'd forced the information from the boy, but he wanted to ask him again about Maia. What they'd talked about. What they'd done together. But he held his tongue, recognizing that these questions exposed his weakness. And he couldn't give in.

9.

Alayna bolted down the hallway, finding a trash can in the corner, near the steps. Unable to make it any farther, she leaned against the wall and retched. The resulting vomit was nothing but bile, as she'd not eaten a thing since the night before. She spat afterward, feeling hollow. The world spun around her.

She felt the chill of a washcloth on the back of her neck. She leaned forward, feeling the cool water trickle down her spine. "You can't imagine how good that feels," she murmured. "Like jumping into a lake on a really hot day."

Lane dabbed the chilled rag higher on her neck. She took Alayna's hand and led her to her hotel bedroom, sitting her on the edge of her bed. Lane knelt down, cupping Alayna's knees and stared up at her. Her eyes were honest and pure. Alayna felt sure they could dig into the depths of her soul.

"Your symptoms are getting worse?" Lane asked. "From the nanites?"

Alayna's fear returned. Anxious thoughts coursed through her mind. She tried to smile but failed miserably. "I'm not sure. Every time I think the stomachaches are gone, they come back with like, triple the force."

Lane tilted her head, and said, "I think there's something else going on," she said. "Remember, after Clay reached this point of his exposure, he started to feel stronger. Like a superhuman. Do you have any of that, at all?"

Alayna considered it. She remembered the weakness that crept through her arms the day before when she'd been trying to carry a box of supplies. Even down to her bones, she felt weak, strung out. She'd collapsed against the side of a house, gasping for oxygen and hoping that Hank and Walt couldn't see, or wouldn't notice.

"No. I don't think so," Alayna replied.

"Then I really think we need to talk to the doctor about this," Lane said. Her fingers stretched out over Alayna's knees. "We can't let this get any worse. I don't think you're contagious, but you can't run yourself into the ground like this. At this rate, you won't be able to eat or sleep, which could kill you, anyway. And just imagine, if you'd run into one of *them,* you wouldn't even be able to get away."

Alayna fell back on her pillow, staring up at a small crack in the ceiling. She was exhausted, her muscles stretched thin. How many times had she thought about death in that room? How maybe, after living through so much of this post-apocalyptic world, she wasn't entirely sure she had it in her to keep going. It was clear that Clay didn't have the capacity to love her. And Megan? She was long gone. Probably dead.

What was any life if Alayna couldn't have love?

"Just promise me you'll think about seeing the doctor," Lane said, sitting at the edge of Alayna's bed. "It doesn't make sense to suffer like this. Not when there could be answers."

Alayna's fear caused her eyes to fill with tears. Embarrassed, she turned toward the wall and curled up into the fetal position. Recognizing that she wasn't up to conversation, Lane went to the door and turned off the lights. "It's going to be all right, Alayna. We've had each other's backs for weeks. Know that I will always have yours," she said softly.

10.

"We should have brought it," Marcia scolded Daniels. She sauntered along, her hips moving hypnotically, left and right. Brandon watched as her ass cheeks almost danced before him: a sight he'd grown to appreciate, despite the fact that they'd been walking for two days.

"I told you. Taking the only scooter those assholes left behind didn't make a lick of sense," Daniels replied, finally growing frustrated with Marcia. "Having one person riding the scooter out ahead would put them at incredible risk. We'd probably find them half-eaten, or else they'd meet us somewhere ahead and try to eat us instead. I wouldn't put that on anyone. We have to stick together."

"So much of the group has split off, it's not like *together* is really a word that works in this context anymore," Brandon said, feeling a strange stirring of anger. He was hungry, starving, and much of their supplies were depleted. He'd been crunching at granola bars throughout the morning and feeling his lips grow dry and cracked beneath the sun.

"Brandon, I don't need your attitude, too," Daniels sighed. "We've got enough issues with Miss Priss up here."

Marcia flipped her greasy hair, waving her half-painted fingernails so that they flashed in the last of the sun. Leland continued to walk silently, having to slide his glasses up his nose every few minutes.

"I think we would have been fine. You worry too much," Marcia said to Daniels, her voice high-pitched and irritating. "Adam, if I had half the gun you do, I could handle this team and probably even gotten us to Earlton by now. But since we have to play by your rules . . ."

That's when Brandon spotted it: a glow at the horizon line. He stopped short, staring at it as if it was a beacon of hope. Stretching his hand across his heart, he squeezed his eyes shut and then reopened them, wanting to make sure he wasn't living out some strange illusion.

"Guys!" he called out.

Marcia, Leland, and Daniels continued to walk.

"GUYS!" Brandon cried again.

Leland swung around, bringing his eyes to Brandon. He followed Brandon's eyes toward the horizon and stopped too; his feet scuffing against the rocks on the pavement. "Holy shit," he breathed.

Daniels and Marcia were speechless. They stared at the glowing light, until, finally, Marcia and Leland exclaimed in unison, "EARLTON!"

Daniels gave them an almost ominous *I told you so* smile, and said, "No. That's not it, guys. The military base is still a couple hundred miles away."

Brandon started back down the road, toward the light. He listened to the others chatter around him.

"That means the town has power. Which could also mean they have a whole lot of supplies," Leland uttered the first words he'd spoken in hours.

"That's a great point," Marcia said. "Maybe a girl

could get a decent shower around here. Although I can't say I'm the one who stinks the worst."

"It seems crazy to just walk into a town like that, without knowing what or who it is," Daniels opined, taking his place as leader once more. His massive form cast a shadow across Brandon's body. "What if we walk in there and it's just filled with the crazed? What if it's a place that's built it up in their heads that the entire rest of the world is to blame for what's happened? I mean, they could be volatile . . ."

"But we're out of supplies. And, like you said, Earlton is still several hundred miles away," Leland said, his voice racked with emotion. "I don't know how you think we'll survive past *this* town, if we don't at least take a chance and stop there."

"And we could maybe find a vehicle!" Marcia cried, smacking her hands together. "Which would could get us to Earlton within a day, Adam!"

Brandon tilted his head toward Daniels, watching as thoughts spun through his mind like a spiderweb. They walked nearly a half-mile more until the highway swung out and met the town. The exit sign read RIDGEWAY, written in cursive. It had been decorated in a cutesy manner: with paintings of trees and wildlife. Beneath it, someone had written the town slogan, "Our home along the ridge."

"Fuck it," Daniels said. He turned toward the exit, leading the others toward the glowing light. "But know this, I'm going to blast anyone that gives us a lick of trouble. I don't want to hear any arguments. Especially you, Marcia. I don't need any more trouble from you."

Brandon felt a wave of apprehension as they left the highway for the shadows of the exit. No one had the energy to speak, not even Marcia. As they drew closer, he felt that familiar fear pulsing through his every inch. Another adventure. How tired he was of adventures.

11.

The following afternoon, Alayna and the doctor were in the privacy of what had been designated as his office, far in the east wing of the hotel. Alayna buttoned her shirt, casting her eyes away from the doctor as he made several notes on a clipboard. She felt just as embarrassed as she ever had back in the old days of doctor's visits. Even at the end of the world, she had her pride. Spreading her legs wide in front of anyone still gave her pause.

"Do you know what's wrong with me?" she asked, her voice tentative.

The doctor's lips parted for a long moment. He seemed to inhale deeply, pausing, and filling Alayna with adrenaline.

But at that moment, the door burst open. Alayna blinked up into the gorgeous eyes of Clay, who seemed wild, manic.

"Well, Clay. I would like to thank you for taking the time to knock," the doctor said, his voice irritated.

Clay ignored him. He reached Alayna and put his hands on her shoulders, staring into her eyes. Her heart fluttered with desire. She yearned to rest her head against his shoulder, to hold him close. But it was clear that Clay's heart was beating a million miles away.

"I've spoken to the others, and they want to track down your lead," Clay said.

Alayna blinked several times, uncertain what Clay was talking about.

"I want you to come along with us if you think you can," he continued. "I can't imagine doing it without you, to be frank. But only if you're feeling up to it."

Alayna felt her stomach lurch, but in a good way. This was the first time Clay had invited her on an actual adventure, something beyond the "safety" of supply runs. Adrenaline pulsed through her, even as the doctor clucked his tongue, preparing to say something—probably that she shouldn't go, that she shouldn't even consider it.

"Of course I'll go," she said, her eyes dancing. "Damn straight." She leaped up from the table, feeling fluttery, wild. She pushed back against the nausea. "I've been waiting for a chance to actually do something around here."

Clay laughed, tossing his head back. Alayna sensed that this joy was merely him getting one step closer his daughter, but she still reveled in it: feeling his happiness like sunshine on her face.

"What do you think, Doc? Think my deputy can get out for some fresh air?"

The doctor didn't answer, merely made another note on his clipboard. Alayna gave Clay a gentle punch on the arm. This was their forgotten dynamic.

"When are we going?" she asked.

"Easy there, deputy," Clay said with a wink. "We're not going till the sun sets. We want to be stealthy."

"But of course," Alayna said, wagging her

eyebrows. "I couldn't imagine it any other way."

"We stand a better chance of not getting caught at night, of course. So we're all planning on grabbing a bit of rest and meeting in the community room at nine-thirty tonight."

Clay eyed the doctor's thin frame. "So what of it, doc? Is she gonna be all cured?"

The doctor sneered at Clay, sliding his clipboard across his desk. "What ever happened to doctor-patient confidentiality?" he asked.

"I figure that went out the window around the time most of our doctors turned into crazed, brain-eating monsters," Clay said, his eyes glittering.

The doctor leaned his head close, so that his long, thin nose was mere inches from Clay's. "I'd say that's an even better reason to honor these things. The further and further away we get from human decency, the more we need it. Wouldn't you say, Clay? Or is human decency not really a part of your lexicon anymore?"

12.

C lay, Alayna, Walt, and Hank headed north from the hotel at just before ten that evening, each armed with three guns and wearing thick jackets, hats, and gloves, against the chill. Clay ranged ahead, sensing something guiding him toward the compound. Something about this mission filled him with hope, and he felt renewed, charged. And even with Alayna—his deputy—there, things felt as if they were finding balance again. As if he was in control.

The team didn't speak throughout much of the trek, which involved a two-hour walk up the highway, crunching over the dilapidated pavement. They were alert, hunting for any sign of the crazed around them. Every shadow moonlight shadow stirred Alayna's soul, reminding her that she hadn't been "out in it," in ages. Perhaps she wasn't as confident as she'd been on their journey to the hotel. Perhaps she'd lost her reflexes.

It didn't help that every twenty minutes or so she felt a rush of nausea. She kept her lips pressed together tightly, ready to swallow whatever came up. Walt and Hank had joked about it frequently at the beginning of the trip. "Where will she vomit next?" they'd joked, teasing her and yanking at her ponytail. "That's the name of the game."

But it wasn't a game anymore. Not now. They were closing in on a source of light coming from what looked to be a large compound. It was surrounded by a six-foot-tall chain link fence, with, as they got closer, what appeared to be campfires billowing from the other side. Clay realized that the fence was paralleled by another line of fencing approximately five or six feet inside.

"Why do you make of this?" Walt asked, his voice low. "That seems like a waste of resources."

"I'm not sure. Maybe added protection from the crazed?" Hank replied. "Why have one fence when you can have two?"

"Sounds unlikely," Walt said. "If the crazed could get through one fence, they could probably get through two. Better to just make the one fence stronger, right?"

"Boys. Can you please shut it?" Alayna asked, glaring at them. "Seriously. We don't have time for this."

She reached into her bag and drew out the walkie-talkies that Sam's tech guy had made and passed them around to the men. As they'd discussed prior to leaving, everyone took a walkie-talkie and split up, to see as much of the encampment as possible.

Clay went toward an entrance marked with a large gate. There were several guards outside, each holding machine guns and stationed on platforms along the top, as well as the bottom. Clay muttered this information into the walkie-talkie, feeling his apprehension rise. If one of those guards spotted one of his crew, he knew they'd be shot in an instant.

"Six guards, all armed, at the gate. Over," Clay said into the walkie-talkie. "Alayna, what do you see from where you are?"

"Lots of fires. People," Alayna said. "Seems to be quite a community in there. But I'm having trouble seeing through some of the fence."

"Maybe I'll hop over this first fence and see if that helps," Clay said. "If I can look through the second one . . ."

"Be safe," Alayna said.

Clay could almost feel the fear in her voice. He heard just how innocent she truly was. Just a small-town deputy, faced with the horrors of this new world. Just like Maia.

With a surge of adrenaline, Clay scaled the first fence and dropped to his feet in the soft mud in between them. He blinked into the darkness. Lifting his walkie-talkie, he whispered, "All right. I'm on the other side. There's no one in here, actually. Bizarre."

In the silence that followed, he leaned against the second fence, staring into the encampment. The first thing he noticed was a fortress-like structure near the far end of the compound. As he watched, someone carried in a tray of what looked like food. Was someone locked up inside?

Clay's heart hammered in his chest. Something was off. But he was too centered on Maia to consider anything else.

As he traced the edge of the fence he heard something rumble. A quick check found nothing out of the ordinary. The grumbling grew louder, more insistent. Clay took a step back on legs which had started to quiver.

As the moonlight broke through the cloud cover and illuminated the run, Clay recognized what the space between the fences was actually for. It was for *them*. The crazed. They lurched forward, their bony and bludgeoned-looking limbs flailing and their tongues lolling from their mouths. Some of them had injuries dripping and flinging tainted blood. And they moved fast, violently, their arms stretched out toward Clay.

Clay jumped at the fence, hitting it high and yanking himself up. Gasping, he pulled himself over the top while the crazed threw themselves in his direction. As they broke against the fence like a wave, Clay realized just how many there were. Fifty, maybe a hundred—even more. They continued to rage through the fenced-in area, after him—or just his stench.

Clay lifted his walkie-talkie to his lips, taking his first breath in what seemed like five bone-chilling minutes. With his hand shaking, he muttered: "Do not, I repeat. Do NOT go between the fences."

Alayna's voice came rapidly, filled with fear. "Why not?"

Clay nearly stumbled again. "They're collecting them. They've got an army of the crazed in there. It's their first line of defense. And it almost fucking killed me."

13.

When Clay's energy returned, he began to pace along the fence—the crazed following his scent, slamming up against the barrier and making it shake. Clay's mind raced, considering the interior of the compound. From where he stood, he could still see the hazy outline of the stronghold, where someone might be locked up. He could also see other buildings, lower to the ground, and campfires blazing further beyond, probably closer to where Alayna was.

Sherman cleared through the walkie-talkie, saying, "I think there's some kind of mess hall over here. Sleeping quarters. And then, beyond that. Near that garrison thing—if you can see that?"

"That's where I am," Clay replied.

"Just beyond that is a larger structure, with lights. It looks a bit more civilized than everything else. I think if I had to guess, that's where your main man would be. That's where I'd be if I were Malcolm."

"Ha. I bet you're right," Clay said. He eased down the fence line, trying to catch sight of this other building. As he passed it, his eyes were drawn to the stronghold once more. He felt a pull from it, a primal feeling he couldn't quite explain.

"I think that fortress is where my daughter . . . I think it's where Maia is," he muttered into the walkie-talkie, feeling galvanized, alive. He thought he could leap over the fence, sprint through the crazed, and find her. It was akin to those mothers you always heard about, who lifted cars from their children with sudden bursts of strength. Something within you was charged and ready to keep them alive, to protect them beyond everything else.

"I'm going in," Clay said, his voice confident, sure.

"NO!" Alayna screamed through the walkie-talkie, making it screech in Clay's ear. "You're absolutely not going over that fence without us."

"I can't wait, Alayna," Clay said, recognizing his own volatility. He touched the fence, feeling vibrations as the crazed approached. Just in the nick of time, he pulled his hand away from the fence, as the crazed stuck their green and decaying tongues through the gaps. They moaned and shrieked in the darkness. "I won't wait another minute more. Not if I can save her now."

"It's against every rule we've made for ourselves. Every rule of safety," Alayna was clearly fuming. "We've been doing this long enough. If we hadn't played by the rules, we'd be dead."

Clay felt the words like a hammer. His optimism began to crack, exposing the depths of the current reality. He tried to visualize what actually would happen if he climbed the fence and stopped cold, sweating.

"Okay. Okay, I'll wait," he agreed.

"Thank you," Alayna said. "I shouldn't have to say that. But thank you anyway."

Clay didn't respond. He continued his trek around the fence, toward the larger structure that Sherman had pointed out. Hank and Walt had begun to banter over the walkie-talkie channel, and Clay turned it to mute, wanting to stew in his own thoughts. As he got closer to the fortress, he felt suddenly as if the world around him was spinning. Reaching out, he clutched the fence to steady himself. A moment of pure, unadulterated, almost animal rage filled him. Trembling violently, he bared his teeth and heard a growl beginning low in his chest. But as suddenly as it came, the anger dissipated. He was left gasping, still staring up at the fortress—feeling very much that this place was the object of his hatred. Feeling so much that he wanted to burn it to the ground.

14.

T hat moment of rage had altered Clay's mode of attack. He felt strangely capable, wild and muscular and animalistic—the fact that the others had come with him to the compound was insignificant. "I've only ever needed myself," Clay muttered, making his way toward the stronghold. He counted the security guards around the building, watching as one marched away, his automatic weapon slung lazily over his shoulder.

"One down," Clay said to himself. This left him only two to handle. From his viewpoint at the far edge of the fence, he was merely fifteen feet from the closest security guard. If Clay could leap down on soft feet, take cover behind the small pile of logs (for burning, he assumed),when the opportunity arose, he could ambush the first security guard, threaten to put a bullet in his head, and then enter, unnoticed by anyone else.

The promise of this plan began to brew in his head. In the silence, without the walkie-talkie crackling in his ear, he reached for the fence. The crazed seemed to have roamed off to another part of the enclosure, like cows going to pasture on another hill. Clay pushed first one foot, then the other into the fence, preparing to vault himself over the top.

In mere moments, he'd be taking the biggest risk of his life. But somehow, he knew. It was his one last fucking chance.

A hand clasped his shoulder, catching the fabric of his jacket and ripped him down. He landed flat on his back, the resulting pain reverberating up and down his spine. Staring up into the darkness, he blinked several times, seeing spots of light from the impact.

"What the fuck," he gasped.

Alayna appeared, staring down at him. The thump of his fall had attracted several of the crazed to them, between the fences. Already, their tongues were lashing through the openings. Alayna was breathing heavily, as if she'd been sprinting. Slipping the back of her hand across her lips, she stared at him, aghast.

"I knew you were going to try to do something stupid," she said, her nostrils flared.

Clay rolled over and pushed himself up from the ground, his head spinning. He glared at Alayna, the woman who was supposed to be on his side. Trying to hold back his rage, he hissed at her, "How dare you keep me from my daughter?"

Fear flickered on Alayna's face. It disappeared as quickly as it had arrived and she stepped into his space, her lips just inches from his. "You were going to get yourself killed. You didn't even care about the rest of us," Alayna said. "Where would we be if you got killed? They'd know others might be here. They'd come after us. And we'd all be dead."

"I could have been up and over both fences without the crazed even seeing me—"

"And then what was your grand plan over on the other side? Who shoots the automatic weapon first?

You, or him? And what if he beat you, Clay?" Alayna's eyes glittered with tears. "Listen. You can thank me for saving your sorry ass now or later or never. But if you try to go over that fence again, I swear, I'll kill you myself."

Surprising himself, Clay felt his lips stretch into a smile. He sighed and leaned back, trying to stretch out his spine. Somewhere behind him, he heard the others approaching; Hank and Walt's whispered banter, along with Sherman's animalistic grunts. His eyes flashed, recognizing that the game was over. That they had to regroup, come up with a better plan, now that they had information to work with.

"And that's an order from your deputy," Alayna said again, her eyes fluttering, making her look absolutely stunning in the moonlight. Her words were tight with fear, but she tried to smile. "It's perfectly clear. I don't want to live through the end of the world without you."

Hank and Walt were beside them now, waving their walkie-talkies. Hank gestured with a long finger, saying, "Clay-ster, we thought you did something crazy. Couldn't hear you on the radio anymore."

"Naw, boys. He didn't do anything crazy," Alayna replied, still holding Clay's eyes. "He knows better than to leave us out here alone."

15.

Rex's massive boot stomped on the gas pedal with force, kicking the truck forward on the gravel road. Megan's arms were crossed over her chest and she glared out toward the mountains. Her gun was braced between her legs, prepped and ready. She reached over and raced through the radio stations, finally landing on one that apparently had been playing the same tape over and over again since the end of the world. It was '80s music, and it was hellish in Megan's ears.

"Turn that damn thing off," Rex said, his voice low and gravelly.

Megan flipped her dark hair behind her shoulder, her eyes flashing. She wouldn't pay attention to Rex or give in to him—no matter how right he was. "Excuse me if I don't want to listen to your labored breathing all the way back to Carterville," she said. "You sound like a dying cow. Didn't anyone ever tell you to stop inhaling hamburgers every single day? Jesus." She glared at his belly protruding over his belt.

Rex didn't answer for a moment. The truck tore down the road, abandoned vehicles in their wake. The sight of each car gave Megan pause, wondering about the fate of her friends. Of Alayna, who she'd abandoned. And of Clay, Daniels, the others . . . how they'd been holed up in that hotel, caught on the other side of the force field. Until Megan ran out on them, taking the remote control device and getting out while she still could. Megan had always been described as a force of nature, never allowing anything to get in her way. For the first time, that selfishness might have destroyed the only person she'd ever loved.

Alayna. The name echoed through her head. She leaned forward, her eyes refocusing on the horizon. "Just drive faster," she said, her voice pointed.

"You know we're wasting our time," Rex scoffed, popping a beer with his free hand. "If what you're saying is true about that bomb, all your friends are dead, Missy, and we're just putting ourselves in danger. That's rule one of prepping. Never think about anyone except yourself."

"Sure, that's rule one," Megan said, fiercely. "But you developed those goddamn rules *before* the end of the world, didn't you? You didn't actually know how stir crazy you'd get roasting yourself at the top of your silo. Did you?"

"They're dead," Rex said, letting out a beer belch. "I can absolutely guarantee that. You wanna make a bet?"

Megan kept silent for the next ten minutes, knowing that Carterville was nearing. She tried to come up with an excuse she could tell Alayna. She imagined the words. "I was just so frightened, and this horrible, belching, belly-scratching asshole took me in . . ."

"That's where the force field is. Watch it!" Megan screamed, recognizing the farmhouse. Rex slammed his foot against the brake, screeching the truck to a stop just in time. On their right, a burnt-out Humvee was all but splattered across the ground, beginning to sink into the grass after what appeared to be a massive accident. Megan slid her eyes away from it, too frightened to see if anyone was inside.

"Poor suckers," Rex said, gesturing toward the area before them. "You know what? I don't see any force field. You're making it up."

Megan reached for the remote control and pushed the button. Nothing happened. She was reminded that the forcefield had previously had a greenish, flickering hue to it.

"I think I'm just gonna drive through it," Rex said arrogantly. "I'm starting to think you made this whole fucking thing up. The force field. The bomb. Everything."

"Why would I make that up?" Megan asked, her voice shaking. "The entire town was supposed to die out. That's why I ran. Why the hell else would I leave—"

"Because you weren't ready to face commitment," Rex said. "Same thing happened with my ex-wife. I made every excuse in the book, but at the end of the day—"

"This isn't about your ex-wife," Megan said. Feeling her brain fizz with fear, she pointed. "Fine. If you want to risk our lives like that, you think you know everything, then drive through. Do it. I dare you."

Momentary fear flickered in his eyes, passing quickly. Megan was surprised to see it at all. The man had spent his entire life prepping for something like this. He'd told her time and time again that if the world *hadn't* ended while he was alive, he would have been disappointed. "Would have blown it up myself,

I reckon," he'd said.

Rex inched the truck closer and closer to the farmhouse. As they passed over the space where the force field had been, Megan closed her eyes, waiting for the inevitable. But seconds later, she felt the truck crumbling over the gravel. A single tear coursed down her cheek.

"Damn," Rex grunted.

As they drove the rest of the way into Carterville, Megan spotted several of the crazed roaming the streets. She pointed them out to Rex, who said, "Guess that bomb didn't work after all." Things were beginning to add up in Megan's mind, with all signs pointing toward devastation. The crazed were still around. The force field was gone. Alayna, Clay, Daniels—surely, without a silo to hide out at, they were gone.

Dead. Another of the crazed.

Rex parked the truck near the hotel. Megan bolted out of her seat even before Rex could stop the engine. Her feet pounded along the pavement, bringing her closer and closer. She pushed the lobby doors and raced up the steps, her footsteps echoed through the empty halls. When she reached the bar, she found herself in a shadowy gloom. Beer bottles, liquor bottles, wine bottles were collected in long rows on the top of the bar, and a thick layer of dust had settled over everything.

Megan realized with a lurch that Rex was right. She collapsed at the edge of the bar, covering her face with her hands and letting out a long, guttural cry. As she wept, Rex appeared in the doorway of the bar, peering around at everything. Megan spun toward him.

"Aren't you going to say it? Aren't you going to

say you told me so?" she gasped.

But Rex kept his lips sealed tight.

"I just wanted it to be a dream," she whispered. "I wanted it all to be fake. Like maybe I'd come back and pick up right where I left off . . ."

Rex's face was ashen. Megan had never seen him so uncertain, so weak-looking. She turned her back on him and walked the length of the bar, taking in everything. She yearned for a just whiff of Alayna's perfume. She wanted a single sign, beyond the booze, that they'd all been there at all.

"Maybe we should head back to the silo," Rex said. "It's bound to be safer for us up there. If we hang out here, the crazed will get to us. It's only a matter of time . . ."

"I know. Just—"

Something flashed in the corner of her eye. Turning her head, she saw a notepad on one of the side tables. Alayna's handwriting—that gorgeous scrawl!

The first collection of words was nothing but a supply list. "Things to bring." On it was water, food, toiletries, soap. Alayna was eternally practical, the perfect travel partner. Megan remembered it well. And then, beside it, was the word "HELEN" written in large, block letters. It had been circled several times.

Megan turned the notebook toward Rex, her eyes wide. She rammed her finger against the page again and again. "Do you know what this means!?" she exclaimed, more tears finding their way down her cheeks. "Rex!"

Rex took the page and studied it.

"This means they left on purpose. They didn't die. Not here!" Megan's words flowed rapidly. "This means, there's still hope, Rex. And at the end of the world, hope is all we have."

16.

A layna struggled up the steps of the hotel as the sunlight began to filter in from the east. Another wave of nausea overtook her. Glancing back at the others, she gave them a small smile. "All right, everyone. We lived through it. Let's get some sleep."

It no longer fazed her how many times she'd had to say, "We lived through it." It was something always echoing around her head, a reminder of how "lucky" they were to have another morning, another night. With the nanites exploding through her veins, taking up residence in the back areas of her animal brain, she knew she wouldn't have full control forever.

The gang behind her grunted in return, Clay returned a soft smile. Alayna remembered the terror she'd felt when Clay had tried to go over that fence. She'd run with the adrenaline of an animal, catching his coat and yanking him back. When he was safely back on the ground, she'd recognized how berserk she'd been. Maybe that was the nanites, revealing themselves? How could it be anything else? She'd never been so physically able. So wild.

As she entered the hotel she saw Lane perched on the lobby couch. She jumped up to meet them, hugging Alayna tightly. Alayna wasn't accustomed to such reactions. Warring emotions were followed by confusion. Lane swiped a tear from her cheek.

"Lane? What's up?" Alayna asked.

But before she could get out another word, Lane had wrapped her hand around Alayna's upper arm, guiding her toward the back of the hotel. She heard Sam's familiar voice greet them, wanting to know what happened. Then Alayna and Lane were out of earshot.

Upstairs in the privacy of Lane's bedroom, Alayna found herself face to face with an overwhelmed Lane. Lane processed whatever she was preparing to tell Alayna; closing her eyes, biting at her lower lip. With a surge of fear, Alayna realized what Lane was going to say.

"It's okay," she said, crossing her arms over her chest. "I already know."

Lane blinked up at Alayna, her lips parting. "What?"

"I'm positive." She allowed the words to fall into the space between them, forcing herself to acknowledge this truth.

"Positive—I mean, yes . . ." Lane began. "How did you—"

"The nanites," Alayna said. "I felt them, when we were out on the mission. I had a surge of . . . I don't know, power? Athleticism, adrenaline, animal instinct—nothing I've ever felt before. I knew then that I must be infected with the nanites. That's what you were going to say, isn't it? The tests came back positive? I'm infected?"

Lane's face fell. Alayna felt her stomach clench with grief, recognizing that this was the truth. What she had dreaded was indeed the truth. She straightened trying not to allow herself to tremble at the horror of her new reality. The nanites. They were taking her body. She was only a vessel for their greater mission.

Someday she'd be nothing more than a shell.

"I thought you said you wouldn't know for sure, though, if you didn't have a full-blown lab," Alayna choked out. "So, I thought I had a bit more time before I had to face this . . ."

"Alayna, no," Lane said, her voice quivering. "That's not the news I have for you. You didn't let me finish. None of you ever let me goddamn finish."

Alayna felt a wrinkle form between her eyebrows. "Lane, what the hell are you talking about? Just tell me. How long does the doctor say I have before— before everything starts changing? Before I can no longer live as—"

"Alayna! No. Stop this," Lane said, pulling Alayna's hands from her face, seeming enraged. "Your blood test showed that you're positive for pregnancy. You're going to have a baby."

Alayna felt the blood drain out from her face. She fell back against the wall, feeling all the air escape her lungs. For a moment, she forgot to breathe. The wave of grief had been replaced with a grey and foggy confusion, a sense that she'd just been forced into another new reality: a place where she didn't really recognize the rules or understand the language.

"What are you talking about?"

"You're going to have a baby," Lane said again, lifting her chin.

"There must be a—a mistake . . ." Alayna whispered.

"Absolutely not," Lane said.

"Does that mean I'm not infected with nanites?" She asked, her voice softer. "Just pregnant?"

"Like I said, we're still not sure about the

nanites," Lane replied. Seeming exhausted, she sank on the side of her bed, rubbing her forehead. Her eyes pulled away from Alayna's, full of their own meaning. "We're going to need to do further tests. But in the meantime   . . ." She gestured toward the window, which showed another unappealing morning in the town. Grey slabs, empty and devoid of people, thrusting against a too-bright blue sky. "But you're bringing a human life into this. Which means you have a bit more to worry about than, well, than just the nanites."

Alayna stewed with that for a moment, feeling the weight of Lane's words. Sliding her hands across her stomach, she understood for the first time: she had a full, human life within her. She was responsible for this boy or girl: for helping them learn to walk, to talk, to live—and, in order to survive, to murder. To shoot a gun. She glimpsed flashes of their future together, traveling through the darkness of this post-apocalyptic world. And the tears began to course down her cheeks.

She'd never really imagined herself with children. She'd always figured to be an experience she, as a lesbian and occasional bisexual, would never have. And now, at the worst time in all of history, she was with child. Brimming with life, knowing, somehow, that this was the antithesis of the crazed monsters outside the hotel walls.

She would fight forever to keep her child alive. It was enough reason to live.

17.

"We better join the others," Lane said, standing and wiping her hands down her front, smoothing out her shirt. She opened the door and Alayna followed her into the hall, in almost a dream state.

"We'll need to get you on a vitamin regime right away. And I don't know what your nutritional intake is currently, but we're going to need to ramp it up. And I mean, exponentially. More protein. More vegetables. Definitely more, more, more . . ."

Alayna drifted into the community room, feeling light, eager. Alive. Clay was holding court over Hank, Walt, Sam, and Sherman, with a rough drawing of what looked like the camp in the mountains behind him. He gestured at it.

"Now, I saw that there's some kind of changeover with the guards around midnight, with one of the guards going in to give whoever's in this tower food," Clay said.

"And you're certain it's your daughter?" Sam asked. "Because I have to tell you, it seems unlikely."

"I don't know what you want me to say, Sam. Want me to say it's father's intuition? Want me to say that I 'just know?' At the end of the day, we're both after the same thing. To kill this asshole. And you weren't actually at the camp this morning, were you? You don't have a clue what you're talking about . . ."

Clay's voice tapered off when Alayna came in. She felt her heart burst just at seeing him. Something between them effervesced, in the same way it had that fateful night. Clay's baby! She touched her abdomen, feeling the weight of this— new family. Nothing else in the world mattered, did it? Just the love between two people, and how that love could create, well, another life.

Clay stuttered slightly, watching as Alayna and Lane sat at the back of the room.

"Out with it," Sam snapped, tossing her foot over her knee and leaning back, almost masculine. Larger than life.

"Actually, is it cool if we take a break?" Hank asked, reaching his hands behind his back and stretching. He looked lankier than ever. "Most of us haven't slept in ages. And I know Walt here's been trying to stay awake for the past twenty minutes. Haven't you, Walt?"

Walt elbowed Hank, making him jump.

Alayna's eyes were on Clay, who continued to stare at her. There was a new kind of communication between them, over the heads of the others— unspoken.

"All right. We can take a break," Clay agreed. He picked up a glass of water and sipped it, his eyes still on Alayna.

The others rose from their chairs, with Sam grumbling about wasted time. Even Lane went, leaving Clay and Alayna alone. Clay closed the distance between them. Their faces were just a foot apart. Alayna felt overwhelming desire. Licking her lips, she waited, sensing Clay was about to say something. Was about to give this meaning.

"Alayna, what's going on?" he asked.

"What do you mean?" Alayna was coy.

"You just look—different," Clay said, looking puzzled. "I can't put my finger on it. I just—are you feeling all right?"

"I feel absolutely wonderful." She stood and brushed past him, walking toward the kitchen. At the doorway she looked back, knowing she had a new kind of power over him. Even if it was just knowledge. Of knowing they were bringing a child into the world together. She didn't yet feel ready to share—to say the words aloud.

"I'm just famished, is all," Alayna said, breaking the tension. "I'm going to grab something and be on my way upstairs for that rest everyone's talking about."

Not waiting for a reply, she ducked into the kitchen, feeling her heart hammering in her chest. Deep inside, she imagined she could feel the baby's heart beating as well, although she knew it was probably impossible.

It was just the bit of hope she needed.

18.

Much like Brandon remembered from Carterville, Ridgeway had a strange energy field around it—a kind of glowing green halo. He, Marcia, Daniels, and Leland were just at the edge of town, staring at the flickering array, none of them able to verbalize just what a blow this was.

"Damn it," Marcia said, digging her toe into the dirt.

They'd imagined so much awaiting them in Ridgeway. They'd imagined food, beds, supplies, a reprieve from the road. After walking for days, their legs were straining and their throats were continually dry, parched. Brandon tried to swallow but he couldn't find the spit.

"Maybe we can find the power source," Leland said, and started along the energy field. His shoulders were slumped, making him look aged, battered. The bald spot on his head reflected the eerie green light.

But as they scouted the edge of the city, they found no such source. Daniels had begun to bark orders as usual—insisting, "It's better we get back on the road right now and find another place by nightfall."

"Fuck that." Marcia sounded snotty, like a

toddler who'd been told to stop. "No way. I know Leland can find the power source. It's time to get smart about this, Daniels, instead of just running all over the world, flitting back and forth without a real plan."

After nearly two hours without finding the source, however, Brandon's heavy feet steered him back toward the road. The others joined him: Marcia didn't have a snarky comment and even Daniels' lips were sealed.

The sunlight reflected off the pavement, bouncing back into their eyes, despite the lateness of the afternoon. As they turned the corner toward the main road, Brandon thought he was seeing a mirage: a million slimy worms, crawling toward them along the center of the road. But he realized with a gasp they weren't worms.

It was *them*. At least nine, perhaps ten of the crazed, swarming toward them on the road. Feeling the adrenaline of an animal, of prey, Brandon turned and ran, Marcia and Leland on his heels. Daniels lifted his gun and blasted first one, then a second crazed, but soon joined Brandon, Marcia, and Leland in their mad dash back toward Ridgeway. Even as he drove his legs forward, Brandon couldn't reason why they were heading back toward the town. Perhaps it was because it was the illusion of safety. He could see a water tank on a hill in the distance, he could visualize the church, the school, the very real structures that had constituted a very real life.

Brandon thought his heart would burst, whether from exertion or emotion he, couldn't say. He'd never in his life wanted to be somewhere more than he wanted to be in Ridgeway. Behind him, he heard the crazed, could almost feel their tongues stretching from their rotting mouths.

On instinct, Brandon reached for a stick from a busted and burnt tree, lifting it into the air.

"What the hell are you doing?" Marcia shrieked.

"Maybe it's not like the others," Brandon said. "It's not as dark as the one around Carterville. You know? Like, maybe not as strong?"

Even as he spoke, Brandon recognized how completely deranged his own thoughts were, fueled by dehydration and fatigue.

"Stop it!" Leland cried, his voice whiny and wild. "You're being an idiot."

Daniels thrust himself forward, trying to catch Brandon's shoulder. But Brandon was sprinting toward the force field with his stick in front of him. He swung it against the forcefield, actually entering it—and seeing the other half of the stick fall. Brandon's entire body was filled with pain. Energy, life, electricity arced up and down his arms and legs, and he was forced back, slamming his head on the ground when he went down. Dazed, he saw stars, wild stars, swirling in the sky.

And still he could hear the crazed, swarming at them.

"GET HIM UP!" Daniels cried.

Brandon felt hands and arms around his shoulders, lifting him. On his feet, he staggered, watching with bleary eyes as Marcia tried to sweep him of dust.

"WE HAVE TO GET GOING!" Leland cried, his eyes nearly bulging from their sockets. The crazed were no more than twenty feet away now. "RUN! And the way isn't FORWARD, Brandon!"

Brandon blinked down at the stick, still fizzing at the end. He shambled into a trot then ran in earnest beside the force field, the others behind him. He heard a ZAP to his right. Turning his head, he saw the force field ripped away, leaving only empty space between him and the town.

Swinging toward where the force field had been, Brandon darted into the town. Marcia screamed, "NO!" But Brandon didn't stop, leaping to safety to the other side.

"What the hell?" Leland cried, and followed him.

With no other option, the others followed. Brandon could still hear the crazed behind them. He gasped, "Are they getting faster?"

Beside him, Daniels huffed agreement. "It's like they're more animal, less zombie these days." He picked up the pace. "We've got to go. The force field doesn't seem to be coming back on."

But just as he spoke, the green orb around the city flickered to life. The first of the crazed crossed the line—his head bounced on the field but sliced into him just at the shoulder blades. His amputated hands hit the ground on the safe side. Green and purple blood splattered the grass, catching the sunlight. Brandon spun at the noise and saw the back of the crazed's torso hit the pavement.

"Jesus," Brandon said.

Marcia, Leland, and Daniels stopped as well, spinning to watch as the crazed continued to splatter their bodies against the force field, seemingly unable to stop. Blood and guts and bits of bone splattered, falling like slop and making large puddles of muck. At one point, Marcia staggered, bent over and gagged. Indeed, the smell was horrible—filling the air around them.

But the noise had drawn still more crazed from the surrounding trees. Flailing and gibbering, they joined the chase. Marcia gasped even as she held her hand over her nose.

"We have to go," she coughed. "The force field. It's obviously not strong enough. We have to get out of here. Hide. Before it flickers again."

"Maybe the force field didn't fail," Daniels said, turning toward the town and lifting his chin. Brandon followed suit, even as the crazed time and time again, flung themselves against the force field. "Maybe they're controlling it. Using it to keep things out. Or to keep things in," he said cryptically.

Brandon's eyes followed Daniels' toward a building at the center of the town. There sat an antenna, forking into the sky and casting a glow. It looked like a news antenna, maybe, although Brandon wasn't entirely sure. Regardless, it looked as if it had been tacked onto the building using whatever tools they had around. It was crooked, wobbling with the wind. And yet, the glowing light from it didn't fail.

"I say we follow that," Leland said. The obviousness of his words made Marcia cackle with nervous laughter. And then, even as the crazed continued to hurl their bodies against the field, they began to walk slowly toward the antenna. Confusion and fatigue blended in their minds, and they fell into a line.

They had nowhere else to go.

19.

I t was three in the morning, but Clay's eyes had already grown accustomed to the darkness. As they approached the compound, he heard Hank and Walt tittering behind him. In spite of that, both were wiry and able, potentially necessary if they had to make a quick escape over the fence.

About fifty feet to the right, Alayna led a team of two, a couple from Sam's party named Tyler and Agnes. Agnes was all-powerful, with bulging biceps and an eagerness to blast crazed through the skull from the back porch of the hotel (something Clay had witnessed several times throughout the previous few weeks). Her husband obeyed her, which was enough for Clay.

Sam led another pair, and Damon, one of her cronies, another. The four groups approached from each side of the compound. The light from the compound almost blinded him, making him blink as if he was staring directly into the sun.

Near the gate, Clay leaned into the fence, careful not to make any noise. From his position, with his nose poking through the holes, he saw that there were even fewer guards awake and alert at this early hour. One leaned heavily against the tower-like building which Clay believed held Maia. The guard was facing the opposite direction and kicking aimlessly at the ground, his head leaning on the wall. He looked like a child.

Scanning toward the gate, Clay realized there were only two guards—one leaning on the gate itself, his chin tucked against his chest. His gun dangled loosely from its strap and. His fingers twitched on the stock, perhaps in synchronization with his dream. His eyelashes fluttered, showing how far from reality he truly was. The main guard shuffled back and forth in front of the gate, facing away. Clay realized that if he approached from the inside, he could apprehend him rather easily. He felt his fingers twitch with adrenaline. He yearned, suddenly, to wrap both hands around his own throat and squeeze.

"Some guards," Walt muttered from Clay's right. "They have one job, you know? Can't even stay awake."

"It's almost too easy," Clay murmured back. Lifting his walkie-talkie, he spoke to Sam, Damon, and Alayna—the others with phones. "I'm going to go over the fence and catch the main guard, eliminate him. We're going to have to be careful. The other one isn't completely zonked out yet."

"Clay. Be careful," Alayna replied. Neither of the others offered anything else. Clay sensed that, even though Sam was in many ways his equal, she didn't care if he lived or died.

Clay pulled himself up the side of the first layer of fence. He found himself in the in-between, in the terrifying territory of the crazed. Stepping lightly through the mud, he crept toward the guard. The man paused for a second, as if his subconscious perhaps had registered Clay's presence between the fences. But after a pause, he muttered to himself,

"Fuck it. It's nothing."

Clay slipped a tranquilizer from his satchel and shot it directly into the upper back of the guard. The guard let out a sputtering gasp and dropped to his knees. In the silence, Clay's ears rushing with blood and adrenaline, Clay swung himself over the top of the second fence and gagged the guard with a strip of cloth, ready for the purpose. The guard's eyes began to roll back in his head, but he couldn't struggle—the tranquilizer was far too powerful. Knowing the tranquilizer wouldn't last forever, especially not on such a muscular, able-bodied man, Clay hogtied and slid him against a nearby shed, out of sight of the rest of the camp.

With the first guard incapacitated, Clay vaulted the gate and did the same to the second guard, not bothering to tranquilize him, but making sure to gag him first. The man's eyes popped open mid-way through the process, and he let out a wild cry choked back by the gag Clay clucked his tongue, fighting down the rising rage in his chest. *This man.* He'd been with Maia the entire time. And he'd allowed her to be locked in a tower, to be treated like slime.

Yanking him to the shed, he left him in a heap beside the other guard. The second guard struggled, scrabbling against the soil

Knowing he was wasting time, Clay opened the gate swiftly. He gestured for the others, muttering into his walkie-talkie, "It's almost too easy," echoing the words to Walt and Hank as they sped toward the opening in the fence. "Just like you said, boys. It's almost too easy."

But as Alayna darted toward him, her legs light and quick beneath her, Clay felt a sudden apprehension. When she was next to him, speaking the first truth of the night, he said, "But just because we're in, doesn't mean you don't have to stay on your guard. I have no idea what's in store for us in there. Just because they have the crazed locked away—"

"I have the device," Alayna said, her eyes heavy with meaning. "And you've got the guns. We've made it this far. We'll stay alert. We always do."

20.

A layna felt the weight of the device bouncing softly against her side as they entered the compound. Clay was in the lead, yet she still wished he was standing beside her, staring into her eyes. There seemed to be something between them again, as if Clay, with some animalistic instinct, recognized that Alayna was carrying his child. And Alayna felt it, too: the need to stay upright, to stay alert, to protect something bigger than herself. Her finger tapped the device, poised to strike.

Hank and Walt were together on the right. As always, their eyes seemed amused—as if this was a grand game to them. Sam shook her head at the men and peeled off toward the other side of the compound.

Agnes and her husband, Tyler, were with her, their weapons ready. Alayna hadn't spoken to them much, but she appreciated their tight-lipped approach. How they'd nodded after each of her orders. "Absolutely. It's the end of the world. We'll do anything we can do to help," had been Tyler's words, as if he were volunteering to help with a silly town parade or soup drive.

Alayna studied the fortress and the attached tower, about a football field away from them in the compound. They were poorly constructed, as if erected hastily. The tower slanted slightly eastward and had raw plywood siding. All the windows were dark and blank, like dead eyes. Alayna tried to imagine Maia asleep behind one of those windows but couldn't. It felt like years since she'd seen the teenager. Thinking of Maia inevitably forced Alayna to remember Clay's wife, Val. Val—who could still be alive. And what would happen to Alayna, to the baby, if Val ever turned up?

Certainly, Clay hadn't forgotten about the love between them. "High school sweethearts," he'd so often told Alayna, back at his desk—dotting his tongue along the side of a donut. "She told me she wanted to see the world, but I told her, hell, I couldn't imagine that there was anything better than Carterville out there. We have everything we need here. Each other. Good schools for Maia. And you, Alayna. I couldn't have asked for a better deputy . . ."

As Alayna spun through memories, Hank and Walt walked a bit too close to one of the buildings. Even as Alayna watched, she sensed a foreboding, a fear. Her throat felt constricted, holding in a scream. She wanted to cry out, to warn them. But it was too late. Hank's tennis shoe touched something invisible on the ground. It buckled him forward, falling to his knees.

The others turned, staring with confusion at his fall. Then, a long HONK ripped the night air around them.

"It was a wire! A trap!" Hank cried.

Everyone froze, watching the uncontrollable unfold. A system of pulleys activated by the wire reached the edge of the fence, creating a horrific, mouth-like opening. An entrance for the crazed.

"FUCK!" Hank yelped, climbing back to his feet.

All of them went for their guns, but Alayna was holding the device. After a long, horrible moment— one that seemed to be an infinity—the crazed began to swarm from their kennel. They poured through the opening, several of them getting hung up on the fence and tearing themselves free, gore spattering wildly.

Hank and Walt backpaddled, lifting their rifles. Agnes rushed toward Alayna, waving her gun. "Hey! Alayna!"

Alayna turned toward her, her eyes wide, swallowing the scene whole.

"It wasn't just that opening. They're coming from over there, as well!" Agnes cried.

Alayna saw this and cringed. On all sides of the compound, the fences had been opened—just from this single mistake. Clay, Sam, and Damon had gathered their groups together, creating small skirmish lines. Clay lifted his walkie-talkie and muttered into it.

"We're still trying to stay quiet, gang," he said into it, showing no sign of fear—even as over a hundred of the crazed approached from all sides. "Use hand to hand combat if you can. We have to stand our ground."

It sounded insane. She'd been out on the road with Clay; had witnessed the crazed's teeth ripping into Ralph's neck. Had seen the horrors of these monsters, and their destruction, time and time again. Keeping the device up, Alayna pointed it toward a mob of crazed who were closing on Hank and Walt, causing them to dive to the ground. The device was silent and was therefore their only mode of attack—other than hands and feet.

Alayna felt helpless, knowing she was the only one with power. She couldn't possibly save all of them. The first line of crazed was close to reaching Clay. Clay swung his fist and connected with a crazed's cheek, causing the bones to bust beneath his knuckles. Sam thrust her boot to the gut of one of the crazed, throttling then casting him back against the wall of the fortress. Even Agnes and Tyler were fighting through the crowd of them—trying to avoid their gnashing teeth. Alayna tried to knock out as many as she could: taking aim, and pressing her finger time and time again against the button.

They heard it: the blast of gunfire. Alayna blinked around her, trying to figure out who from their party had finally said, "fuck it," and decided to protect themselves for real. But she realized it wasn't one of theirs. Instead, one of Malcolm's goons—all in black, wearing a dark helmet and wielding a rifle, was marching toward them—easing through the crazed like a ship in the night.

21.

A fter the first blast from one of Malcolm's men, other guards began to press forward, shooting at both the crazed and members of his team. Clay swung his rifle toward the guard who seemed to be their leader, aiming at his chest. But as he let the bullet fly, a crazed lurched in front of the guard— exploding in a flurry of bloody fireworks and splattering all over the guard's face.

The guard was unfazed. Clay realized the seriousness of the situation he'd brought his crew into. Adrenaline pumped through him. He drove his rifle forward and into the chin of another crazed, breaking bones. A bullet whizzed past his ear—from one of Malcolm's men or one of his own. He could no longer say for sure.

All hell broke loose. Agnes took a shot at a crazed. Its brains splattered across her husband's chest. Another leaped, trying to get his teeth into Tyler's neck. Again, Agnes fired. Nobody could prepare you for this. Nothing could.

Sam wielded her gun like the master she was, dropping three crazed in three shots and then ripping a bullet through the heart of one of Malcolm's gang. The guard cried out and fell to his knees with a gloved hand against his chest, blood geysering through his fingers with his final heartbeats.

Alayna used the device to knock out crazed after crazed. Clay was grateful knowing that she could take care of herself. She pointed the device at a crazed moving to attack Agnes, then another after Walt. Sam pumped a shot through another of Malcolm's guards, but Damon fell to the ground with a bullet of his own. The chaos continued to spin.

But Clay knew he had a bigger job to do.

He found a small path between two buildings which guided him toward the stronghold on the other side of the compound. As he swept through the darkness he encountered another four crazed, cut off from the rest of their horde and lost. Clay shot the first one in the head. When it went down, it knocked down the pair behind it. Clay slammed his elbow into the wide gap of the fourth crazed's mouth, busting his nose and shattering teeth.

Clay bolted toward the tower where he felt sure Maia was. Two guards saw him and gave chase. One of them shot at him; Clay responded in kind. He felt anger, adrenaline rushing through his veins. In the back of his mind, that little voice—all but stamped out these days—told him, "You're meant to serve and protect, serve and protect. Not murder!" But he forced it away, knowing that killing these men— human or no—was the only path to his daughter.

The last man blocked the doorway into the fortress, his rifle aimed at Clay's chest. His arms shook, showing his fatigue. Clay couldn't see the man's eyes beneath the helmet, but he caught a glimpse of his curly blonde hair. This wasn't a man who'd ever wanted to go to war. Something about him screamed of youth.

This wasn't his world.

"Just step aside, man," Clay said, his rifle still aimed directly at the kid's stomach. "I know you don't want to be here."

But the guard didn't move an inch. Feeling oddly invincible, Clay took a step forward, almost daring him to shoot. A single bullet wound wouldn't stop him from finding his daughter. He took another step, and then another, until his own rifle was pressing into the guard. The guard jerked and dropped to the ground. Clay looked back at the guard he'd already shot and said, "Don't make shoot you, too," He stared at the darkness beneath the guard's helmet, hoping he was staring into his eyes. "Just let me get to her. She's my daughter."

The guard dropped his rifle. Wordlessly, he raised his hands, then ran from Clay's aim, disappearing into the darkness. In the distance, he could still hear gunfire and the wails of the crazed. But for the time being, he was alone.

Clay crashed through the door and barreled up the steps, feeling his muscles ache. At the top of a winding staircase was a single door, wooden and crooked. Inside, he found a small, dreary room with dusty floors. A small, emaciated girl was cowering in the corner, her dark hair streaming down her back. She wore a white dress; her legs bare and dirty and her arms wrapped tightly around her knees. She was shivering, malnourished and underdressed.

But it was Maia.

"Daddy?" The word was tentative, shocked.

Clay allowed his arms to fall, still holding the rifle. Emotion overtook him and his eyes filled with tears. "Maia," he whispered. "My God, what have they done to you?"

Clay dropped to his knees and wrapped his arms

around her. In the silence that followed—a small forever—Maia found some strength and hugged him back, her string-like arms around his neck and clinging to him tightly. She shook as she sobbed, whispering over and over the heartbreaking words, "I didn't think you'd find me. I didn't think you'd ever find me, Daddy."

22.

M aia was weak and so fragile that Clay found it easy to lift her—much like he'd done when she was a much smaller girl—and walk toward the door. She continued to shudder, muttering nonsensical words at times. "I heard all the gunshots outside. Thought for sure the monsters got out of the cage," she said, her voice raspy. "I knew it was just a matter of time before one of them got through and came up here and got me."

"They're not, Maia," Clay said, his eyes burning with ferocity. "You have to trust me, kiddo. We'll get you someplace safe. My team's downstairs handling Malcolm and his guys right now."

"God, Malcolm," Maia whimpered, her tears still falling. "He's not gonna be happy—"

"Let me worry about that," Clay said. He hurried down the steps, making sure that Maia was comfortable in his arms. At the bottom, he stood her on her shaky legs, asking, "Can you walk? I need to use my gun, just in case . . ."

Maia gave him a wordless nod, her eyes wide. She gazed out the door, at the two guards who'd bled out. Clay sensed, then, that Maia had spent a good deal of time with the men. That they'd been her jailers, the ones who ensured she didn't escape. Her eyes burned, almost orange with anger. And then she ducked her head and slipped out into the night. Clay had a million questions but held them, although he felt no anguish for taking the lives of her guards.

It was a level of rage Clay had never experienced, ever in his life.

He guided Maia through the grass, and down the path. As they moved, Clay realized that the gunfire had dissipated. Silence stretched over the compound, except for a single voice—calling out, sounding almost like an animal. Wild. Maia blinked up at Clay, her eyebrows stitching together.

"Who's that?" she asked.

Clay recognized the voice. It was Sam, but louder, angrier, and with more power and volatility than he'd ever heard from her. When Clay and Maia stepped into the wide clearing at the center of the compound, Sam was standing tall, gun in hand. It wasn't a gun that his team had brought. It had clearly been taken from one of Malcolm's people.

There was a man before Sam, on his knees. He was wide-shouldered, with rugged, fat cheeks and a thick, dark blonde beard. The man gazed up at her, fear in his eyes. Sam stormed back and forth like a wolf on the prowl. Her gun stayed on his skull, a constant warning.

"If you fucking move an inch—and I mean a single inch—your head will be all over the grass of your stupid little compound," Alayna said.

Clay glanced around, taking stock of what had happened since he'd abandoned the fight. Crazed, bleeding out, detached limbs and severed heads scattered on the ground. Tyler, Agnes' husband, was dead, with a wound to the neck and a wound to the head (one, Clay found out later, was a mercy shot from Agnes herself, who didn't want Tyler to become a monster). Agnes sat next to him, tucked in a ball and staring into space. About twenty feet behind her, Hank had Walt's head in his lap, trying to wrap a bullet wound. Damon's face had been covered with a sheet. He hadn't made it, either.

The gates had been closed, keeping the rest of the crazed between the fences. Alayna regarded Clay and his daughter and gave Clay a small smile, although the smile didn't spread to her eyes. She had one hand on her stomach, an awkward stance.

Sam continued her tirade. She kept the gun pointed at Malcolm, but made sure to look at all of Malcolm's men, on their knees in the grass with their leader.

"And if any of YOU move, know that I won't spare you," she said, all but screaming it. "I'm prepared to tear into all of you, to rip your guts across this compound. Malcolm . . ." She stopped in front of him. "What kind of animal are you? To do this to people? What kind of egomaniac . . ."

Malcolm gave her a strange, crooked smile. A new kind of rage twisted inside Clay. It felt almost like someone else's. He pushed that idea away. He recognized the evilness of this man. His eyes glittered with indecency, with the ability and desire to use people for his own personal, horrible gains. *At the end of the world*, Clay thought. *That's when you see the real evil.*

"That isn't what you said to me a few months ago, baby," Malcolm said, bringing his tongue along his bottom lip. It was revolting. It made Clay's stomach clench.

Sam put the gun at Malcolm's forehead, pressing it into his skin. Clay rushed forward, his heart surging with a sudden realization. Seeing the bodies strewn around, including the ones he'd shot he knew: if he could help it, he wouldn't allow another person to die. Not in front of his daughter. He couldn't yet know what she'd seen, what kind of horrors she'd witnessed. But it was up to him to fight for another reality. "Serve and protect," echoed through his mind. "Not murder. Not murder. It was never meant to be murder."

He reached Sam who was twisting the muzzle against Malcolm's forehead, digging a red groove into the skin. Malcolm grimaced but continued to stare into Sam's eyes. Clay put a restraining hand on Sam's arm.

Sam turned her head and glared at him. "What is it, Clay? Can't you see I have some unfinished business to attend to?"

He'd always known she burned with the kind of ferocity you challenged at your own, very real, peril. Slowly, he eased his hand away from her arm.

"We got what we came here for, Sam," he said.

"You did. I didn't," Sam said, her eyes darting momentarily toward Maia. "We're meant to be equal, Clay. Don't be so selfish." She dug the gun deeper into Malcolm's forehead, giving Clay a wry smile. "Or you didn't think I was really this kind of person?"

Clay stood his ground. "No one else is dying here today, Sam."

"Listen to your little boyfriend, Samantha," Malcolm said. "He's the one giving the orders around here. I always knew you couldn't hack it, being the leader."

"You aren't helping your case," Clay snapped at Malcolm. His hatred began to boil. His fingers twitched.

"Malcolm, I've dreamed of this day a very, very long time," Sam said, enunciating carefully. "I've thought about you, about how I wanted to blow your brains out and make you pay for what you did to me. But dammit—" her shoulders shook as she allowed a small, surprised laugh to escape. "Now that I'm here—Well. You were never enough for me. Not even now."

"Sam, think about this. If you do this, you're no better than he is," Clay pleaded. "You'll have to live with it the rest of your life."

Sam's finger ticked against the trigger. Then, after a long, tense few seconds, she dropped the gun to her side and turned toward the exit of the compound. Clay's squad began to follow, with Hank pulling a bleeding Walt over his shoulders. Clay tugged at Maia. And slowly, like a flock of wounded dogs, the ones who had survived marched into the wild once more—leaving Malcolm and his horrible compound behind.

23.

"Huh. It's just a goddamn tractor-trailer." Daniels said with bewilderment as they approached the center of Ridgeway. The town was incredibly small, allowing them a view of the green energy field down every street. Brandon held his gun at the ready, walking next to Daniels, his eyes scanning, scrutinizing every dark corner. Every shadow.

"A military tractor-trailer," Marcia said, correcting Daniels.

"Well, thanks for that, Marcia," Daniels sighed. Although it hadn't been obvious, the tractor-trailer did have military insignia and was painted a dark green. Brandon didn't know what to make of its peculiar design. It had a single person cab where the engine should be, and no smoke-stack exhausts he'd been accustomed to seeing on the big trucks. The flatbed trailer carried a large spiraling obelisk-shaped spire with catwalks on two sides.

"What do you think the antenna's for?" Leland asked.

The antenna attached to the trailer bed spilled glowing light, illuminating the town. As the sun sank behind the horizon, it was their beacon: the only destination the four of them could see.

As if on cue, the clock tower in the center of town began to blare. Brandon's terror erupted and the blood drained from his face. Marcia pointed at him, snickering, "Is the top of the hour some kind of fear trigger, kid?"

Before Brandon could muster up a sarcastic response, they heard it: gunshots. Brandon dropped to his belly, gazing up at the bell tower. From just beneath the clock, he spotted a single rifle . . . pointed right at them. Bullets began to ricochet off the pavement all around. Daniels reached down and yanked him up. "We have to MOVE kid! NOW!"

Brandon dove behind a compact car parked nearby. The bullets continued to pepper down around them. The others had fallen in line behind a row of parked cars, some of them with their glass already shot out. Marcia quivered against a bumper, speaking to herself. Saying the same words over and over again. Brandon wondered if she was praying.

When the gunfire stopped, Daniels raised his arms over his head and yelled, "HEY! WE'RE HUMAN!"

Brandon felt a moment's reprieve, as if this could possibly be over. But again the bullets rang out—punching holes in the cars and busting out the rest of the glass.

"WE'RE NOT INFECTED! HEY! WE'RE HUMAN! WE'RE SAFE!" Daniels tried again, slowly rising from behind the car. The shooting tapered off. "DON'T SHOOT! H-U-M-A-N," he spelled out, waving his hand.

After a long, horrible pause—during which Brandon felt sure that the bullets would come streaming down again, Daniels yelled, "I'm coming out! Hold your fire!"

Daniels exchanged a look with Brandon. With an exaggerated movement, he stepped out into the open, waving his arms—trying to make himself look conspicuous. Without warning, bullets were raining down once more. Daniels dove back behind the cars. Marcia sputtered with involuntary laughter, pulling her own hair and all but screaming at him, "NOW WHAT?"

"I'll have to go in through the back," Daniels said. "It's the only way."

"Don't be a fool. You can't go alone," Marcia said.

"Well, I'm not gonna drag you along. I can't take care of all of us right now. And if you stay out of sight . . ." Daniels trailed off, as if he assumed what he'd said was enough. He picked up his rifle and slinked down the shadowy sidewalk to a small gap between the street-facing buildings. Once there, he darted out of sight. Another hailstorm of bullets fell around them, chilling Brandon to the bone.

Silence, and a feeling of foreboding blanketed them over the next few minutes. Marcia, Leland, and Brandon continued to exchange petrified glances. Knowing that the next shot they heard could very well mean that Daniels had been killed. It wasn't clear how many people were up there, and it certainly wasn't evident if they were "good," anyway—even if Daniels was somehow able to get to them and try to explain.

"What the hell do you think he'll say to them, anyway?" Leland asked, his voice quivering. "He's not exactly who I'd send over as a diplomat, if you know what I mean."

"Who would you send, then? Marcia?" Brandon replied, frowning at them both.

"And I suppose you think we should have sent

you?" Marcia spat. "You're nothing but a child. Look at you. Seventeen years old?"

"I'm eighteen," Brandon said, feeling rage stir within him. "And I know I'm way less crazy than all of you put together."

Brandon was unaccustomed to speaking his mind. He felt himself grow taller with it, even as Leland and Marcia exchanged glances—rueful, angry.

They heard what they'd been waiting for. Gunfire erupted from within the bell tower, the sound echoing throughout the town square. Brandon hunched down, waiting. His blood rushed in his ears. A million questions came to mind. What the hell would they do if—God forbid—Daniels had been on the wrong side of a bullet? For the first time, he imagined himself, sprawled on the roadside with Marcia, bleeding out. He remembered his sister: how rowdy she was, how angry she could get. How she would have put Marcia in her place on day one of her outrageous complaints. How she'd have said, "Who gives a fuck what you think, Marcia?"

Then it was silent again. Brandon squinted, trying to see into the darkness beneath the clock. The bell began to toll again—a warning, perhaps? Brandon glared at Marcia and Leland, suddenly blaming them for the fact that he might have to die beside them. How dare they be the only people around at the end of his life?

A bullhorn squealed with feedback, a familiar sound, scratchy but shrill.

"All right, team. That's an all clear," Daniels' amplified voice said. "Meet me on the steps of the church."

Incredulous, Brandon bounced from his hiding

spot and stared up at the clock. He waved his arms, leaping up and down with the kind of adrenaline that only comes from escaping death—again. Brandon was growing accustomed to it. It was becoming his fuel.

At the church, Brandon saw Daniels tugging a large man—similar in stature and muscle to Daniels himself. The uniformed man dragged his feet as he walked. Blood dribbled down his forehead, oozing on his lip, and he spat on the carpet just inside the church, giving Brandon a demonic, slant-eyed look. Marcia gasped as Daniels pushed the man forward.

"Check this out," Daniels said, his eyes sizzling with energy. "Seems that our military isn't here to protect us after all."

"What the hell are you talking about?" Marcia asked, her voice quivering. She began down the steps, her shoulders shaking. Her eyes wouldn't leave the bludgeoned face of the military man. "What did you do to him?"

"I had to neutralize the other one," Daniels said, still holding the man's shoulder. "But after a knock to the head, this feller here seemed to be in a more cooperative mood, if you catch my drift."

"Barbarians. You're all barbarians . . ." Marcia muttered.

The man in Daniels' clutches remained silent. Daniels had tied his hands together, and he strained at the bonds. His eyes were downcast, filled with self-pity. Brandon was too experienced to believe that the man felt remorse for anyone except himself.

"Tell them what you told me, Sonny," Daniels said, shaking him. The man whipped around. "Tell them."

The man's voice was one accustomed to

addressing a crowd. He looked directly into Brandon's eyes—something that made Brandon start.

"We're the only two at this outpost, manning the relay tower," the man said.

"And you've got supplies, you said. Over by the police station . . ." Daniels coached him.

"We've been positioned there, yes," the man said.

"Well, it looks like we'll be heading there!" Daniels said, his eyes wide, manic. He started down the steps, dragging the man with him. He was all but whistling, with a skip to his step. This was his element, the kind of war he always yearned to fight.

It was a better war. One with two sides. So unlike the war against the crazed, Brandon thought.

As they walked toward the police station, the man sputtered, "I should tell you, we do have a special guest in the jail cell. We have 'em on special orders, straight from the lieutenant."

"Oh, goody," Leland said sarcastically. "Another wild person who should be locked up in prison, who is, for some reason, going to be a part of my life." He glared at Brandon for a moment; Brandon's hands clenched into fists.

"Just thought you should know, so you don't try to blow their brains out first," the man said, grunting as he spoke.

When they arrived, Daniels reached forward and pushed open the door. And sure enough, there— seated in the dank jail cell, perched at the edge of their seat, was a person that everyone—Marcia, Leland, Brandon, and Daniels—absolutely recognized. Someone they hadn't seen in what felt like years.

24.

"You really think tying them up is going to be enough?" Sam scoffed. She was darting around the compound as Clay and the others wrapped tape and rope around wrists and ankles, sitting them along walls and fences. "Because I'm telling you, this man—this man right here—" she pointed at Malcolm, "He's a fucking monster. He's far more dangerous than most of the crazed beasts wanting to eat our flesh."

But Clay carried on, his mind one-track at this point. He'd decided that there would be no more murders, and he was resolute in this decision. As he worked, he kept looking back at Maia, who was with Alayna—holding her close. The sight warmed him and made him work with more ferocity, faster, biting at the tape and wrapping it tight.

"You're an idiot, Clay," Sam said, gesturing wildly. "You're all idiots if you think some tape and rope is going to keep this crew back. I can't imagine how you've all made it this far, actually, if you're so unwilling and unable to fight for what you need. And that's elimination, Clay." Clay continued to work.

"We don't have much time," he told her. "I want to get Maia home."

"Home. As if that's something that exists in this

world," Sam scoffed.

When Clay reached the final woman, she was noticeably shaking: her shoulders rocking back and forth. She looked up at him, revealing her youth. She couldn't have been more than twenty-two or twenty-three years old. With a soft voice, she said, "If you tie us all up, we'll just die here. You know that, don't you?"

Clay realized the truth in her words. He glanced at Alayna. A memory of his purpose warmed his heart: he was meant to protect. He was meant to be an honest hand of the law. He reached down and helped her to her feet. Sam uttered a groan that turned into a scream.

"You'll walk out with us," Clay told the woman. "All the way to the exit. Then we'll close the gate, and you'll go back and untie everyone. You can go back to the way things were, but without my daughter. All right?"

The woman nodded, biting at her bottom lip. Clay dropped her hand but gestured for her to follow. He, Alayna, Maia, and Sam left the compound to join the others. Agnes was sobbing over the death of her husband. "We weren't supposed to do this alone!" she shrieked to the sky, pounding her fists on her legs.

The sun was rising. Clay closed the gate between him and the stranger. He gave her a firm nod and turned back to his team and started back toward the hotel. Hank carried Walt over his shoulder. Walt groaned with misery, but Hank had wrapped it well and the bleeding had stopped. Hank muttered to himself as they walked, "I shouldn't have fucking tripped. All my fault. All my . . ."

Clay was grateful for the chance to carry his daughter. Feeling her relax in his arms was one of the most beautiful feelings of his life—the way she nestled her cheek against his chest and closed her eyes, her eyelashes fanning against her porcelain-like skin. Alayna kept up with him, walking without speaking. The rest of the team followed this cue, except for the occasional outburst from Sam. "I can't believe this. I just can't—"

At the hotel, Clay set Maia down at the lobby entrance. She peered inside with tentative eyes. Holding the doorframe, she glanced back at Clay— worry making her eyes heavy.

"It's okay," Clay said, coaxing her. "The hotel's clear. None of them are here. We've been sleeping here for weeks. And there's plenty of other people ... a little community of sorts."

Sam stomped up behind him, her boots landing heavily and making the porch quake. "Right. Safe. Safe until that monster comes back here to kill us all, you mean?"

Clay spun toward her, frowning. Hank clambered up the steps with Walt still over his shoulders, breaking the tension. "We're gonna need the doc!" Hank cried. "Doc? Hey?"

The doctor barreled down the steps into the brightness of the morning. He helped Hank lift Walt onto one of the lobby couches. With a flourish of his knife, the doctor cut through Walt's jeans, exposing the gunshot wound. He ordered Lane to grab his medical kit, and the others to clear out.

"The community room," Clay called, going in that direction "We'll talk about our next steps."

Sam grumbled. The people who'd stayed behind scampered down the steps, falling in as they walked toward the community room. Clay felt, suddenly, like a God amongst men. He'd guided them through a most treacherous rescue—and had done so with very few casualties. Above all, he'd found his daughter. And now he felt charged, energized, ready to proceed. With an entire company of people at his back, he felt he was building something. It wasn't Carterville, no. It was a new kind of society, for a new world.

Once in the community room, Sam stormed to the center, in full view of everyone. She tried to stare Clay down. Clay stood his ground, sensing that letting his guard down a single time in front of this volatile woman could lose him respect.

"Nobody died and made you leader here," Sam said, her voice as charged and angry as it had been with Malcolm. "Least of all, I didn't die."

Clay raised his voice to speak over Sam—to address everyone else. "It was a great group effort out there in Maia's rescue," he said. Maia peered up at him from an oversized armchair, all skin and bone in the purple fabric. "In the wake of it, and after losing Damon and Tyler, it's important we rest up and think about next steps. How we'll proceed in this, shall we say, brave new world . . ."

Clay was astonished by the way they looked at him: with the eyes of followers, seeking answers. Several of the people who'd come with Sam continued to look at him with distrust, especially as she stormed across the room, enraged. She jabbed a finger into Clay's chest, trying to shove him toward the wall.

"Let me repeat myself," she said. "You left a full-on maniac alive, and pissed off, and he's probably on the way here to kill us as we speak. Do you understand that? That if we stay at this hotel, it's only a matter of time before he finds us? I mean, that's abso—"

"You're going to need to calm down," Clay cut her off, speaking in what he hoped was a leaderlike voice. "I think what happened back there was handled . . . well, responsibly. Malcolm knows what he's up against."

"You're delusional, Clay. This is the end of the world. Nobody like Malcolm lets bygones be bygones," Sam snapped.

Sam turned back to the crowd. "If any of you assholes want to follow this man to the ends of the Earth—play nice and die of your own stupidity, then stay right here. But if you want to keep yourself alive, then come with me. We'll have our own meeting in the other room. Just a warning: It won't be all lovey dovey, nicey-nice, sunshine and puppies in there. We have to be realistic about what this world is, and what it takes to stay alive in it. You hear?"

A few people rose from their seats, most were looking at one another, incredulous. After weeks of relative harmony at the hotel, it seemed their world was shattering. But since Sam had been their leader for months, they trudged after her—knowing no other way. Clay watched them go, but was surprised that Sherman—Sam's supposed right-hand man, had remained with him.

Clay realized that Maia's eyes had closed. She was curled up in the armchair, eyes darting back and forth at a nervous dream. He scooped her up and carried her toward the lobby, where the doctor was administering aid to Walt's leg.

"Doc, this is my daughter," Clay said, feeling humbled at the words.

The doctor looked up at the undersized teenage girl. He straightened, his hands still holding bandages.

"She needs fluids, right away," he said. Snapping his fingers, he alerted Lane, organizing medical supplies across the room.

Lane came over and placed her hand on Maia's cheek. Appalled, she helped Clay walk her up the steps to a bedroom. Maia continued to shiver, making Clay forget, if only for a moment, about Sam. About Malcolm. About any of them. This was his flesh, his blood. His world.

Maia's eyes fluttered open when he and Lane tucked her beneath the sheets. She gazed up at Clay, her chapped lips parting to speak.

"Hush, now. You need to rest, honey. Let yourself sleep," Clay said, stroking her head. "The doctor's going to make sure you get what you need to feel right again. It'll take no time at all."

Maia's eyes closed again; she was asleep almost immediately. Clay marveled at it: all the times he'd spent, watching Maia trying to fall asleep in her crib. Always, when she'd finally dropped off, he'd felt relief. But this relief was something else. It was something deeper. It was as if he'd been given a new chance at fatherhood. He would take it.

25.

C lay awoke just after eight to a knock on the door. He lurched up from his bed, feeling suddenly apprehensive. He shouldn't have left Maia alone like that, all night! In the crack of the door, he saw the doctor peering at him behind thick glasses.

"What happened. What is it?" Clay demanded, jogging into the hallway, already halfway to his daughter's room.

"Slow down! Slow down," the doctor said, straining to keep up with him. "I just wanted to tell you. I've been monitoring your daughter's vitals, and they're looking better and better. She just needs a bit of sustenance, something good: protein, fat. Nothing sugary. Let her sleep as much as she can throughout the next few days. I reckon she'll be back at it in no time."

Clay's relief was palpable. He thanked the doctor who marched away to tend to Walt. Clay trotted down the steps toward the kitchen, remembering the frozen sausage they'd been keeping in the freezer. As he went in the kitchen, he nearly stumbled into Alayna, who was nibbling on a cracker. Her eyes, which had been gazing off into nothingness, immediately looked electric, charged. Excited. A small smile stretched her cheeks.

"Morning, Clay," she said.

"How are you? I haven't talked to you since, well . . . since everything happened," Clay said. He gave Alayna a short hug.

Alayna swept her dark hair from her eyes. "I'm, well. I'm good," she answered, sounding vaguely awkward. "And Maia, how is she?"

"Doc says it shouldn't be too much longer till she's back on her feet." He headed for the freezer on the far side of the kitchen, pep in his step. "I'm just going to make us some breakfast. And it looks like you're hungry, too. I can cook us all something . . ."

But as he passed the counter between the kitchen and the community room, he stopped short. On it was a large piece of paper, with the word CLAY on it. His brow furrowed; he reached for it.

"What's that?" Alayna asked. "Jesus, it's—"

"She's gone," Clay affirmed. "Sam left. And she took some people with her."

The note read,

Clay. Sheriff Clay. You'll have awakened this morning—probably worried about your daughter (of course, how could I blame you?), but you're about to learn that I've—shock!—taken half of the supplies. A good number of us left in the night, all dramatic-like. It's kind of my thing, I suppose. At least that's what ex-boyfriends (like Malcolm) have told me. You'll be happy to know that Hank, Walt and Sherman all stayed, but I've taken able-bodied men and women with me, to ride out this strange journey called life. Or whatever we're calling this, now that life seems to be scarce. Clay, our encounter was brief, strange, and bright. I'm glad I got to know you. And I'm sorry I wanted to rip your head off more than once. That's also one of my things.

All the best, and I hope we never see one another again. I would have enjoyed knowing you, honest roots and all, in a different life.

Sam.

26.

C lay half-chuckled to himself, reading the letter. The words didn't seem to be written by a delirious, maniacal woman—certainly not by the woman who'd shoved a gun into the face of a man just the day before, ready to kill. Rather, they seemed like words from a person with compassion. A person with a sense of being, of self.

"She would have been different if this all hadn't happened." Clay spoke half to himself, half to Alayna. "Maybe even a sensible person. Who knows."

"So, she just left, then?" Alayna asked, crossing her arms in front of her. "Who all went with her?"

"We have to figure that out," Clay said. "Let's gather everyone downstairs. Community room. We can figure out who's here, what they need, what they're capable of, and how we can proceed."

"But you don't even have a plan in mind," Alayna said, her eyes widening. "Shouldn't you think of something? Plot something out before—"

"I don't know, Alayna. I just don't know!" Clay flung his hands skyward, shaking his head. "I just lost half of this community. And half the supplies. Just—just grab everyone."

Alayna backed toward the doorway, hunting for the right words to say. She eyed Clay with some trepidation, as if she suspected he might explode. "We don't need her. She was a wild card," Alayna said. "You know that, don't you?"

But before Clay could answer, Alayna was gone. Clay leaned heavily on the freezer door, his head swirling. Sam had been a force of nature, a kind of secret weapon—and certainly not one he'd wanted to give up quite yet. He believed they were stronger together. And now, faced with the open road, he couldn't be sure whether either of them would fare as well on their own.

Of course, he couldn't be sure any of them would live through tomorrow.

Hank wandered into the kitchen, then. He reached for a cup of coffee, greeting Clay with sleepy, half-opened eyes. Clay clapped him on the shoulder. He had a million little, loaded things to say. But, "Thanks for sticking around, man," was all that came out.

Ten minutes later, the six or so people who'd stayed, including Sherman, Hank, Quintin, another of Sam's men, and Walt—who grimaced from the pain in his leg, but seemed to be returning to normal, Alayna, and Lane gathered in the community room. Clay assessed them, realizing that the doctor was with the children upstairs. From where he stood, he could see droplets of blood at the top of Walt's bandage.

"You probably realize we lost a few of our crew last night," Clay said, his voice seeming to echo back at him from over their silent heads. "And I'd like to thank you all for sticking around. You came here with Sam, but you seem to see a benefit in staying with me. I was sheriff of my town, I know how to protect you. I can promise you that."

Several members of the crew glanced at one another—perhaps missing friends, the ones who'd left them behind. The room was tense.

He continued, "Our ultimate goal is to reach the military base in Earlton. That's where much Carterville was sent. I'm assuming they have supplies, places to sleep, and a safe place for us, not so exposed, like we are here. We can't last in this hotel forever, as good as it's been for us."

In the back of Clay's mind, he recognized that really, the goal for going to Earlton was to find his wife, Valerie. He turned his face away from Alayna, making sure not to make eye contact. The tension between them still sizzled, making him sexually alert, almost wild. Still, his heart remained steady for Val.

"But on the way to Earlton," he said, "We have to pass through Helen. It'll give us a chance to resupply and rest. And when we get to Earlton, well, I reckon it'll be a bit more like civilization. They'll probably have their own rules. Their own practices. Who knows? Like us, you might have some people to reunite with there." His eyes lingered on Agnes, who'd left the love of her life behind in that field. Bled out and cold.

"Sam left the transport," Sherman said from the back row. He stood, speaking directly to Clay. "The old bus I used to drive when I belonged to the nearby church. Back before. We can load it up and should still fit all of us."

"Good," he said as Sherman pulled the keys from his pocket and jangled them. "That'll get us there. Let's find as much gas as we can before we load up and get on our way."

The people began to chatter. Agnes, looking weak, joined Clay and put out her hand. She shook

Clay's with a surprisingly firm grip, looking into his eyes.

"We're putting our trust in you now, Sheriff," she said. "Don't lead us down any road that puts us at risk, all right? We're not all fighters. We're just trying to get by."

Clay knew Agnes was speaking about her deceased husband. And Clay's heart grew heavy with the fact that he couldn't protect everyone, not even if he tried.

27.

C lay gently guided Maia to the bus while Sherman secured the last of their supplies in the rear storage compartment. The rest of the crew was already on board the bus—which had the words "LUTHERAN CHURCH, LOVE THEY NEIGHBOR," painted on it in big, block letters. Maia curled into one of the front seats. Her color had improved a bit since the night before, with a rosy flush on her cheeks.

"Where are we going?" Maia asked, her voice far away. It reminded Clay of when she'd been just a child, asleep on one of their family road trips. They'd tucked her into the back, beneath a blanket. All snuggled up, with just her brown hair poking from the top.

"We're going to find Mom," Clay told her, his voice low. "Try to get some sleep now. You still need your rest."

With Maia situated, Clay sat by Sherman, hunting for a map in the passenger seat compartment. Sherman's large hands tapped the steering wheel. "What are you looking for?" he asked.

Clay closed the compartment, disgruntled. "I don't know the best route to Helen."

Sherman gestured toward the road. "It's pretty

simple. If we take the highway—"

"You remember the last time we were on that highway, don't you?" Clay said. "Malcolm's compound."

"Right." Sherman pressed his lips together. Clay half-expected him to criticize, tell him he should have murdered Malcolm. That all their problems would be over, if not for his "act of compassion." But he kept his mouth closed.

"We have to find another way," Clay said, rummaging through the glove compartment.

Hank came forward, looking a bit less manic than he had carrying Walt back from Malcolm's compound. He stuck his head between Clay's and Sherman's, saying, "I know another way. My dad and I used to go hunting up there, and it avoids that stretch of highway. But it'll add another few days to the trip. Don't know if that's something you're okay with."

"I think it's our only option," Clay said, glancing back at Maia. Her eyes had closed and her chin was tucked into her chest. A few seats behind her, Alex was sitting up, another blanket wrapped tightly around his shoulders. He was similarly skeletal. Alex's head tilted to the side, trying to get a view of Maia.

"All right then," Sherman said, turning over the engine. Clay felt the bus shake around him. "I guess we'll settle in for the long haul, then. As much as I like a good road trip, I can't say I wanted this one."

Clay tried to chuckle at Sherman's joke. He turned his eyes toward the hotel, remembering when they'd first found it—weeks, but what felt like years, ago. It had been a haven. A welcome reprieve from the hell of not knowing what was next in this world.

Clay leaned his head against the back of his seat, his thoughts chaotic. Sherman drove with steady hands, leaving Clay to scout his side of the road. Despite Sherman's apparent switch to Clay's side and away from Sam, Clay decided to remain cautious. There was always the possibility that Sherman could be awaiting a signal from Sam. Some sort of revenge.

But at this moment, with his daughter slumbering behind him—and an entire crew of people in the bus—Clay had no option but accept. Outside, the mountains slashed the blue sky, and the sun crept skyward. They were miles and miles away from Helen—and days away from Earlton. But what did time even mean at the end of the world?

28.

"The gas mileage's a piece of shit," Hank said, easing the bus into the right lane, and tapping the glowing light.

Sherman leaned over, grunting, his eyes on the dash. "It's always been that way. But with the church, hell. We were never driving much farther than the park for a picnic, then back. You know what I mean?"

It was nearly eight hours since they'd left the hotel. Clay felt his stomach grumbling with hunger. He, Hank, Sherman, and Quintin, had been rotating the driving, with Clay mostly manning the passenger seat during his off-duty times—scouting their route. He scanned ahead of them for a gas station. They'd had good luck when the first of the gas had run out. But after that, they'd hit a dry spell—finding only stations long-since out of gas. Morale was sinking.

"We shouldn't have taken this long-ass road," Quintin grunted from behind Clay. He was dark and wrinkled, his jowls sagging down to his neck. He grunted acknowledgment and gnawed at what seemed to be chewing tobacco, which made Clay's stomach turn. Clay had half a mind to ask Quintin why he hadn't gone with Sam, if he was so certain that Clay's decisions were ill-informed. But he held his tongue.

Maia's head popped up behind Quintin's arm. She was bleary-eyed, rubbing at her dark circles with small fists. Clay's heart leaped at the sight of her. He stood up, nearly bumping his head on the bus's roof, slipped past Quintin and slid next to his daughter. He exchanged a glance with Alayna, who was seated near the back of the bus. It was strange that she'd been so quiet. She wasn't even talking to Lane— someone he'd assumed was a confidante.

But he was soon lost in Maia's company. She seemed more alive—a bit like her old self. She pulled a notebook from a small bag, maybe something Lane had put together for her, and showed Clay a picture of a woman with long, curly brown hair. She gave Clay a half-smile. "I just don't want to forget what she looks like, you know?"

Clay understood immediately. In the portrait, Valerie had her head tipped back laughing, wearing that familiar checkered dress, which she'd worn until it had holes under the arms.

With a surge of emotion, Clay lifted his eyes to Maia's, realizing that he hadn't yet asked her about what had happened when she'd been separated from her mother. He took her hand and looked at her, the question written large on his face. Her eyes filled with tears.

"I didn't get to say goodbye to her," Maia whispered. "They took me away so fast. I could hear her screaming my name, but I couldn't get back to her. It was—" She paused, unable to find the right words. "Daddy, I didn't know that people could be so cruel. Why did they do this to the world? Why can't they stop it?"

Clay felt helpless at his daughter's questions. As

he gaped at her, hunting for a response, he felt the bus begin to slow down. They eased off the highway onto an exit ramp. A few of the passengers began to fidget, stretching their hands above their heads. But Clay was glued to his seat, his attention on Maia.

"I don't know why they did it, honey," he whispered, his voice jumping with emotion. "I reckon people do a lot of things without thinking how they could destroy the lives of so, so many—"

"But Daddy," she blurted, her voice catching. "What if we don't see Mom again? What if we can't go back home again? What if—"

Hank cut the engine and rose from his seat, looking toward Clay. Quintin and Sherman did too, waiting for his directions. For a moment, Clay gaped at them—almost not recognizing them.

Sherman's eyes flicked toward Maia. After a small nod to Clay, he tipped his head at the door and said to Hank and Quintin, "We can sort this out ourselves, boys. Let's get the gas. Check on the situation."

Hank raised his arms to address everyone, calling out, "We're going to check out the gas station. If the coast is clear, we'll come back and let you out a few at a time. You can walk around. Go to the bathroom. See the sun for a bit before we get back on the road. But it's essential that none of you get off the bus before we give the go-ahead. Is that clear?"

The passengers grumbled agreement, slightly reminiscent of caged animals. Quintin muscled closed the bus door behind them. Maia was speaking again, in an almost conspiratorial whisper.

"And how do we know we can trust any of them?" she asked. "I mean, some of them were working for— for that woman who almost blew Malcolm's head off.

Daddy? They can't be good people."

"We have to trust them," Clay heard himself say. His gut told him to grab Maia's hand and run, run, run away from whatever kind of civilization this was, to build them a cabin in the middle of nowhere and protect them forevermore with his rifle and his killer aim. "We're all each other has, now."

Sherman appeared in the window directly beside Maia's head. Clay leaned over, opening the window to hear Sherman's report.

"Gas pumps aren't working," Sherman said. "But there's some cans in the shop. We can siphon fuel from some of the vehicles that were left behind. It won't get us far, but, hell. It'll help, won't it?"

Clay nodded. "Guess there's not much else we can do."

Sherman's eyes got stony. "Got ourselves a murder-suicide inside the shop, though, so I don't think the crew do any scavenging. Hank's salvaging all the food he can."

With that, Sherman disappeared. Quintin guarded the bus, watchful of the passengers exiting one by one. Holding his rifle at the ready, with his grizzled black and grey hair wild around his ears, he looked dangerous.

He heard Maya say something, but it was drowned by surging adrenaline. Voices, other people's—people he had never known, nor would ever know—began to echo through his brain. Clay burst up from his seat, his hands on either side of his head. He thought his eyeballs would fall from his skull.

"Dad! Daddy!" She shook at his bicep, forcing him to look at her. "Dad? You're scaring me."

Clay blinked several times and reality was back. He gave Maia a smile, gesturing with his head at the door. He could still sense voices in his skull, but he shoved it away. It wasn't something he could mention without sounding like a complete lunatic. The feeling was similar to how he'd felt at Malcolm's compound, yet more heightened. It was like a physical response to some kind of trigger.

"What do you say we take a quick walk?" Clay asked. "I think it's about time we stretch out our legs. It's still going to be a long drive, we'll regret it if we don't."

What he said was so normal, so regular, that it made Maia forget the terror she'd seen on his face. She took his hand and followed him from the bus into the afternoon light. He prayed he wouldn't feel what he'd just felt. Not again.

29.

"I can drive, dammit," Lane said, glaring into the rearview mirror at Hank, who'd been trying to tell her she was "moving a little too fast, given the curves of the road."

"Just because I'm the only woman who's up for driving," Lane continued, her eyes flashing, "doesn't mean you get to stand back there and tell me what to do. I'm a scientist. Didn't anyone tell you that, Hank? I've done things in labs you can only dream about. What was it *you* did before, huh?"

"Before what?" Hank asked, looking genuinely confused. He held up his hands, his fingers spread wide as if he was surrendering to the cops.

"You know. Before this hellhole happened. That's what—"

"Let's all calm down, now," Clay chimed in, knowing that both Sherman and Quintin were too indifferent to try and keep the peace. It hadn't really been their duty in Sam's crew. They'd been the muscle, like Damon and Al. Clay sensed there hadn't been much room for compassion. That's what differentiated Clay from people like Sam, he reminded himself. His level of compassion.

He had let Malcolm live for that reason. Because he still saw value in human life, even at the end of the world.

"Besides, we need to stop again," Lane sighed, gesturing to a rest area sign. "The tank's running way too low, and I see a lot of cars up ahead—hopefully, some with fuel in their tanks. And I think some of us needs to pee."

With a jerk, Lane brought them off of the highway and toward the parklike rest area, which looked shadowy and strange against the backdrop of the trees. At nearly eight in the evening, the sun was setting, which made Clay immediately apprehensive about getting through the night. He stood and addressed the everyone after Lane cut the engine, explaining, "Listen, gang. I don't know if it'll be safe to let you off the bus overnight. This will be it for a while. We'll scout the area to make sure it's safe, and then I want all of you to do your business quickly. Then spread out and see if you can scavenge any supplies from these abandoned cars. We're going to need them. We always do."

After Sherman gave a thumbs up, Clay led everyone from the bus. Once out in the open, Clay reached for Maia's hand. Maia was taking stock of the other passengers. Alex was among them, walking with a slight spring in his step. Their eyes met and held each other's briefly, then Clay led Maia further toward the bathrooms. Her hair swung forward, and Clay was unable to read her expression.

He wondered if Alex reminded her of the bad times, locked up in the hotel with Malcolm. He still had so much find out about his daughter's ordeal.

Then Clay felt it. The voices, hammering away in his mind. Some of them seemed more articulate this time, calling out for help. "I'm still here," one of them came, sounding almost demonic, raspy. "I'm here—"

Clay bent over at the waist, gripping his knees as the voices rang through his mind. Maia stopped and stared fearfully at the expression on his face. Her own had was a sour green color. "Daddy? Are you— are you all right?"

With all the strength he could muster, Clay forced his face to relax. He pressed back against the darkness in his mind, trying to drown out the voices. He nodded and straightened up. He had no idea what this chaos was, but he had to learn to control it, to push it away when he needed to. Whatever it was, it couldn't affect his life.

"Sure. Just a little queasy from the bus," he lied, reaching again for her hand. "You know I always got sick on long car rides."

Clay walked Maia toward the woman's bathroom without speaking. He could still feel the voices in his head. Maia continued to look up at him apprehensively.

"Wait here," Clay told her, reluctantly releasing her hand. "I just have to make sure it's clear."

As he pushed into the bathroom, he saw a flash of light in his mind's eye. Then it felt as if his skin was on fire, a lighter tracing his forearms and his neck. With the burning sensation, the voices were more insistent. He knocked the side of his head with his fist.

"Fuck off," he muttered, the epithet echoing off the tile. He kicked at each of the bathroom stalls, finding only unused—a bit dusty—but overall clean toilets. The crazed hadn't been here. And with the only other entrance a small window near the highest corner of the room, he felt safe letting Maia in.

While he waited for Maia outside, the voices began to escalate—words streaming one on top of the other, like water in a cascade, coursing through Clay's mind. "Get out of here. Get out—get away!" the voices cried. Bringing both hands to his ears, Clay stepped toward the men's door—just a few feet away. He tapped on the door. Immediately after the tap, he heard the stirring of bodies—seemingly all pressed together, like some sort of maggot hive. The moaning echoed across the cinderblocks. He backed away from the door; The crazed were inside.

And that meant he would leave it alone. Not bother them. The attention span of the crazed seemed to be rather short. Seconds after the knock, they would surely forget it ever happened and return to their hive mind.

Clay heard rustling behind him and spun around. It was Lane, her large backpack over her shoulder. Her face was preoccupied, frustration on her crinkled brow. When she saw him standing in front of the women's room door, she gave him a silent wave and headed for the men's bathroom.

Clay caught her just in time. But before he could explain, wooziness struck and he was shaking at the growing anger of the voices inside his head.

"What's going on?" Lane asked him, raising an eyebrow.

"The Men's is . . . out of order," he said. "You can use the women's as soon as Maia's done."

Lane cocked her head inquisitively. "Clay, everything's out of order. It's the end of the fucking world."

Clay's eyes closed as another wave of horrible voices clamored. His stomach clenched and he nearly vomited. The crazed inside the men's room began to howl again and Lane immediately reached for the neutralizing device in her backpack. Clay tried to stop her. But before he could, Lane kicked the door open and a dozen crazed boiled out of confinement.

Without a second of delay, Lane cranked the device, forcing each and every one of the crazed to fall to the ground—their grotesque green tongues flopping around their chins and cheeks, blood oozing from small slashes in their arms and legs. Lane's eyes were flat, soulless as she returned the device to her backpack.

There was instant silence, both around him and inside his head. He realized that the voices had stopped when Lane neutralized the crazed. His eyes searched the bodies—really analyzing them in ways he hadn't since the first few kills. Three women wearing ratty-looking, plaid dresses. One of the men was Amish, bearded and garbed in black. People. Clay reminded himself of it. These were people.

Clay, Maia, and Lane were back on the bus ten minutes later. As Clay climbed up the steps, Maia hung back, speaking with Alex. Clay sat in the driver's seat, his hand on the wheel, watching Alex. He was holding up a necklace. The metal glinted in the last of the setting sun. As Clay's eyebrows furrowed, Alex hung the necklace around Maia's neck, clasping it under her hair. Maia offered a small smile, a secret smile, to the boy.

"What are you waiting for?" Sherman grunted at Clay from above his left shoulder, interrupting his thoughts.

Clay turned back toward the road. He felt the bus dip and creak as Alex and Maia and the other stragglers boarded and got situated. He turned over the engine and drove them out of the rest area.

It was almost dark.

30.

I t was just after eleven and Clay was wide awake. Most of the group was slumbering in the darkness of the bus behind him. Above, the stars sparkled at the tip-tops of the trees, and the mountains were dark shadows against the night sky. With the voices no longer invading his mind, he felt almost meditative.

Maybe this was the first peace he'd felt in years.

Alayna appeared beside him, perching at the edge of the passenger seat. Surprised to see her after not speaking the entire day, Clay greeted her with a smile, gesturing for her to come closer. She did, bringing her body against his. Her warmth was calming, making Clay's muscles relax He felt her sigh. But before he could grow used to it, the hug was over, and she pulled back, a full foot away.

"Maia finally fell asleep," Alayna told him, her voice a whisper. "She looked better today. Stronger."

Clay nodded. "I'm making sure she eats. I don't think she really wants to, but who would after what she's been through?"

Alayna nodded, sliding her hand along her stomach. Clay's eyes drew back to the road for a particularly curvy stretch of highway; the bus lurched side to side for a moment, the heads of the passengers lolled back and forth in the rear-view mirror.

"We've got enough gas to get us there, if my calculations are correct," Clay said, tapping the gas gauge.

"Good thing, Sheriff," Alayna said. "And it looks like we're making excellent time, as well."

"Should be there by dawn," he replied. "And when we get there, we can get those tests run on you. See what kind of nanite damage we're dealing with. Shouldn't keep us in Helen too long. But I think it'd be better to know. Don't you?"

"Right," Alayna said, her voice hesitant. "I wanted to ask you about your symptoms. Have they gotten worse? Better?"

"In the last week or so, the rage has subsided. I'm no longer trying to tear Alex's head off, for example," he said, trying to lighten his own mood. "But the strength and endurance has come on tenfold. I feel like I could run twenty miles right now. Up a mountain, even. I could drive all night, and I will. But there does seem to be one side effect . . ." he began, trying to find the confidence to tell her about the voices. It was hard to describe without being suspected of poor mental health. He imagined Sherman and Quintin pushing him aside, explaining to the crew that he'd grown "schizophrenic." That they couldn't trust a leader like that.

But as he searched for the turn of phrase, Alayna blurted, "Clay, I need to tell you something," her voice low, and heavy with meaning.

Oh God, he thought. *Alayna's hearing voices, too.* Soon, perhaps, their brains would be mush—nothing but the chaotic voices of the crazed, trying to take them over. He squeezed the steering wheel tighter.

"I'm pregnant," she said, staring at the road.

In the silence that followed, an absolute physical reaction tore through him. He bumped the bus toward the side of the road, nearly sliding off the edge of the pavement. He got the bus back under control, his heart bursting in his chest.

"Please, be careful, Clay," she whispered.

Clay heard emotion behind her words. He glanced at her and saw a single tear glitter down her cheek. He recognized, suddenly, that he'd been pushing to find Maia, to fulfill his own selfish life, and he hadn't noticed that Alayna's "illness" was, well, very much related to him.

"Wow." He paused, hunting, and gliding his tongue along his teeth. "How are you, um . . . how do feel about it?" he finally managed.

She shrugged slightly and rested her chin in a palm.

"Are you sure it's not just the nanites?" Clay asked. "Like, could it possibly be them making you feel this way?"

"Lane and the doc ran the test," Alayna told him, her voice small and childlike. "There's a strong chance, though, that I'm both pregnant and infected . . . and that the baby will be infected, too. I don't know what that means. I don't know what it means to bring a baby into this world like that . . ." She trailed off, her shoulders shaking.

Clay pressed his lips together, another layer of worry falling over him. With his daughter sleeping behind him, he'd felt safer, sure. But now, with another child, his child, growing inside Alayna—preparing to enter a world he didn't fully understand—he had no words to explain his fear, even to himself. Silently, with one hand still on the steering wheel, Clay took Alayna's hand and squeezed it, letting her know—no matter what—that she wasn't alone in this. But still, he was silent. He couldn't imagine what words could possibly mean enough.

31.

C lay drove the bus into Helen at dawn the
following morning, his eyes still wide open—
nearly popping from his skull as he set the
emergency break in front of the Helen Diner. The rest
of the drive in, he hadn't spotted a single crazed. In
fact, Helen was a portrait of normalcy. The lines and
lines of suburban-looking houses, all matching in
light brown bricks and safe, slabbed roofs, was
reassuring. Alayna slumbered beside him, still
holding his hand. Her unconscious mind still needed
him.

But with a stab in his gut, Clay realized that—
despite their circumstances—he was still committed
to Valerie. He had to find her. He didn't know what
would happen then, with a baby coming. He could
explain, maybe, what had happened between him
and Alayna. It had been the end of the world. Maybe
infidelity didn't matter anymore, not the way it had
before. And a new human life was never bad.

Although a human life, infected with the
nanites? He had no idea what that meant.

Clay's ever-changing ragtag crew stood at the
entrance of the diner, peering out across the town.
Helen was bright in the new sunlight, like a bubble
of hope in an otherwise rocky hellscape. Alex

maneuvered through the group, getting closer to Maia. He was just a few inches taller and looked meek, almost alien beside her. Lane alone, stoic, while Agnes and Alayna were talking to one another. Walt hobbled along next to Hank, an arm over Hank's shoulder and holding onto him tightly as they fumbled toward the door. Walt cackled, pointing at the sign outside the diner.

"Think they still have 50-cent milkshakes on Tuesdays?" he asked. "Because damn, I could really use one."

After Walt's wisecrack, they went in, Alayna and Agnes busying themselves at the coffee maker. The place filled with the nutty scent of brewing coffee. Clay found himself at a booth alone, while Sherman and Quintin took a booth near the door. Their hands remained on their rifles. It was clear the rest of the group felt vaguely apprehensive about Sherman and Quintin. They were almost overbearingly masculine, eliminating any chance for light chatter. The rest of the team sipped their coffee quietly, with the light of day streaming in from the large pane window, casting ominous shadows throughout the diner.

It felt like it had been ages since Clay had been in Helen. Since they'd parted ways with what now felt like lifelong friends—even though their fellowship lasted only a handful of weeks. But, when time spent together was as arduous as theirs was, time is exaggerated completely. Damn, he missed them.

"Clay, this place seems perfect," Agnes said, her eyes bright as she settled a cup of coffee in front of him. "I didn't see a single one of *them* on the way in. I was thinking, well . . . Why don't we secure the perimeter here? In Helen?"

Clay felt the truth of her words. He leaned

heavily against the back of the booth, considering her words. Her bottom lip quivered, showing her nerves.

"I mean, it just seems silly to head out to someplace we might not get to, when we could just be safe here. And goodness knows, I like all of you," Agnes said, slapping her hands lightly on her thighs. "We could build something here, for God's sake. Something we could be proud of."

Clay sipped his coffee, closing his eyes. He felt the others' agreement. Still, Sherman and Quintin didn't speak.

"I understand that mentality. I really do," Clay began, wondering how he should verbalize such a selfish feeling. "But I have to make it to Earlton. I have to find my wife. Valerie."

He could see the way words affected Alayna. Her shoulders slumped, and she stared at the ground. But in the silence that followed, it was Alayna who agreed with him.

"Actually, I want to get to Earlton, as well," she said, addressing the crowd. "My . . . girlfriend could be up there. Megan. I wouldn't mind making sure she's all right. Not that I have my hopes up. But . . ."

Maia spoke up from her seat beside Alex. "We have to find mom. Wherever you go, Dad, I go," she said.

"I think we should head to Earlton, yeah," Alex agreed, sounding more assured than he had in the weeks since they'd found him. His voice was even more masculine, rather than the child-like squeaking when they first found him near death.

Others nodded their heads. Lane muttered something about finding Marcia and Leland—her people. Agnes made peace with it, returning to the coffee machine to brew another pot. Sherman and Quintin remained in their own booth, neither voicing an opinion. The road with Sam had been a far different trail, he supposed. But they were outsiders in a world where all of them—each and every one— were outsiders, outliers. They had to band together. He couldn't cast doubt on them just for not being sociable.

"All right, guys," Clay said gruffly. "We'll settle into Helen for a day or two. Gather supplies where we can. Then we'll head up to Earlton."

Over the tops of the heads, his eyes connected with Lane's. With a distinct nod of her head, she turned from the diner, tugging Alayna along as they headed toward the lab, Lane steering Alayna with her hand in the small of her back. Alayna looked meek, fatigued, with her chin tucked down. Clay wanted to run after them—to be there when Alayna found out her true fate. But he stayed where he was, sipping his coffee. Trying not to feel.

32.

T he next morning, Clay and Alayna sat across from one another at the diner, digging into biscuits and gravy with a side of silence, each lost in thought. Several of the others were still slumbering at the hotel across the street; Sherman and Quintin had taken it upon themselves to scavenge for supplies. Clay had discovered Sherman lacing up his boots around four-thirty that morning, muttering to himself. "We have to get a move on," Sherman had told Clay, his eyes dark. "I don't trust this place. Not without a perimeter. Not without a plan."

The diner door jangled in an almost overly friendly way, forcing Clay's eyes up. Sherman and Quintin came in.

"Guys," Clay said, standing to greet them. Their allegiance to him was generating still more strength in him. "How did you make out today?"

"Filled the tank," Sherman said. "And found about twenty gallons of gas cans at various houses, which we strapped to the back of the bus."

"That should get us the rest of the way there," Clay said optimistically. "What about supplies? Food?"

"All packed in the back of the bus," Sherman said. "We're good for a while, and we'll have stuff to tide us over when we get to Earlton . . . if the worst has happened."

The worst? Clay felt the truth of these words. That they had no possible way of communicating with Earlton before they arrived. They could be heading toward a ghost town.

"I guess we have to hope for the best," Clay said, feeling his throat constrict.

Lane bolted through the door, holding a large file of papers. Her eyes were on Alayna, who seemed to scrunch into a ball. "If you're looking for supplies," she said, speaking directly to Sherman and Quintin, "There's loads more in the lab. We barely touched it when we were locked down there. Now, if you could get the hell out of here? I have some information for Alayna, here. And I prefer confidentiality."

Without even a glimmer of curiosity, Sherman and Quintin removed themselves from the diner, pressing the door closed so that it didn't jangle. Lane sat next to Clay, across from the deflated Alayna and straightened the papers on the table in front of her. She had an air of professionalism, as if she'd often sat down with patients, preparing to tell them their fate.

As if on cue, Alayna began to cry. She wiped at her eyes then laid her hand on her stomach, feeling at the heaviness growing within.

"Just tell me," Alayna said. "I can't take it anymore."

Lane reached forward and caught Alayna's hand, giving it a reassuring squeeze.

"Alayna, it's going to be okay," she murmured. "I promise you that."

Alayna sniffed. "So, I don't have the nanites?"

Lane's shoulders sagged. "No, you do have them,

Alayna. I'm sorry to say. But they're the same variety that's pulsing through Clay right now. And look at him. He's a portrait of fitness."

Alayna snickered, clearly unsure if she should feel frightened or relieved. "Interesting assessment of our sheriff," she offered.

"Alayna, you're going to be fine. We all will, as long as we keep away from all those assholes out there trying to eat us," Lane replied.

"So, what now?" Alayna asked. "I mean, I'm pregnant, and I have the nanites. But the baby's going to be fine? The nanites won't affect the pregnancy? I mean, I've never even been pregnant before. I don't know what's normal, in any capacity."

At this, Lane hesitated. "The truth is, we don't really know how the nanite technology will affect the baby. As you know, the nanites are incredibly new to the human ecosystem, and we have absolutely no tests or even reports on the effects on fetuses or pregnant women. That was never a part of the plan."

Alayna's eyebrows furrowed. "So, what are you telling me? What should I do?"

"That's all I can tell you," Lane said. It was clear she wouldn't tell Alayna anything else. Lane cleared her throat. "I better get to packing up the lab. I'm not going so far without my instruments this time around. No way."

Lane rose from the booth, giving them both a firm nod. When the diner door closed behind her, Clay turned his eyes back to Alayna, ignoring the half a biscuit getting cold next to her.

"She hardly told me anything at all," Alayna said. "I already knew I'm pregnant. And now I know I'm definitely infected. But she hasn't told me how to handle it. How to live, to protect this baby . . ."

"You just have to do what you've been doing," Clay said, putting both of his hands over hers. He felt certainty as he spoke. As if he could convince her that she could defeat an entire pack of the crazed single-handedly if she had to. "Getting sleep. Eating well. Caring for our baby. I'm sure Lane will monitor you, even if only for the strange scientific experiment of it all."

Alayna chuckled at the truth of this. "Even if it all falls apart, Clay. I'm glad it's yours," she confessed.

Alayna stood from the booth, and left, leaving Clay alone, staring into the dregs of his coffee.

33.

W hen it was time to get back on the road, Alayna volunteered to drive. Her eyes were resolute, her thoughts collected. She said to Clay, "I just need to get my mind off it somehow. Driving helps. It always has."

Sherman sat beside her, radiating a kind of quiet confidence, while Clay sat one row back. To his right, Maia and Alex were talking quietly together. Clay assessed them without speaking. He hadn't witnessed his daughter socializing in months, and the thought that she needed anyone else gave him a strange feeling. The spoke in the colloquialisms of young teenagers, hoping to take on the world. Even at the end of it.

"I mean, you know what he was like. That guy, Mark? Back at the hotel?" Alex asked Maia about people Clay would never hope to know. "He was always so shy and distant, right? But then when my dad told him to tie me up, you'll never guess what he did. He didn't even hesitate. He was like an obedient dog, the ropes were so tight they dug into my skin. Look, you can still see the rope burns."

Maia's face blanched. "Jesus," she whispered. "I didn't know he had it in him."

"Weird, how we'll probably never see those

people again," Alex said. "Like, I'll never see my dad again. The idiot raised me, you know?" Alex's eyes turned toward Clay; Clay pretended he wasn't listening. "You're lucky, with the dad you got. Came all the way to save you. He went at me for weeks, trying to figure out where you were. I thought he was gonna kill me."

"Him? His bark is worse than his bite," Maia laughed.

"Maybe to you," Alex said, sounding almost accusatory now. "Well, it doesn't matter. We're all safe now."

"And we're going to find my mom." Maia sounded confident. "And you know you can stay with us, probably. When we get there . . ."

Alex appeared bewildered by that. His Adam's apple bobbed as he swallowed. Before he could speak, Alayna yelled, "Hey, Clay. Look, gas station, off to the right!"

Clay bounced up and peered through the bus's windshield.

"Are we stopping?" she asked.

Feeling anxious, Clay nodded. Alayna curved down the exit ramp to the station below. As they slowed, Clay heard Alayna mutter something to Sherman and jerk her chin. A single moped sat ghost-like, leaning near one of the pump islands.

"What the hell?" Clay gasped. He sprang toward the door, opening it as Alayna braked. He barreled toward the moped. When he reached it, his heart sank. He knew this moped. Remembered it from when they'd split off from their old friends.

"Oh my god," Alayna said from behind him. "I can't. I can't even." She bent forward, almost retching.

Clay slid his hand down her back, trying to comfort her. But his heart was heavy, wondering who might have died. Why else would they leave a moped behind?

"Daddy? What's wrong?"

Maia's voice brought him back to the present. He waved at the crew, trying to hide the fear in his eyes. "Maia, honey. Alex. Please, stay on the bus until we figure out if the coast is clear, all right?"

Maia obeyed. Alex followed suit. They pressed their noses against the window, curious.

Sherman and Quintin joined Clay and Alayna. "It's fully gassed," Sherman said, tapping the tank. "Must have just gassed up."

"But no supplies with it." Alayna shook her head. "God, this doesn't look good, Clay. I don't like it at all."

"I know. But we can't . . . we don't know what might have happened. We can't go there. Not now. Lots of things happen on the road." He scanned the perimeter of the station, where the pavement met the trees beyond. Clearing his throat, he said, "Let's just get the gas and get on our way, all right? It's all we can do. It's all we can ever do—move forward."

34.

"Ridgeway. Never heard of it," Clay said from the driver's seat. From the highway, they'd spotted the small village—only a half-mile across, maybe—with a stark green energy field sizzling around it. The roadway seemed to dive all the way through the tiny village; the small town nothing more than a speed bump on their path to Earlton. "Get Lane up here. Stat," he told Sherman.

Lane joined Clay and said, "You can see all the way through that town," and leaned closer to the window. "I wonder why the hell they would keep something . . ."

"Something like what?" Clay asked.

"You remember. The reason Carterville had an energy field was to protect the device. But Carterville's a decent-sized place. This little village—what is it? Ridgefield?"

"Ridgeway," a now awake Alayna corrected her. She blinked sleepy eyes, trying to take stock of their surroundings.

"Right. Whatever. It's far too small to hide anything important," Lane said, folding her arms across her chest.

"And there's no candy store slash lab in Ridgeway?" Clay asked apprehensively. If their only person connected to the world of energy fields didn't know why there was one in Ridgeway, it was probably something they should refrain from investigating.

"Not that I know of. And trust me, they gave us a run-down of the other labs, just in case," Lane said, flipping her dark hair behind her shoulder. "I think it's best we go around it."

"That'll put us almost a day off schedule," Quintin said. "This is the most direct way to Earlton off the interstate. We don't want to run out of gas again, do we? Put us in a bad situation, somewhere on the road—some ten hours away from our destination?"

"If you want to take that risk." Lane shrugged.

"I kind of agree with Lane," Alayna said. "Even if we do get through the force field—which, mind you, is something that almost killed us before—there's no way to know who's on the other side. I mean, it could be filled with *them*, you know? And how will we get back out? Too many variables."

Quintin leaned toward Alayna, a snarl on his face. "And you're saying we can't handle more of those fucking crazed, after all we've been through?"

Alayna didn't reply. Clay recognized the sizzling tension, an inevitable side effect of the road. Characters, butting heads. He couldn't imagine adding another hour to their trip, let alone ten or more. And on top of that, the bus hadn't been maintained very well. It was beginning to grunt and belch fumes, chugging when Clay pressed the gas pedal too hard.

"Going around might kill the bus," Clay said.

"The trip through the force field definitely would," Alayna replied.

The bright green energy field flickered and

dimmed. Clay's adrenaline surged. He pressed the gas pedal with a bit too much pressure, and the bus chugged in protest. The energy field came back up. But within another second, it shut down altogether.

"I guess the town has made up our minds for us," Clay said, his grip on the wheel tightening. "We go forward."

35.

C lay slammed his foot on the brake when the bus was just a few feet away from where the energy field had been. He'd had a sudden image of Ralph, devastated after his wife had splattered across the energy field outside of Carterville when it turned on.

"Keep going!" Sherman all but ordered.

But Clay cut the engine, directing his finger toward the door. "We're going to walk across the barrier," Clay said, not looking at Sherman. He refused to explain himself. He felt Alayna's eyes on him and she whispered a single word, "Ralph." Clay knew then that she felt the weight of the memories just as much as he did.

"All right, everyone," Clay said to the crew behind him. He noticed Walt's head lolling against Hank's shoulder: he was in and out of consciousness. "We're going to walk just a short distance. Hank, can you help Walt across? When you're safe on the other side, I'll hop on the bus, and drive it over. Then we'll drive to the other side of town."

Maia blinked up at him, her jaw set. Alex, beside her, looked less brave—his eyes glittered with fear. But Clay was sure. He wasn't going to make the same mistakes again. That was a part of surviving.

The ragged-looking crew straggled across the boundary. Sherman and Quintin weren't armed, looking vaguely naked without weapons. Alayna's hands remained on her midriff, but her step was cautious.

When everyone had crossed the invisible threshold, Clay started the bus over the line— holding his breath until he was on the other side.

"All right, folks. Looks like we've made it. Now, let's get back on, and get through the town," Clay said. "Not too much longer now."

"Look!" Alex shrieked, pointing a skeletal finger.

The others turned to see ten or eleven of the crazed charging at them.

This pack of crazed was off somehow. Their legs were literally worn down, apparently from friction. Their teeth were cut out of the tops of their mouths, a horror Clay had seen before. Clay leaped in front of the team, herding them back to the bus.

"We should have stayed on the bus! Goddammit! Clay—"

"Not now, Alayna!" Clay exclaimed. "Jesus. We don't have time for this!"

Then they were surrounded by the crazed. The monsters formed a ring seven or eight feet out from the team. Oddly, the crazed didn't seem to be in a hurry. They'd lured Clay's people into a trap, and they seemed to be savoring it. Their puss-covered tongues lolled over their chins and their eyes rolling wildly. Maia clung tightly to Clay's arm.

Clay reached for his holster and pulled the only weapon he was carrying. His revolver only held six bullets. "I gotta make these count—" he grunted.

Maia let go of him, huddling close to Alayna. Agnes' face was stony. Sherman and Quintin were grim, preparing to fight hand and foot for survival. Clay imagined they could tear a few of the crazed in two.

Clay shot at a crazed between them and the bus, punching a hole in the monster's forehead. The crazed dropped, leaving a gap in the circle. Another crazed filled it immediately. With no better option, Clay shot that one, and then the next, hoping that the gap in the circle would remain long enough to let someone through to the bus.

Sherman leaped across the buffer and put his fist through a crazed's head. The crazed flew back, taking three others to the ground with him. But within seconds, the monsters were back up and were flying toward Sherman with more ferocity. Clay shot down another one. But that was four of his bullets—and he sensed the impending doom.

Before he could think, before he could really recognize what was happening, the gunfire started outside of the kill box they were trapped in. On cue, crazed heads exploded—splattering blood and brains everywhere. Maia screamed, closing her eyes tightly. The carnage continued, crazed dropping around them. The horrible groaning, moaning, and howling of them tapered off.

After what seemed a horrible eternity—twenty or thirty seconds, not a single crazed was standing. A voice Clay recognized blared from a megaphone.

"HEY! IDIOTS! GET THE HELL BACK ON THE BUS AND GET INTO TOWN."

It was Daniels. Clay grinned. He'd made it. In this wild and horrible world, one of his own had made it. Laughing, he dropped his arm over his daughter's shoulders, bringing her closer to him.

"I SAID STEP ON IT," Daniels squawked. "BUT

ALSO, YOU ARE IDIOTS. CLAY, YOU ESPECIALLY. IT'S GOOD TO SEE YOU, DAMMIT. IT'S REALLY GOOD TO SEE YOU."

36.

C lay parked the bus in the middle of the square, near a bell tower. His passengers were silent, still stunned at the ferocity of the crazed—and their unlikely demise. Daniels was waiting for them, his hands on his hips, and his chin high. One by one, Clay's crew climbed off the bus and vied to shake Daniels' hand.

"My God, Alayna!" Daniels cried when he saw her. He wrapped his arms around her, hugging her tight. They met like old friends, or like family members. Not like people who'd fought and bickered throughout much of their journey.

After a long moment, he was on to the next person—shaking Agnes' hand, introducing himself. His voice was jovial, almost childlike. Clay wondered where the others were. Perhaps Daniels was manning the town alone?

"Maia!" Daniels cried, seeing Clay's daughter. He swept her off the ground into a hug and said to Clay, "You did it, my man. You found her. That must have been a wild ride. I'm sure you have quite a story to tell."

"Not one to be told now," Agnes smiled at him. "We're exhausted."

"And what of you strapping guys?" Daniels

asked, offering his hand to Quintin and Sherman. They shook his hand. Both were a full head taller than Daniels, who was usually the tallest person in any group. "Where did they find the two of you?"

"Where else?" Sherman not giving anything away. "On the road. Where we've been since this all began."

Daniels' smile faltered. Releasing Sherman's hand, he turned at last to Clay, his emotion at the reunion plain to see. They came together like brothers.

Daniels said, "I really wasn't sure if I'd ever see you again, my friend. But now I know I was foolish to ever doubt you, wasn't I?"

"You should have made it to the base weeks ago," Clay said, releasing Daniels' hand. "What happened? And where is everyone?"

Daniels cringed. "We ran into a few snags along the way, not unexpected."

Alayna interjected, "We saw one of the scooters, abandoned at a gas station. What—who?" She faltered under the weight of the question.

"Ah, yeah," Daniels looked embarrassed. "We got boosted, is all. We went in to gather supplies and someone stole all but one of the scooters. We've been on foot ever since. But, yeah. We found this place along the way, as you can see."

"This place, it safe?" Clay asked, looking at Daniels with an element of distrust. "The minute we got in, the crazed were on us. We wouldn't have been able to stop them, even if we were all armed. Not without the device."

"I saw you coming up the road miles away," Daniels said. "I Didn't know it was you until you were practically at our door. A Lutheran bus? Ha. The irony's not lost on me, at the end of the world. But anyway, the energy field is powered by twin generators. I had to let you in, but I saw the crazed coming. No more than we could handle, though." Daniels winked. "We've got this place pretty well sealed. Any crazed that get in get their heads blown off. Well, you saw it."

"That we did," Sherman agreed.

Clay tried to parse this new information, feeling like it couldn't possibly be reality. Ridgeway. Their next stop on a path to—what? What kind of future?

"What about the others?" Clay asked again, turning back to Daniels. "Brandon? Marcia? Jacobs, even?"

"They're all here," Daniels said solemnly. "We're all safe. And, imagine this. We have a special, surprise guest for you to meet. C'mon."

37.

D aniels led the others up the steps and into the church. The building was historic, made of limestone, with a lobby featuring several stained glass depictions of Jesus, the Virgin Mary, the shepherds, and the Wise Men. Clay stared at one of the shepherds tending his flock. He felt such a kinship with him. To the dedication in the man's eyes. Back then, surely, with wolves howling in the hills, highwaymen poised to murder you, death seemed just as imminent as it did now.

"It's the safest place for us right now," Daniels said. "Or the place where we can all kinda do our own thing. Plus, who wouldn't want to live in a church for a little while. Gang, look who's here!"

Clay saw scattered people in the pews—not in any order and keeping a healthy distance from one another. Brandon's head poked up from between the pews. His hair was long and straggly, and his crooked smile lit up his face. He leaped from the pew toward Clay, who was surprised at the maturity he'd found in just a few weeks. His muscles were firmer, his cheeks were gaunter, his eyes were older.

Clay hugged him tight, slapping on his back. "Good to see you, kid," Clay said sincerely. "I bet she wouldn't recognize you."

"Yeah, sure," Brandon laughed. "I haven't changed that much."

"You'd be surprised how much," Clay said.

Clay found Marcia, then Jacobs with relief. They'd made it this far. He nodded at them both. Lane wrapped Marcia up, crying and laughing at once, kissing her on the cheek.

Brandon shook hands with Sherman, Quintin, Hank, and Walt. When he reached Maia, he stopped, his eyes dancing.

"Well, well, well. Where the hell did you come from!" he asked, raking his curly, wild hair with his fingers.

Maia giggled like the teenage girl she was. She adopted a flirtatious pose, youthful and vital. Behind her, Alex's eyes burned with anger and confusion.

"Brandon! What the heck?" she exclaimed.

But Clay's eyes were drawn across the pews, toward the corner of the church. There, seated alone, was a woman he hadn't seen in months. A woman he'd worked alongside for years, ever since he'd first taken the sheriff's position in Carterville. A woman he'd trusted, confided in, and followed blindly, even as it seemed she'd moved their town ever closer to the ends of the Earth.

"Lois Washington," Clay's voice echoed.

The mayor of Carterville—or ex-mayor—Lois, got up as quickly as her sixty years would allow. Her jet-black hair—dyed, surely, made her look almost demonic. Her eyebrows were dark lines that gave her a perpetual frown. As she got closer, Clay realized with a start, that while he knew his people's stories, and he knew Daniels' situation generally, he couldn't begin to comprehend Lois'.

Maia and Brandon were giggling together. "I have to admit, I thought about you a few times on this weird journey," Brandon said. "Course, I knew you were Clay's daughter. But I didn't—well. I wasn't sure—"

"If he'd find me?" Maia asked. "But he's my dad, Brandon."

Brandon assessed Clay. "He looks a bit different than when I last saw him. Stronger, maybe. Stands up straighter. He seems, I dunno, angrier?"

Maia tilted her head, as if she were seeing her father for the first time. She wondered how much her disappearance had changed him. If he was angrier, more volatile because of the stress of trying to find her. Brandon gazed at her with large, hungry eyes— eager to hear her speak.

And Alex's face was bitter. He steeled himself to meet this interloper.

But then Clay's voice thundered across the pews. At Lois Washington, the ex-mayor of Carterville.

"You must have seen her, Lois. You must know where she is," Clay's rage was palpable. "Where is my wife? Where is Valerie?"

38.

"Oh, Clay," Lois's pose was prayerful, her expression beatific. "Clay, I never imagined I'd see you again. I thought you were gone, like so many others. God, we've lost so many. It's why I love being in this church. I spend all day praying to *Him* to save the ones who've become . . . changed. What a terrible, horrific situation—"

"Lois," Clay cut her off. "Out with it. What's going on with Val? Where is she? Is she all right?"

"It's just . . . it's not what we thought would happen, Clay. You have to understand that. But you also need to know that I did everything in my power to save her, Clay. But it was too late. Everything about this life has been too late . . ."

Clay tensed, stunned. Still, he tried to make sense of her words. "She's . . . gone?" he gasped, shaking his head. The rage began to flood his veins. The sensation was similar to the initial nanite infection—anger rising and powering him. "What the hell do you mean, *save her?*"

Lois unclasped her hands, licked her lips, then smiled warmly. "You remember the colonel, don't you, Clay? Colonel Scott Wallace?"

Clay remembered. The man had a boorish manner when he'd marched into town, demanding the impossible and ordering his townspeople into buses to be taken away. Clay remembered, for sure. The chaos was unforgettable.

"What the hell did he do?" Clay spat. "Tell me!"

"Well, the colonel obtained a device that the scientists had been working on—" Lois gestured at Marcia, Leland, and Lane. Clay's eyes didn't waver. He remained focused on Lois. "I'm not sure how he found it. But anyway, he had heard that the device would be an appropriate way to control the crazed. That he could manipulate them—make them walk, or run or even duck. Which, I know, sounds absolutely nuts! But apparently, they really *were* cooking up something like that—"

"It's the whole reason this happened, you idiot," Marcia snapped, her eyes burning. "We've told you that countless times this past week. We wanted to make a better, more useful weapon—"

"Let her finish." Clay glared at Marcia. The silence that followed was punctuated by Maia sobbing quietly at the loss of her mother.

"We were here in Ridgeway, working," Lois said. "And the colonel had this idea to bring some of the crazed into the town square, to test it. To see how well the device worked. The crazed were corralled at first, but each test the device passed made the colonel more reckless. He decided to introduce humans into the testing and surrounded the field with people. Valerie was there. She didn't have a lot of fear at that point. She was behind the fence and for the most part, her mind wasn't on anything around her. She'd been separated from your daughter, and . . ." Lois trailed off.

She took a deep breath and continued. "At first, the device worked well. The general could control the crazed like they were like his personal puppets. It was almost funny, really—yet eerie. I remember in particular, even Valerie laughed when the general had the crazed walking backwards, their arms flailing around. It was odd. When the device was controlling them, their eyes were still wild and alive-looking—as if something completely different was going on in their head.

"But the general got sloppy," Lois's tone shifted. "He marched the crazed a bit too close to a few of the survivors. And just like that, their teeth were out. They tore into the people. I was in the bell tower, and—" she wiped her nose, "one by one, the crazed knocked the survivors to the ground. And from up there, the only thing we could think to do was—well . . . eradicate the whole lot."

Alayna and Agnes gasped. Clay staggered and caught the back of a pew. He imagined it, over and over again: his gorgeous bride, his Valerie. Her face, being ravaged by the crazed monsters. The blood soaking her dress when one of them tore her throat out. Bile filled his mouth.

But his eyes burned with anger. He knew, with a single tug, he could break Lois's neck. If he wanted to. And, God, he did. He yearned to twist it, until there was no resistance—no pulse.

The world was growing fuzzy, blurred. Clay felt a scream escape his lips. And then, for a long while, he felt nothing at all.

39.

P ain.
   Aaaaah! I scream, but there is no sound.
It's only in my head.

   I open my eyes and everything I see is tainted .
. . stained red. I'm lying—lying on the floor, and
there's a halo or an aura around my vision.

   Where am I? Who . . . am I?

   Aaaaaah! The pain is so bad and I don't know
why. I'm burning —my blood is boiling inside.

   What's the last thing I remember? I—I can't
think with . . . all this . . . HUNGER!

   I try to get up and run away from this confusion,
but I can't balance. I sway from side to side, trying to
make sense of my surroundings. I only see fire. Or is
that the blood in my vision?

   It's heat, and it's making my eyes bleed. Jesus,
the hunger is scalding my gut. I tear at myself,
ripping through my clothes.

   MAKE IT STOP!

   Teeth pierce my lips, and I stagger forward,
HUNGRY. HUNGRY. STARVING. I chase her. *I can
smell you . . . don't run!*

   I lunge for the neck—latching on and feeling—
tasting the blood. It gushes—the blood—into my
hungry maw. It pours across my cheeks and I lick it.

The body crumples, no more than a sack of bones and guts and brains, and I fall on it, ripping at the flesh.

Sustained, but only for a moment.

Through my hazy vision I see a woman. *Who are you?* I ask, but only I hear my words. I am silent.

She doesn't answer. Not because she cannot hear me, but because she is dead. Death, I can smell it.

What is this? Who am I? I know nothing but hunger. I am wild.

What is this? *I can hear you. Don't run! I NEED YOU! HELP! I MUST* . . .

I MUST FEED.

40.

C lay tightened his hands on the wooden pew and yanked it free. A scream erupted from his throat and filled the church with echoes like demons. Pieces of the floor became flying debris exposing the darkness of a cellar below.

Clay threw himself at the wall on the opposite side of the nave and ripped an ornate crucifix down, the splinters tearing into the skin beneath his fingernails. As stared into the dead wooden eyes of the savior, the voices in his head returned—louder and more insistent than before. FEED. FEED, they cried out to him, although he had no hunger for anything but violence. He drove his fist through a stained-glass window, not caring about the blood running down his arms. Again, he screamed. He couldn't control the rage.

Only a few feet away, Maia had curled into a ball, rocking and sobbing and screaming in turn. Brandon tried to comfort her, to calm her down, but she kicked at him like an animal. "NO. NO, NO!" she cried. "STOP! NO!"

Alayna was terrified. She implored Sherman, Quintin, anyone. "Someone. Please. Stop him. He's going to hurt himself. He's going to destroy himself . . ."

Clay was bleeding from his forehead, his nostrils, his arms. He grunted as he tore another vestige from the wall, ripping his clothes along with it. Being the only one who was big enough to even try, Daniels raced forward and finally wrapped his arms around Clay's shoulders, trying to stop his tirade. Clay slammed his elbow into Daniels' nose. Blood exploded from his face, pouring down his lips and chin. But Daniels was not giving up.

Clay was blind to anything but his rage, deaf to all but the voices in his mind. When Daniels grabbed him again, Clay slammed his forehead against Daniels' cheek. This brought him the same rush as breaking anything else, and he drove his fist at Daniels' chest. But this time, Daniels caught it, using the momentum to drive Clay toward the wall. Clay overbalanced and staggered, trying to regain his footing. But before he could, Daniels sent his own considerable fist into Clay's nose, putting him on the ground.

Clay landed like a stone. Daniels was already on top of him, pinning his arms to the ground. Clay spit out scream after scream, devolving into sobs when he recognized he couldn't overpower Daniels.

He finally surrendered, and tears fell as he began to grasp the enormity of his loss. This life. This life that he'd been trying to build. It had been for his family. For Valerie, for Maia. And now Valerie was gone. His first love. The woman to whom he'd pledged his life.

"FUCK! FUCK!" Clay screamed with finality. With a final surge of energy, he pulled his pinned limbs away from Daniels and pounded them against his own thighs, coming back into his human mind. "NO. NO. TELL ME IT'S NOT TRUE!"

No one spoke. No one knew what to do, faced with such devastation. Even Agnes, who'd only just lost her husband, was unable to find the words. She knew, better than most, that nothing worked. Nothing was ever enough.

41.

Finally, Maia rolled over and crawled to her father. She collapsed against him, hugging him close. Clay wrapped his arms around her slim frame, feeling her sob. This, beyond anything, reminded him that he was still alive. That there was still a purpose.

Maia pulled away from Clay's shoulder for a moment, revealing her blotchy cheeks. "Daddy, no. No. No," she begged. "It can't be true."

Clay cupped her face, marveling at the softness of her skin. He remembered what an angelic baby she had been. How he and Val had stared at her with incredulous eyes, as she'd slept in her crib. In certain lights, he could see Valerie's nose on Maia's face. Her eyes, so dark and forceful and alive. In so many ways, his wife lived on in the angel in his arms. But so much of his soul felt dark.

"I really loved her. You know that," Clay said, scarcely able to believe that he'd found the words. "You know she was my entire world. You and her . . . for so much of my life. It was just us."

Maia nodded. "I love her, Daddy. I never stopped."

"And you won't, baby. Will you? Promise me you'll never stop." Clay rocked his daughter. Blood continued to dribble from Daniels' punch. A wooden splinter was embedded above his eyebrow. He sniffed and swiped at the blood under his nose. The voices had filtered out, replaced with the comfort of Maia's.

"I promise, Daddy," Maia whispered.

As they sat together, holding one another close, the rest of the team moved away. Daniels studied his hand, looking at the already drying blood on his knuckles. The adrenaline from seeing the wild and frenetic energy in Clay's eyes took a long time to dissipate.

Alayna appeared beside Daniels, gripping his upper bicep. Daniels flinched at first, looking at her almost incredulously. She had a hand stretched across her abdomen, cradling herself, then threw herself forward and pulled Daniels close.

Daniels couldn't have imagined why. He couldn't have imagined that Alayna was brimming with a strange mix of sadness and relief; that it had been a horrible thing to watch, as Clay had smashed through the church.

One by one, the group stepped out into the sunshine. Clay and Maia found themselves alone—with the high ceilings of the church returning their voices, without anyone else to hear. His voice quivering, yet certain, said the only thing on his mind.

"I'm not going to let anything happen to you."

Maia's eyes held his. "I know."

"For as long as I live, Maia," Clay said with more grit, now. More passion. "For as long as I live, nothing is going to happen to you ever again. And that's a promise."

42.

Several hours later, the entire team was spread out in the pews. They'd been fed, watered—like cattle, Clay thought uncharitably. The devastation of Valerie's death made his head spin. Still, Maia was with him, her head on his shoulder. She wouldn't leave his side. Not now.

Daniels got up and paced nervously. He strode toward Clay with his hand out. Clay shook it, giving Daniels a firm nod.

"I see Lane patched you up," Daniels said, gesturing at the bandages. "Good thing. You really tore yourself up there."

"Thanks for stepping in," Clay said. "The only thing I could see was red. I couldn't have stopped myself . . . not without—well, you. That punch. Man, you've really got a right hook."

Daniels didn't laugh, but Clay sensed that the tension had dissipated. Walt and Hank began to speak in a more upbeat tone, as if the stress of the afternoon was now only a memory.

"So, I take it your plan was to head up to Earlton, wasn't it?" he asked.

"Course it was," Clay said. "To find Val, sure. But maybe to set up camp, possibly. To find some semblance of a life, off the road. I imagine that's where the only civilization is around here."

Even as he spoke, he recognized that his words were wishful thinking. That, much like he'd pinned all his hopes on finding Valerie, he had also been building up what Earlton might bring for all of them. He'd been so sure of it, he'd promised it to the others. Telling them all things would be much better for everyone if they would only help him get there.

"Tell me what happened," Clay said, the question represented all he didn't know, or understand. "There's a reason you didn't carry on, isn't there? A reason that you're here and not in Earlton."

As he waited for a reply, Clay's eyes drifted toward Lois, whom he'd come to loathe. She was the one who'd last seen Valerie alive. He could blame her for that. As if she felt his eyes, she rose from her pew and turned to meet Clay's eyes.

"He thinks he's in control of the world," Lois announced, addressing everyone. "The General, that's what he calls himself now. The minute he got ahold of that device and had so much power. He stopped listening to the other members of his brigade—to the others around the world—when he thought he was the only one left. He's let the power go to his head."

Clay sat up. Maia slid away from him and was watching like a frightened child.

"You mean, more so than when he just went by "Colonel'?" Clay asked sarcastically. "Because there was a whole lot of power hunger where he was concerned."

"It's ten times worse," Lois sighed. "Of course, our initial plan was to get to Earlton. But when we got here, and everything happened with—with Valerie and the others . . . I made my voice heard. I wasn't about to stand aside and allow him to continue. Not with my people. I was meant to take care of my constituents. And I know I failed them."

Clay heard the semblance of an apology but held his tongue. He stared at her unmoved, waiting.

"But of course, my protests fell on cold ears," Lois continued. "And then, the self-appointed general had me thrown into the brig before they left for Earlton. He left two soldiers to guard the relay tower and babysit me, until they decided what to do with an old lady. Of course, I know all human decency is out the window. But I was battered and bruised and left to rot in that jail cell."

"That's where we came in," Daniels said. "We arrived here. Got attacked by the assholes in that bell tower. Only one of them made it. The other? Well, he's out there on his own. Let him get to Earlton alone, for all I care. The guy tried to kill me in my sleep more than once, and we sent him to the wolves, with only two guns to his name."

"And you've all decided to stay? Not go rest of the way to Earlton?" Clay said. "Because it's too dangerous? You're not sure what you'll find?"

"Honestly, Clay, I don't see how it would be any better up there than it would be around here," Daniels said. "We can build something here if we want to. And we won't have to make ourselves known to the general. He's a monster, Clay. He used your wife like some sort of pawn in some weirdo game he knew he would always win."

Clay's hands clenched. Again, the adrenaline began to pulse against his eardrums, making his breath come in chaotic puffs. Lois and Daniels watched him like a time bomb ready to explode.

"We can't just let him be, not in the place we

want—a place that's safe. We can't just let him have it without a fight," Clay exclaimed. Everyone from Agnes to Walt was completely mesmerized.

No one spoke for a long time. Clay's skin felt itchy and wild, craving the adventure of revenge. "Think of the others," Clay finally said, turning his eyes toward Lois. "The women and men and children of your town. Our town. Carterville," he said. "They're up there with him, at his mercy. Who knows what other atrocities he'll try, Lois. We can't trust him. And I think not giving it a chance, not fighting for something we believe in—even at the end of the world—is the worst possible thing we can do."

43.

C lay's speech galvanized them. Every inch of him screamed for retribution, but he knew he had to explain it differently. In a way that wasn't so selfish. In a way that showed the world. What was right. And, in the small part of himself still connected to his law enforcement roots—a time when he'd genuinely cared about everyone—he knew fighting the General was the right thing. A madman, power hungry and wild, with every kind of weapon in his arsenal (including the potential ability to control the crazed) wasn't someone you could just leave alone. He wasn't like a rat you avoided in the basement.

"I just think you're underestimating him," Lois said. "I don't know if we could handle him at his worst. I can't imagine how much he's changed since he's taken over Earlton. It must be exponential, in the previous few weeks—"

"Lois, we've been through a hell of a lot," Clay said. "Maybe your little rendezvous with the General seemed intense, but we've been out there fighting the crazed, watching our friends die, and struggling to stay alive out there. If we can kill hundreds of those crazed monsters, I think—" he swallowed hard, the voices tickling the back of his mind again. They echoed in his ears, and he clung to the edge of the pew in front of him. A bead of sweat tracked from temple to chin.

"Then I think we can take out the General," he finished.

"That's something I cannot get on board with," Lois said. She glanced at the scientists. "It seems to me that if the General can control the crazed, use them to attack us—how the hell can we possibly fight back?"

Clay turned toward Alayna. This was the first time he'd looked at her, really looked at her, since learning of Val's death. She was small, retreated into herself, alone in the back of the church.

"Lois, I've been infected," Clay said, speaking directly to Alayna.

"What are you talking about?" Lois asked.

"The nanites. They are inside me," Clay said, speaking slowly. "I've been infected for months now. Alayna's infected as well. And I'm still here. She's still here. Which means we might have more control over this epidemic than we think, even without the General's device."

Lois took a step backward, covering her mouth. She stared at Clay like a sideshow freak. "But how you both not one of them?" she asked, her fear audible.

Clay shrugged. Lane said, "We initially monitored Clay's symptoms. Over time, the symptoms changed a great deal. Rather than becoming one of *them*, he got stronger, wilder. Meaner, in some respects—"

Clay closed his eyes against the flashing memories of tearing through the church, much like he had back at the hotel in Dearing. The anger he'd felt—it was unparalleled in his experience. It was a high he couldn't explain.

"We've speculated that the reason for this immunity is the radiation he was exposed to before leaving Carterville. It's possible it allowed the nanites to be more adaptive within him, working with his body's cells instead of against them."

Lois nodded, tipping her head at Alayna. "And what about her?" she asked. "I don't suppose she was exposed to the same radiation."

"She wasn't," Lane affirmed, "And no, she isn't one of them either. Thank God."

"Then what is it?" Clay demanded. "How is it that she's okay?"

Lane turned toward Marcia and Jacobs. They whispered, almost conspiratorially, while the rest of the crew waited impatiently. Clay contemplated going to Alayna. He had an idea of how fragile she was but he couldn't bring himself to take that first step. Then, the voices swelled in his ears. Louder, more insistent, clamoring. Then Alayna was beside him, her hand on his upper back. He felt it, just as he could hear the three scientists whispering several pews away. But the screeching in his mind continued, tugging, pulling him away from his reality.

"It could be a variety of reasons," Lane finally said, sounding to Clay as if she was at the end of a very long, black tunnel. Clay had to really concentrate to hear her over the screaming, violent chorus in his mind.

"A variety of reasons?" Clay asked putting his hands on his ears. "What—"

"It could be because of the pregnancy," Lane offered tentatively. "The female body has many, many ways to protect the fetus through development. In fact, it was one of my areas of research in college. But

I digress . . ."

Alayna's hand gently traced Clay's spine. The room continued to spin around him. He swayed, feeling himself falling into the spiral in his mind. "Okay. Okay."

"But it could be, that you—well. The fact is, you're the one who impregnated her," Lane said, her eyes boring into him. Clay half-wondered if they were accusing him. If people were whispering amongst themselves, "He cheated on his wife. He deserves this misery."

"So what?" Clay couldn't make the connection through the torment. "So what . . ."

"The point is," Lane said, "Is that your sperm carries the nanites. And theoretically the same mutation caused by the radiation. That baby in there, well. It's got—Clay, what's going on?" Lane looked at Clay fearfully.

Clay backed away from Alayna, away from Lane, suddenly feeling that everyone's eyes were on him. The voices continued to inundate him, making him tremble.

Clay didn't want to be made to feel this way. He was fine. He had it handled. His wife was dead, but he'd get revenge. The world was falling apart, but he'd keep his daughter safe through it. No matter what, he told himself. No matter—

44.

H unger.
  God, always so hungry. My tongue drapes over my parted lips, scraping my chin—my face, feeling—searching for just one more morsel . . . of flesh. Yes! I taste the brain matter and it's glorious, but it's . . . *GONE! I need more!*

The world around me is grey, foggy, like a rain sweeping down all around me, and all I can do . . . all I can think of is—

FLESH!

Wild thoughts lead to confusion, which in turn leads to turmoil. I'm lost, I don't know where to go. I . . . know something, but . . . what's that sound?

My limbs flail as if they have a mind of their own. I stagger on, aimless in my pursuit . . . toward a sound I cannot see. With each labored step, the pain—oh, the horrendous agony—stabs at my inner soul. The ache is deep, penetrating my bones. I tear at the skin—feeling the folds of it come apart, feeling the cartilage beneath. I yank, to stop the suffering.

But God, I can't . . . stand it. The world tilts in front of me, the sun falling through the sky until— BOOM—I slam my face against the pavement. I feel the blood oozing from my ear. I can do nothing, I am nothing—I feel . . . NOTHING, and everything . . .

But I hear it. The world, it's here, still. And the blood, it continues to pump through my veins. I remember . . . something! Something I was meant to do . . . before. Before what? Before I was blindsided, taken. Taken from where? Taken from this once-blue sky . . . before it turned this insanely horrible grey . . .

Hunger. And pain.

Aaaaaah!

Still on the ground and my tongue searches, past my lips, to my nose. I chew at my bottom lip. I want to taste myself, and this . . . blood-soaked gravel, and this world.

I know if I don't eat, I will starve. But will I die?

But what am I? And why am I so—

What is that? That sound again, just out of sight? I drag my face around, toward the noise. The pavement scrapes chunks of my skin away, blood oozes.

BUT WHAT IS THAT FUCKING SOUND—

I flail, until—

45.

C lay came to on the floor of the church, his face pressed into his hands. He heard Maia's screams as if they were far away. He dropped his hands to find Lane's face inches from his. Her lips were pressed together, and she was as white as a crazed. She passed him a glass of water, which he accepted, but only held it in front of his lips until he could catch his breath.

"Clay?" Lane finally said in the motherly tone that he'd heard her use when caring for Alex. "Clay. What just happened? Where did you just go in your head?"

Clay gulped water. He could still hear the voices—wild, manic, angry, but they were distant. He still yearned for flesh. But he recognized these weren't his thoughts. They came from somewhere else.

He was beginning to understand—*them*. Even as the rage stirred; even as his blood pulsed with strength and vitality, he had an undeniable urge to destroy, to strike out, even at Lane if he had to, he recognized that it wasn't coming from *him*.

"Clay?" Lane leaned closer. "Clay, if you don't tell us what's going on, we can't help you."

Clay used the pew to regain his feet, finding his

knees were still weak. Several feet away, Maia was clinging to Brandon. Clay could see the brightness of her bones, pressing against her skin. The sight filled him with anguish. This feeling—this pain, reminded him to remain grounded, here with the humans. If he could.

"Shit, I'm sorry," he sighed

"Clay," Lois said firmly, "tell us what just happened. You were rolling around, yelling things we couldn't understand."

Clay shook his head; he didn't have the strength to answer. He certainly couldn't explain the truth.

But what else could he do?

"It's been getting worse," he admitted to Lane. "The voices—"

He heard Alayna whimper. Lane's face was inscrutable

"Voices?" she asked.

"I didn't know what they were before. But they're clearer now. Louder. Calling out for . . . for flesh. They're confused, angry, hungry. They don't understand what's happening to them, or why . . . why they're so hungry." The words tumbled from his lips now. Fast without measuring their cost.

"They?" Lane asked. "You don't mean . . ."

"I don't know." Clay fought the rage. "I can hear them. And their anguish, as well as my anger, it's worse. Much worse. As you can see," He gestured at the mutilated pew, at the torn-apart walls. "It's like they're communicating with me, or I'm connected to them in some way. Or maybe I'm just going crazy. Take your pick."

Lane turned to see what her colleagues made of Clay's admission. Marcia shrugged, Jacobs just frowned. Recognizing that this was new territory for all of them, Clay spun toward Daniels, an idea burning to get out.

"Adam," he said excitedly. "What's powering the energy field out there? I think, well . . . it feels like they're getting closer, and I want to make sure we're protected. We need that thing to stay up, at all costs."

Daniels spoke carefully, as if he didn't want to trigger the rage he'd witnessed. "The energy field is powered by twin diesel generators. We have to fill the tanks every twelve hours or so, to keep them up. It's some new military-grade generator, left for the communication tower. They repurposed it for the energy field."

"Is there enough fuel to keep it powered up?" Clay asked.

"Right now, we have enough diesel to last us another week or so. Ten days, maybe."

"And then? What's the plan after that?" Clay asked sharply.

"Clay," Lane said. "Please tell me more about these voices. Can you control them? Or do you feel yourself wanting to give in?"

Clay sank into a pew. He remembered the world disappearing when the voices invaded his mind. He wondered just how much he could take before he lost complete control.

"I'm not sure, Lane," Clay answered, his heart heavy. "I'm not sure I can trust myself much longer. I don't know if—if I'm dangerous. If any of us are safe now."

46.

Jacobs led Clay toward the front to join Lane, Marcia, and Jacobs. Clay imagined he could hear them saying, "Should we really trust this guy to be our leader? He's either going crazy, or he's being taken over by them."

"When did you first notice these voices?" Jacobs asked. "And why didn't you say something?"

Clay remembered back to the first inkling of them in his mind. Scratching at the bandage on his face, he muttered, "I guess the hotel. But they've gotten stronger since we've been on the road."

"Stronger in what way?" Marcia asked.

"Back at that rest area," Clay began. "I was waiting for Maia. I heard them—an entire horde of crazed in the men's restroom. I heard their wails, their screams of pain. You know, not just the way they communicate now. Not the screeching. It was like there were real thoughts there."

"So you felt connected to them?" Lane asked. "And when I used the device?"

"The voices went away," Clay affirmed.

The three scientists exchanged glances, disturbed. Daniels joined them. He appeared to be nervous. He wiped sweat from his forehead. "This is bad. Really fucking nasty," he muttered to himself.

Clay half-wondered if Daniels thought the best idea was to put a bullet in his brain. Get it over with, then and there. Get it over with, before he gave in to them.

"This is fascinating," Jacobs muttered.

"But why? Why start now?" Clay asked. "I mean, why didn't I have the voices in my head back in Dearing, or Carterville for that matter? I've been infected this entire time. It doesn't make sense."

Marcia turned away and reached into her pocket. She drew out a pack of cigarettes—a practiced motion Clay hadn't seen in what felt like years. Without an apology, she lit up. She was a portrait of beauty—blonde hair, an impenetrable stare. And as she smoked, she gave the only answer any of them could think of.

"Must be this fucking general," she blew out a cloud of smoke. "He's got the device, doesn't he? And you're getting closer to him all the time. If he's trying to control the crazed, chances are, since you're infected, he's getting to you, too."

Lane and Jacobs both nodded, as if this added up in their minds. Rage spun within Clay, making him see red. He imagined the general up north, tapping his device's buttons—and making Clay a monster.

"Is that really possible?" Clay asked. "All the way from there?"

Marcia continued to smoke, her face tense despite the nicotine. "Well, he probably amplified the output. He thinks he's ruling of the world, so I can't imagine why he wouldn't want to control all of them from where ever he happens to be. But, Clay . . ."

Marcia dropped her half-smoked cigarette, crushing it out with her foot. Clay could smell the nicotine on her.

"Clay, there's a good chance you'll continue to experience these—erm—episodes, forever," she said.

"Unless we can get up there. Unless we can stop him," Daniels insisted.

For the first time, Clay felt a flicker of hope. He sensed that they were beginning to come to terms with the need to go after the general. He would have his vengeance. He rose and said—in no uncertain terms, "You agree, then. We absolutely have to go to Earlton. We have to stop him—"

In the silence that followed, Clay thought he had won. Then, in the distance, an incredible boom, an explosion, rocked the town, shaking the church. Clay felt it in his bones. Everyone turned toward the stained-glass windows, at Jesus on the cross, the many shepherds, their sheep.

And they waited, knowing all too well devastation was upon them.

47.

The shockwave blew the stained-glass into the church. Shards exploded inward, potentially deadly collateral damage. Several people screamed. Maia ran straight to Clay and pressed her face into his chest. Clay felt her rabbit-like heartbeats and held her close for protection.

Clay called, "Is everyone all right?"

Weak replies filtered back to him as everyone pulled themselves together. Glass fragments blanketed the church, colorful missiles that miraculously killed no one. Feeling his throat clench, he called, "Alayna! Where's Brandon?"

Overhead, a megaphone squawked on.

"CLAY! It's Brandon. Up in the bell tower. We've got trouble coming at us fast!"

"What's happening?" Clay yelled.

"The force field just went down!" Brandon called back. "And we've got a pack of *them* coming on strong."

"Shit," Clay muttered. His thoughts raced and his brain mapped out what he'd seen of the square outside, trying to plot a safe zone. It was clear they couldn't gather everything they needed from the bus—the supplies, the gas, the people—before the attack. "Brandon, get your ass down here!" he called.

"And let's head to the police station! Across the square!"

As if on cue, the voices battered him once more. Trying to control them, he took Maia's hand and drew his gun. Brandon flung himself down the final flight of stairs, pulling his own gun. Everyone who could handle one had weapons ready, and they raced toward the door and out into the sunlight.

At the far edge of the square, Clay could see a pack of sixty or seventy crazed. Their arms flailed as they sped forward, and their calls were wild and guttural. Even as they cried out, Clay could feel their very real thoughts crowding his own.

HUNGRY! EAT! RUN! BLEED!

"We have to go!" Clay said, starting across the square. He pointed his gun at the crazed, moving as fast as a team of horses, and dropped one, then another. They fell forward, their blood splattering across the ground. The rest of the horde trampled the bodies, indifferent. They were no longer human; they had no empathy.

Behind him, Alayna fired at targets of her own among the monsters. Daniels, Brandon, and even Lane were next. Quintin and Sherman were last, protecting everyone else and making sure no one was left behind.

HUNGRY! FLESH! MUST . . . EAT . . .

Trying to remain in this reality, rather than fall into theirs, Clay tried to push the crazeds' thoughts out of his mind. "NO!" he thought, concentrating. "KEEP AWAY. STAY OUT!"

As he pushed their chaotic, stirring, murderous thoughts away, the crazed slowed down. No longer a galloping herd, their movements resembled an undead pub crawl. Shocked, Clay gaped at the drunk-appearing, sloppy crazed, shambling now. Lane scrambled up beside him, breathing hard. Her eyes were wide.

"Do you see that?" She was stunned. "They're slowing down! Clay—what are you thinking about? Is it you? Are you doing something?"

Clay kept his eyes on the crazed, still concentrating. But he allowed her a small nod. Lane smacked her hands together and laughed.

"YES! Keep it up, Clay. You can control them! You're buying us time. We're going to make it!" Lane cried.

Clay slowed to a walk, still staring at the crazed. His crew continued to shoot them down, on their way across the square. It was an oddly beautiful moment. Clay had complete control. From the corner of his eye, he saw his people make it to the station, Daniels and Brandon taking sentry positions outside. To his right, Hank and Walt were side-by-side, their rifles lifted. Walt still limped; not fully recovered. But his eyes glittered with anger and concentration, keeping him in Hank's shadow.

"OH SHIT!" Hank cried, pointing beyond the sea of crazed. "Is that—is that who I think it is?"

Clay turned to see a veritable fleet of large, roaring trucks. One of them was honking its horn spastically. Clay went cold. He recognized the vehicles.

It was Malcolm. Malcolm had found them.

Clay shoved Maia toward the police station, screaming, "MAIA! RUN!" Maia did as she was told, Alayna hot on her heels. In all the commotion, Clay lost his footing and his concentration slipped. The crazed sped up—their strides grew longer, and their lips smacked hungrily.

He'd lost control of them.

The crazed were upon them. Hank leaped back, unknowingly leaving Walt in their path. Without hesitation, one of them pounced, sinking its teeth into Walt's upper arm, ripping into his flesh. Clay felt a surge of adrenaline, of joy.

FINALLY. FLESH. YES. FEEEEED!

Clay watched on with a mixture of conflicting emotion: fear and anger blended with glee; Walt fell to his knees, howling. Hank let several bullets fly, but it was too late. Walt was on his back, gripping his arm, screaming as the crazed began to feast on him. Hank screamed, turned toward the station and ran.

"FUCKKK!!" Hank cried. "GO! GO! GO! THEY GOT HIM! THEY GOT HIM!"

48.

C lay stood outside of the police station, Lane beside him. Less than a quarter-mile away, Malcolm's caravan was inbound—their vehicles near military caliber, and thus protected from the crazed that they were driving forward.

Clay and Lane continued to take down the crazed closer to their proximity. Clay with lead and the smell of cordite, Lane with the push of a button, knocking down ten, fifteen, at a time, depending on where she pointed the device.

"They're still coming. Look—" Lane pointed. "Just behind Malcolm. Can you feel them? Their thoughts?"

Clay could. But he couldn't control them—not anymore. Not with so many. His brain was stretched thin from the struggle with the voices. He could still see Walt's body—what was left of it. In the distance, more voices, more words, were streaming into his head.

FEED. FEED US. FLESH.

Then the bullets came. They ricocheted off bricks of the station, one just missing Clay's ear. He grabbed Lane's shirt and dragged her back behind the pillars for cover. There was no mistaking Lane and Clay were the targets, rather than the crazed.

"They're monsters!" Lane cried. "Can't they see— why won't they help us?"

This was a predicament. All of Malcolm's men— in armored cars, no less, on one side and all the crazed approaching from, well everywhere, Clay knew it was over. For now, at least. He dropped his rifle to the ground. He'd never been the type of man to surrender. But he had to do the best thing to save his people. To protect Maia.

"What the hell are you doing?" Lane asked hysterically. "What—"

But Clay raised his hands and stepped out from behind the pillars even as the last of the bullets spun around him. He felt like Jesus on the cross—trading himself for everyone else. At Malcolm's mercy.

Lane raised her arms and set the device at her feet. They waited together at the top of the steps. Seconds later, Malcolm's trucks halted ten feet or so from the station, with the sunlight glittering across their windows. Silence fell around them. Clay waited, apprehensive, knowing that any second, one of Malcolm's guns could blast through them both.

The passenger side door of the biggest truck opened. A single, dark green boot dropped to the pavement, between two of the crazed. Malcolm. Standing tall, his shoulders broad and thickly bearded. He stared directly at Clay, a slight smirk on his face. He kicked at the crazed, nearly booting Walt, and started toward the station. Several of his men followed, rifles in hand.

"Well, well. I bet you didn't expect me so soon, did you, Clay?" He drank in Lane's curves with his eyes, then turned his attention back to Clay. Behind the armored cars, the crazed were coming up fast—a river of the damned behind a dam.

Clay refused to be afraid of this man. "I don't know what you're here for, Malcolm. I wouldn't even guess," he said.

Malcolm chuckled. A few of his men turned toward the crazed and began to spray them with bullets. But more and more of the crazed streamed into the square from every direction. More of Malcolm's men began to fight, slaughtering the crazed wholesale.

"I reckon we should talk inside," Clay said.

"Is that so?" Malcolm asked, almost seeming to dare Clay to do something wild. To challenge him.

But most of the crazed had been slaughtered.

"Because I think we'll probably be all right without that talk," Malcolm said, crossing his hands over his chest.

A lone crazed burst from between buildings, charging one of Malcolm's men. The man dropped his weapon and let out a wild, guttural scream. Even from fifteen feet away, Clay could see the whites of his eyes.

Without hesitation, Lane grabbed the device, and in a smooth motion, dropped the crazed. Malcolm's man huffed, still wailing, looking down at his arms, his legs. He seemed to be checking for injuries.

Malcolm raised an eyebrow and said, "Well, well. What's that you have there?"

Lane didn't bother to reply.

Malcolm cackled. "Cat got your tongue, don't it, girly?" In three quick strides, he clambered up the steps and lumbered up to Lane. He held out his hand. "Come on now, hand it over. That magic wand of yours. This world is just one surprise after another, isn't it?"

49.

I'm not alone. I'm surrounded by those like me … of them—hungry, my tongue lashes out, searching for something. Anything to taste—to bite. Around me, the others' eyes are wide and bulging. Big, purple drops of blood fall to their necks, their chests. I reach out—I can't control my hands, can't grip—I want to grab them. To take them. But as my tongue grazes skin, I taste nothing but bitterness. Sour. SOUR.

They won't satisfy this hunger. They're not what I need. And yet—they're here. And I want them. I want them more than I can—

Aaaaah!

I scream inside my head, but my voice is unheard.

The pain is unbearable. Like light searing my eyes. I blink into it, my mouth still open, my tongue still lolling. I hear muffled voices, screaming. I need to reach it. My legs are sluggish, but they carry me forward. The world spins; the horizon shifts back and forth.

Them, those around me: they reach for me. Rotting nails dig into my skin. They sniff at my arms and lean forward, trying to sink their teeth into my torso. But I swing at them with my elbows. Blood oozes from my eyes, and I feel—I feel—RAGE. HUNGER.

I am spinning, I am wild, I am inhuman I am inhumane. Nothing is right. Everything is HUNGER. I NEED FLESH!

50.

C lay, Lane, and now Daniels faced off against Malcolm and two of his men just inside the station. Lane still held the device, though the crazed seemed at bay for the moment. Her eyes were dark, searing into Malcolm. Clay knew that if she'd had a rifle, Malcolm would be a corpse.

Clay recognized that they were in trouble. If they shot, Malcolm's men would return fire. And there were more of Malcolm's men still in the trucks. Waiting for something to go wrong.

Outside, the crazed continued to filter into the square while Clay struggled against the constant awareness of rage and hunger, coming in from the monsters. He focused on Malcolm, trying to direct this rage.

"Look at you, Clayster. You look like you're about to explode," Malcolm said with a titter. "It's a real joy to see the man who got the drop on me looking so nervous. Isn't it, men?"

His two accomplices chuckled obligingly. All three were at least six feet tall, Malcolm's men in the 250-pound range. Daniels, Quintin, and Sherman could probably have taken them in a fight, but it wouldn't have done any good.

"Get their weapons. I'm tired of feeling like we're

about to duel," Malcolm snapped.

Malcolm's lackeys relieved them of their guns. All that remained was the device, still in Lane's hand.

"All right. Now that that's over, we can get on to the comedy portion of the evening," Malcolm said snidely. "Tell me, Clay. What's more amusing to you? Is it that you didn't kill me when you had the chance? Or is it that nothing really matters, now that I have the tables turned? Such a useless, meaningless thing, this life. Wouldn't you agree?"

Clay's brain pulsed with anger. He took a small step forward, his hands clenching into fists. "I should have let Sam murder you where you stood."

"Ha. Old Sam, wanting to kill me. Now, that was a trip, wasn't it?" Malcolm said, seeming genuinely cheerful. "You should have seen her in bed. Quite feisty."

Malcolm's men cackled again, as if they were all in some kind of melodrama in the afterlife.

"But really, Clay, I need to thank you for that. For saving my life. I mean, if you hadn't insisted on letting me live, we wouldn't be having this talk right now. And I, for one, am really enjoying this conversation. I think our little girl here is enjoying it, too. Aren't you?" Malcolm leered at Lane.

"Leave her alone. She's doing what you asked her to do," Clay said. "Jesus, can't you just—"

"What's your name, baby?" Malcolm asked. Clay could smell his foul breath. "What should I call you? A pet name?"

"Fuck off," Lane said.

Malcolm tilted his head back and laughed. "Jesus, she's good. She's way too good."

"What the hell do you want?" Clay barked. "We've given you our weapons. We don't have anything else."

Malcolm's smile widened. After a long, dramatic pause, he reached for Lane's hands. But instead of touching her, he pulled the device up to his chest. "Isn't it obvious, Mr. Sheriff? This thing right here. It has everything I'm looking for."

Malcolm inspected it: the buttons, the gleaming metal. He sniffed and turned with a surprise. Alex—scrawny, skeletal Alex, stood in the crowd, his thin arms crossed over his chest. The two—father and son—held one another's gaze for a long moment, until Malcolm began to chuckle.

"This must be it, isn't it, Alex?" Malcolm said. Clay realized then that Alex looked far more like his father than he'd thought. They had the same leering stare. "Tell me this is it, Alex. Tell me."

Alex straightened and took a small step forward but remained intermixed in Clay's group. Foreboding made Clay feel like he might vomit. Maia's lips parted with sudden understanding.

"That's it, all right," Alex replied.

"What the hell," Lane muttered. A tear slipped down her cheek.

"Very good, son," Malcolm purred. "That's very, very, good. Better than I expected from you."

"And you know what? They have an extra battery," Alex added, seeming to gain more strength as he spoke. "I'm not sure where it is, but that's—that's good for you, right, Dad? That's gonna be helpful?"

51.

Malcolm raised his gun and aimed it at Lane's face. Clay felt like he'd been struck by a giant fist. He held his breath—cognizant that if he made a single noise, Malcolm might blow Lane's head off. He swallowed slowly, his nostrils flared. Focus, he told himself. In the silence, his eyes went once more to Alex, who seemed incredibly pleased with himself.

"All right, girlie," Malcolm said. "Where is this extra battery my son here's telling me about? You know you should tell me. You know you WANT to tell me, even. It's in your best interest. And it'll get me and my men out of your hair just like that." Malcolm snapped his fingers, still leering at her.

Seconds ticked along. All the while, Clay was in a struggle with the voices in his head—spurring him, making him hungrier, wilder, than he'd ever been. He clenched his fists so tightly, his nails pierced his palms and blood began to flow.

"Come on, girlie. Out with it," Malcolm said.

Lane's chin shook with apprehension. Her eyes glittered with tears. But as Malcolm moved the gun closer to her face, pressing it to her cheek, she whispered, "It's in the bus."

"The bus, huh?" Malcolm sneered. "Where is this friendly little bus, baby?"

"It's—it's a few blocks away," she said. "To the west."

Keeping his eyes on Lane, Malcolm directed one of his men to retrieve it with a jerk of his chin, but not before passing him the device. Malcolm's man tore from the police station, allowing the screams and wails of a pack of crazed to echo in. Clay felt that he knew every nuance of their cries, now. And for a moment, he had far more compassion for the crazed monsters outside the door, than for the man pushing the barrel of a gun into Lane's cheek.

"All right," Clay said. "You got what you came for. Take the device. Take the goddamn battery. And leave us the hell alone."

Malcolm removed the gun from Lane's cheek. She gasped with relief, her hand rising to her cheek. Malcolm slid his gun into his holster and turned toward Alex, who was with Clay's people.

"I'm not just here for the device," he said. "Just one more thing. Alex? You ready?"

Alex gave his father a joyful nod, his face glowing. As he pushed through the crowd, he knocked against Alayna, shoving her to the side. And he went out of his way to pass Clay, shoulder-checking Clay's bicep. Clay and Alayna had risked their lives to get medicine for Alex. They'd sacrificed to care for the boy, giving him everything they could find. Even when Clay had screamed at him— demanding to know where Maia might be, he'd recognized the boy as an innocent in the game. But now he knew he himself was the stooge.

When he got to Lane, he thrust his hips against her. Clay nearly bolted forward, wanting desperately to beat manners into this asshole kid. Daniels put a warning hand on his arm, though, keeping him in check. Alex joined his father, and they hugged. Alex's eyes closed, he was clearly savoring this moment.

He'd probably been plotting it all along.

"Alex. Have you—did you plan this?"

Alex sneered at Clay, without speaking. From his pocket, he retrieved a small radio and held it up triumphantly. His grin matched Malcolm's perfectly, making him look like a rat.

"Well, as fun as it is to stand around this pretty little village and chat," Malcolm said, "It really is time to go meet this general you're all up in arms about."

"I don't know what you're talking about," Clay said, glaring at him.

"Oh, I think you do," Malcolm retorted. He wrapped an arm around his son, jiggling him from side to side. "The strong and powerful general up in Earlton, isn't that right, Alex?"

"Earlton. That's right, *Dad*," Alex said, clearly relishing the word. Clay could hear his joy. It was sour in his ears.

"Wonderful," Malcolm said. "Earlton. I know precisely where that is, son."

"And what the hell do you think the general will do to you if you confront him?" Clay asked. "You can't trust that monster. He isn't human any longer. The ego—"

"Ah, my poor, misguided Clay," Malcolm said, clucking his tongue. "It does seem like such a pity, that moral code you can't shake, even at the end of the world. Think how powerful you could be, if only you could ignore that big, selfless heart of yours. How boring.

"But I think an alliance between that General and myself would help us both prosper. Don't you agree, Alex?" Malcolm turned to leave, Alex following him like a dog at heel. "Someone's going to be the ruler of this new world. And I imagine the two of us will get along just fine."

"You can't leave us like this," Clay said. The crazed were ravenous—he could literally *feel* their hunger. And they were waiting.

"Oh, I certainly can," Malcolm grinned manically. "I'll leave you just the way you left me. Completely defenseless, surrounded by the crazed. Imagine just how angry you'll be—if you get out of this, Clay. Maybe you'll be angry enough to shed your useless morals and give me a real run for my money."

Malcolm and Alex slipped out. The door clicked closed behind them, leaving Clay and his group in complete silence. They listened as gunshots ricocheted outside, clearing a path for Malcolm and his son to fight to the trucks. And then, seconds later, there was the sound of revving engines, before they ultimately faded into the distance.

52.

T he police station was dark, shadowy. In the minutes after Malcolm had sped away, no one had spoken. Clay leaned heavily against the front desk, trying to parse the direness of the situation.

He was meant to be their leader. He was meant to guide the way. And yet, he felt hollow. He'd trusted the boy. And yes, sure: he chose the moral high ground. He'd assumed, with his sheriff, "good guy" mentality, that if he followed the "rules," everyone would be all right. But now they were trapped in the police station, without even a gun to their name. And they were about to be dinner.

"I wish there was a goddamn window," Daniels said. He made his way across the lobby, placing his hand against the door. "We can't even see how many of them there are. And we're losing light."

"It's worse than that. We've already been through the station, and there're no weapons to speak of. And we don't have any supplies," Marcia said. "My god. We're going to die here. Jesus. I'd rather be torn to bits out there—"

"Stop," Alayna said curtly. "We can't dwell on things like that. We'll drive each other crazy."

Clay covered his ears, trying to tear his mind away from the hungry thoughts of the crazed.

"Dammit. I'm sorry, everyone. I'm so sorry. I shouldn't have let Malcolm live. I put us in this position . . . I shouldn't have gone down without a fight. We have nothing to save us, and we're trapped . . .we're defenseless—"

Daniels snapped his fingers, interrupting Clay's melancholy. He slid up his pant leg, revealing a small pistol. His eyes twinkled as he pulled it from the ankle holster, saying, "Not completely defenseless."

Clay smiled sadly. The pistol was no bigger than Daniels' palm, and Clay knew it could take out only five or six of the crazed before they were overrun. He sighed, patting Daniels' shoulder.

"If only," he said.

"Hear me out," Daniels said. "This pistol here, it's enough to get me to the clock tower. And you know what's up there?"

Brandon stepped around Maia, his eyes dancing. "Of course. The sniper rifle."

"It's still there?" Clay asked.

"Of course it is," Brandon said, smiling at Clay. "Left it up there when you ordered me down. If we run, I think we can make it."

Clay had a sudden flash of little Brandon, teenaged, bratty. That Brandon had died along with so many others, leaving this strong, impassioned warrior in his place.

"While you clear a path to the bus, I can guard the trapdoor to the bell tower," Brandon said. He rummaged in the desk and came up with a nightstick.

Daniels nodded. He looked at Clay, seeking approval. Clay shook his head. "No. If anyone's going to do that, it's me, not Brandon."

Brandon swung the baton like a baseball bat,

warming up. "Sorry, boss," he said, his smile widening. "But you know as well as I do that you have to stay here and protect the others."

Clay wondered what he could say to convince the kid that it wasn't worth it. That he didn't want him to end up like Walt, like Ralph. His eyes fell on Hank, in the back of the room. His face was in his hands, sick from the memory of watching his friend die. Clay didn't have the heart to say anything to him. Walt was gone. There was nothing, no band-aid, to heal that.

"Okay," Clay said, nodding "But goddammit, if you're not careful . . ."

Brandon gave him a confident smile—cocky, brave. Like the football star, just before he tossed the winning touchdown.

"You've been out of my hair for a while, Clay," Brandon said, sounding like a much older, much wiser man. "And I think I've grown up a bit. You don't have to watch out for me anymore." Brandon glanced back at Maia. It wasn't lost on Clay. "And we're heading to Earlton, right? Just get on the bus and pick us up on the way out. Don't forget."

Clay grabbed his walkie-talkie and passed it to Daniels. "Okay. We can communicate with this. Lane still has hers. Be careful out there. And I'll do my best to control the crazed. Think happy thoughts. I'll slow them down as much as I can."

53.

C lay closed the door behind Brandon and Daniels. He sighed, sliding his hand across the doorframe, and tried to focus his mind on the crazed outside the door. He shoved at the insane, flesh-hungry thoughts.

PAIN. HUNGER. MUST EAT FLESH—

And tried to replace them with his own. He thought of Maia and Valerie: birthday parties, that vacation they'd taken to the Gulf of Mexico. Cozying up in bed with the two of them and reading, Maia's small head sliding lower and lower on his shoulder.

Images of the past. They were stronger than anything from the present. And as he pulled these thoughts to the forefront, he could feel the crazed out front slowing. Their wailing tapered off.

After several minutes—more time than was necessary to make it across the square—Clay tipped his head back, closed his eyes and began to count, knowing that if he didn't hear the sharp crack of the sniper rifle soon, either Brandon or Daniels was probably toast. *Three. Four. Five.* He heard the soft prayers of someone behind him. *Nine. Ten. Eleven.* Was it Agnes? *Thirteen. Fourteen. Fifteen.* Someone else was crying softly. Suddenly, Clay reached twenty—no sound.

"What's going on out there?" Alayna asked. "Do you think—"

Clay lifted a finger, telling her to wait.

The first report cracked across the square. He turned to Alayna, shaking his head incredulously. "I can't believe it. They made it."

Alayna wrapped him in a joyful embrace, one that felt spontaneous. Agnes' hands were still folded in prayer, Quintin and Sherman were sentinels, their thick arms crossed over their chests, looking ready to take on any challenge.

Their chance would come.

Clay cracked open the door to find the town square teeming with the crazed. Still intent on controlling his own thoughts, Clay was pleased to see the difference in them. They were slower and more disjointed, but their hunger—and the sheer numbers—would destroy his team in seconds.

But the sniper rifle was direct and accurate. Each of Daniels' shots put down another one. One, two, three in a row created a small path through the crowd of crazed—one that filled up in a few seconds. But as Daniels grew more confident in the bell tower, his shots rang out faster, creating larger pockets in the pack.

"He's forging a path!" Clay cried. "Get up here, guys. Two at a time. You remember, the bus is two blocks that way—and we're going to have to run. Hank? You good?"

Hank got up, forcing his eyes to meet Clay's. Without speaking, he nodded, joining Agnes. All of them were anxious. Maia bounced from side to side, squeezing her hands together. She was next to Alayna, just behind Lane.

Daniels cleared a space in front of the station.

"Okay. LET'S GO!" Clay cried, charging into the square, pulling Lane. Alayna and Maia held onto each other. All around them, Daniels' expert shots shattered skulls, splintered bones and sprayed guts. Several times, Clay felt chilly fingers latching onto his forearm, then growing slack as Daniels executed them just in time. It was incredible that Daniels didn't accidentally shoot one of their own. But Daniels was a professional. An artist painting in lead and gore.

In a haze caused by adrenaline, Clay saw the bus—only half a football field away. He called out, "WE'RE ALMOST THERE!" But he knew they could hardly hear him over the squeals and wails of the crazed, and the popping noises of the sniper rifle. In the final stretch, he shoved his elbow against the wide, gaping mouth of a crazed, poised to bite down on him. And then, he opened the door, pushing his people up the steps as they reached him. First Lane. Then Maia, Alayna, Agnes, Lois, Hank, Marcia, Jacobs. Quintin and Sherman were last in, both of them stained with pus and bleeding from their knuckles. Without looking twice at Clay, they clambered aboard and went for their guns, but they were nowhere to be found. Sherman whirled and planted the heel of his boot in the chest of a crazed trying to get on the bus.

"What are you waiting for?" Sherman asked. "Drive!"

Clay fished the keys from his pocket, dropped into the driver's seat, and revved the engine. Sherman stood in the stairwell, holding the door closed. Clay stomped on the gas pedal, driving straight through the crowd. He could feel bones and skulls crushing and popping under the tires. It turned his stomach, watching the crazed get pulled under the bus.

The noise was deafening. But still, Clay kept going, checking his group in the rearview mirror. They looked petrified, staring out the windows on either side. It was like Clay was driving a submarine. Even the blood splattering across the windows was oddly beautiful—if you ignored the source.

"ALAYNA!" Clay yelled as the bus neared the bell tower. "CALL THEM. TELL THEM WE'RE THERE IN THIRTY SECONDS!"

Alayna shouted into the walkie-talkie. He kept motoring forward. And within seconds, they were stopped in front of the bell tower, the remaining crazed—seemingly hundreds, at this point, throwing themselves against the bus and rocking it. Sherman slid forward, doubling his pressure on the door. Quintin joined him, throwing his upper body against one side, while Sherman held the other. But still, the crazed were wild, banging against the bus.

"THEY'RE GOING TO ROLL IT IF THEY DON'T HURRY!" Quintin yelled. "We have to move."

But Clay couldn't leave without everyone. Standing at the bus driver's seat, he saw Brandon dart from the church, pistol in his hand. In quick succession, he blasted the first half dozen crazed in the head. The gunfire from above stopped. Clay's heart soared, knowing that Daniels was on his way down.

Brandon stomped up the steps, panting and spattered with gore. Clay gave him a hearty slap on the back and was rewarded with a smile.

"Adam was right behind me," Brandon said, sliding in next to Agnes. Huge beads of sweat poured down his forehead, and his eyes were wide, sizzling with adrenaline. "But we gotta move. Daniels said that we're completely surrounded on all sides. We don't have a lot . . ."

Daniels' voice cut in from Alayna's walkie-talkie. "CLAY. ALAYNA."

Clay took the radio and yelled, "YOU NEED TO GET A MOVE ON, ADAM. WE'RE DOWN HERE WAITING."

There was no reply. He stared at the gaping darkness of the doorway, waiting for Daniels to appear. But still, nothing. A row behind him, Quintin cut his hand across his throat, alerting them that he'd run out of bullets. "Nothing left," he said.

"DANIELS?" Clay tried again.

"You have to get out of here, Clay," Daniels replied firmly. "There's no way for me to make it out. I'm out of bullets. I just have one grenade. That's it."

Clay sputtered. "No fucking way, soldier. We're waiting down here for you. Brandon still has bullets. We can cut a path . . ."

But, much like Quintin had, Brandon raised his gun and shook his head. The crazed continued to blast against the bus, rocking harder, like a boat caught in horrendous, never-ending waves.

"FUCK!" Clay cried into the walkie-talkie. "It can't end like this, Adam. We've been through too fucking much."

Clay felt so angry, so helpless, he could hardly breathe. Quintin slid into the driver's seat, ready to crank the engine. Clay stared up at the bell tower, looking for Daniels.

It was the last time he would see him.

"We have to save him," Clay protested. "We can't just leave him like this. No man left behind . . ."

"Get out of here, Clay," Daniels cried into the

walkie-talkie. "I swear to God, if you don't get those people to safety, I'll come down there and kick your ass. Don't be an idealist, Clay. Get the hell out of here, and don't look back."

The wheels of the bus began to churn over the bodies of the crazed, taking them back toward the highway. Clay could no longer see Daniels at all.

"It's been a pleasure knowing you, Clay," Daniels said. "Signing off, now."

"No," Clay whispered to himself. He felt sure he would vomit. But he pressed his lips together, knowing he had to remain strong for his team. As he turned his attention back to the front of the bus, he heard the grenade.

This was the nail in the coffin.

Clay clenched his fists and felt the blood filling his hands. The pain seared across his eyes.

It was a rage he couldn't control. A feeling unmatched.

And then he saw nothing but red.

54.

C lay collapsed into the passenger seat as the bus pulled forward, unable to breathe normally. He squeezed his bleeding fingers, staring out at the crazed—at the whites and purples and strange, oozing greens. He had no compassion for them any longer.

There was nothing but rage.

Startling everyone, Clay let out a gut-wrenching scream. Hatred, anger, blood and fire pouring from his throat. And, at the pinnacle of his outcry, the head of one of the crazed—some five feet in front of them—burst apart. Blood splattered across the windshield. Clay's scream hung in the air as he channeled more and more hate at the crazed.

Then, it happened again. Several more of the crazed in front of the bus exploded. Gore filled the air, fouling the bus and the crazed around it. Agnes let out a guttural wail and covered her face. Alayna and Lane gaped at the impossible, gory spectacle. In the last, dying note of Clay's scream, Lane put her hand on Clay's shoulder.

Clay turned, rage in his red-tinged eyes. "What the fuck just happened?" he snarled, barely able to articulate his words. "What the fuck did I just—"

"Whatever you did, try to do it again," Lane said

firmly.

Clay shook his head wildly. "I can't. I don't know what I did," he said. He knotted his fingers in his hair, tugging at it. "I have no clue—"

"TRY, GODDAMMIT!" Lane shouted and shook him. "OR WE'RE GOING TO DIE."

Clay leaned forward, bracing his bloody hands against the dash. Still gasping for air, He tried to concentrate, find his rage and inflict it on the crazed bumping into the bus.

"TRY!" Lane ordered.

And he did. But he couldn't bring back the pain that ignited him before. It had been replaced by unfathomable loss. Daniels—who'd been with him from the beginning—was gone.

Enraged and unable to control it, Clay slammed his fists on the dashboard. He growled at Quintin who promptly vacated the driver's seat. Clay slid in and pressed his foot on the gas pedal and plowed ahead and over the crazed. He ripped into the crazed, one after another, and his heart began to calm. After another few minutes, the pack was thinning out— Clay only crunching over one of the flailing once-humans every twenty seconds or so.

But with the silence, Clay felt the heaviness of the bus's morale. In the rearview mirror, he could see them staring forward silently, varying degrees of shock on their faces. Agnes was still crying. Hank's skin was a strange grey color, which made his bright hair all the more cartoonish. Alayna had her hand on her stomach and her other arm around Maia, holding her close. Brandon was in the far back now, his knees up against his chest. He still held the nightstick, twirling it slowly.

Clay steered the bus toward the edge of the town.

The energy field was no more, leaving just the open road stretching before them. A large truck appeared, cutting directly toward him.

"It's them!" Lane gasped, leaning toward the front window. "Malcolm stuck around, just in case we got out!"

"I don't think so," Clay said, stabbing the gas pedal. "Looks like a different kind of vehicle. But we haven't got a single bullet to our name. If it's him ..."

"What the—" Alayna gasped.

She barreled forward. Her eyes were huge, filled with child-like wonder. She perched at the edge of the passenger's seat.

"It can't be," she said.

"What are you talking about?" Clay demanded. "Alayna—"

It was then that he recognized the person in the passenger seat of the large truck. The dark, curly hair, falling forward across her face. The smirk.

Megan.

Megan slid out of the truck, her hair flipping in the wind. The look on Alayna's face: one of adoration, of incredulity, was enough to make Clay forget the blood, dripping from his hands. It was enough to make him hope—if only briefly—for a future.

55.

F UCK! I cry out in silence, smashing my fists through the air. My legs can hardly hold me. They're like weird splinters I toss forward as I lurch ahead. Blood oozes from my eyes—or at least, I think it's blood—and I feel my nails growing longer, sharper.

"FUUUCCCKK" I try again, but this time, it sounds like a groan, a grunt. I'm some kind of animal in this afterlife. This strange, concrete wilderness. Around me, the others flail, groan, grunt. They sound just like me. Their hair is matted with bits of blood and bone. Are they the bones of our once-friends? Have we ever been anything but this?

FLESH. I smell it. I inhale it. I can think of nothing else. My tongue throbs with hunger for it.

In the distance, I hear gunshots echoing through the buildings. The smell of flesh is stronger, and I'm panting now—wanting to feast, to tear it with my teeth.

To the right, I see it: the blast, the explosion. Skulls shattering, with blood splattering across us all. We're drowning in our own blood. It's not the taste we want. A huge, shining beast crushes some of them, smashing them against the ground. I flail, unable to control anything but this urge—

This desire—
To feed.

56.

"Stop the bus!" Alayna screamed. She cranked open the door, not waiting for the wheels to stop turning. She flew across the gritty and cracked pavement between the bus and the pickup.

Clay heard mutterings behind him. "Where is she going?" Agnes asked.

"I think that's someone we used to know," Brandon said apprehensively. "Clay . . . is that?"

Clay stood and watched it unfold. Alayna had stopped a few feet away from Megan. Her shoulders were shaking. Behind him, Brandon said to Agnes, "She betrayed us. Left us at this hotel back in Carterville. I think the two of them had a thing—but, should we really forgive someone like that?"

Clay felt a similar conflict. Megan and Alayna finally wrapped their arms around one another. Clay wondered if Megan could feel the baby growing in Alayna's stomach—the small curve above her belt. Proof of what they'd done, when Megan ran away.

As Clay approached, he could hear fragments of what they were saying. Whispered, lovely things that he might have wanted to share with Valerie, had he gotten to her in time.

"I never thought I'd see you again," Alayna said. "I thought you were gone. Like so many others . . ."

"I was trying to find you this entire time," Megan told her. "I made Rex here leave his silo, to come out here and try to find you. I realized how selfish I'd been. How absolutely horrible it was to leave you like that."

"Don't talk about it now," Alayna replied. "Please. It's in the past. And nothing matters now."

Clay remained several feet away, crossing his arms over his chest. Behind him, his group trickled out of the bus. The man driving the pickup slid out onto the pavement. Even a few feet away, Clay could smell the alcohol on his breath. His eyes were bloodshot. Clay half-wondered if he was drunk: just tearing across the abandoned landscape half out of his mind.

Rex stuck out his grubby hand for Clay to shake. "What on Earth are you doing out here?" Rex asked. "Of all the people I'd expect to see this far from our neck of the woods, you're the last, Sheriff."

Clay's memory flashed with recognition, but at the moment, he wasn't particularly in the mood to rekindle the old relationship. "I'm sorry? We've met?" Clay said, playing dumb, if for no other reason to make Rex work for it. Clay clearly remembered the old farmhouse on the outskirts of Carterville where Rex prepped for the apocalypse. The weaponry, the food, the gear—it had all been beneficial. Just another stepping stone on the road of survival.

Rex was nonplussed, his hand still out, but he didn't reply.

"Of course," Clay said, giving Rex a sincere, if unenthusiastic, smile. "I see you fell in with Megan."

"Oh yeah. She's been driving me insane for quite a while now. Meg—" Rex turned toward her. Alayna and Megan still had their arms wrapped around each other. "Guess these are the assholes we've been looking for?"

"A few more of them than when I last saw them," Megan said, her eyes scanning the group. "A few new faces. And a few missing . . ."

"What kind of bus is that?" Rex guffawed. "The Lutheran church? Are you building some kind of cult, Sheriff Clay?"

"All we had for transport, I'm afraid," Clay said. "But we're fresh out of weapons at the moment. Supplies are lacking too. We got trapped back in Ridgeway by a pack of them—hundreds and hundreds, I mean. On all sides. Had to drive over them to get out."

Rex assessed the front of the bus, which was splattered, seemingly painted, with the purple and green, puss-like blood of the crazed. Clay forced his eyes away.

"Ridgeway, huh?" Rex nodded. "We were scouting a farmhouse back there, and heard an explosion coming from that direction. By the time we got to the truck, a caravan went barreling by. Maybe thirty or so vehicles, speeding down the road. That got anything to do with you?"

Clay nodded, suppressing rage. Alayna explained, "That's Malcolm. He thinks he trapped us with the crazed. But we escaped."

"So fucking many of them," Rex said, shaking his head. "Where are they all off to?"

"We have to go after them," Clay said, his voice urgent. "We're utterly defenseless, without our weapons, but we have to destroy them. Somehow. Some way."

A strange smile stretched between Rex's ruddy cheeks. Clay held his eye contact for a long moment, sensing that this man's level of crazy was exactly what he needed. Rex cackled and jerked his head at his pickup.

"I've got enough on hand to supply a small army. What do you say we go back to that farmhouse and figure some things out?"

57.

C lay rode with Rex in the pickup, with Alayna and Megan in the back seat. Sherman followed them with the bus as they drifted down country roads, snaking through the trees. "How did you even find this place?" Clay asked, peering through the pines. The farmhouse sat in a bright green yard, boasting loose clapboard siding and shabby shutters swinging gently in the breeze. A truck in the driveway leaned crazily on its two remaining tires under a basketball hoop. If Clay hadn't known better, he'd think the owners were still there. That they were tucked away, drinking coffee and chatting in the breakfast nook.

"I got a nose for places like this," Rex explained, cutting the engine. "Places where people like me pack away some good supplies. It's not like these people came into the countryside for no reason, you know. They were hiding from something."

As the group filtered out of the bus, Rex equipped each of them with a gun—excluding Maia, of course. Agnes adjusted the sling on her shoulder, determination on her face. Rex spoke up, "We didn't have time to do more than a cursory sweep. So, we're going to need to do a more thorough search of the property. Clay and I will go over the weapons I have, and he'll fill me in on this Malcolm you all keep carrying on about."

Clay watched as his group split up and disappeared through the trees. He felt a sense of obligation to them, stemming from this new reality, and their new sudden intake of weapons. Even Hank, strung out after the death of Walt, seemed to have a spring in his step. He walked beside Agnes and spoke conspiratorially—almost as if he were sharing an inside joke.

Alayna and Megan hung back with Clay and Rex, their rifles slung over their shoulders. Megan couldn't seem to look at Alayna enough. But Alayna set her chin, turning toward Rex.

"There really is an urgency in going after Malcolm," she said, taking over for Clay. "And we need you to understand it before we proceed."

Rex slid his fingers into his shirt pocket, removing a cigarette. He stuffed it between his lips and eyed her, curious. "Proceed," he said, as he lit the tip.

"The General's up north," Alayna said. "At the military base. He's on a massive power trip, because he believes himself to be the only military man left in the world. And he's got support to back him. A device that can control the crazed. Or so we think."

"It's imperative that we try to get to Earlton before Malcolm does," Clay said, leaning against the pickup truck. "If only to stop an alliance between Malcolm and the general."

"I see," Rex said, puffing on his cigarette. "Two powerful, evil forces. Damn. They always find each other, don't they?"

"It could mean the end of us if we don't find a way to fight back," Clay agreed.

In the distance, Clay heard members of his crew calling out—clearing the area. There was a sunny quality to the afternoon, as if the horror in Ridgeway hadn't followed them here.

"Listen, Rex," Clay began, "I know we weren't very . . . close, back in Carterville—"

"That's all right, Sheriff," Rex cut him off, "I know how it is, you bein' a man of the law and all. No hard feelins."

"Thank you, Rex. But I can't very well ask you to fight our fight. I appreciate your help, and your guns, more than I can say, but—"

"Well, I ain't gonna sit around here by myself. And I certainly ain't going down without a fight," Rex said. "Meg, you ain't been target practicing for nothing, eh?"

Megan didn't answer him.

"See? We're good to fight. We're with you—shoulder to shoulder," Rex said with a grin.

"All right. Much appreciated. Now that we've got ammunition and weapons, we have find food and fuel," Clay said, scanning the farmyard. "You said this place was well stocked?"

"Eh, it's not perfect in the fuel department," Rex said.

"We could head back to Ridgeway, maybe?" Megan asked. "The crazed have probably cleared out, and you said you had a ton of fuel back there."

"Naw," Clay said, his stomach turning over. The image of a sea of mutilated crazed with more hiding around every corner shook him. "There's got to be a better way. Somewhere between here and the base."

"There's another farmhouse up the road," Rex said. "More trucks out front. Seems like maybe they'd have some fuel. Maybe we could split up. Send a few over to investigate. Hell, I'll go myself."

Clay nodded, despite his hesitation about separating. He sensed courage in Rex that he appreciated. A feeling that everything would be all right, if only they continued to push on—without fear.

58.

C lay watched as Rex, Quintin, and Sherman crunched down the dirt road toward the other farmhouse. The three burly men looked comical, jammed in the front seat of Rex's pickup, but their faces were stern, like they'd been chiseled from stone. Behind him, Alayna and Megan were whispering again. Although he was curious about their conversation, Lane's hand pulled him away.

They joined Marcia and Leland near a stand of trees. Leland leaned toward Clay, almost examining him. "We all saw you do it, Clay," he said. "We all saw you make them—erm. Explode."

Clay sighed. At that moment, he was mostly himself—nothing was trying to invade his thoughts.

"I can't describe how it felt," Clay said. "It was like a wave of anger, and then suddenly—" He splayed out his hands, imitating an explosion. "That was it."

"But it wasn't just that," Lane said. "You were able to slow them down back in Ridgeway. This connection you have with them . . . I don't think you should avoid it. Maybe you can learn to control it."

Clay glanced back at Alayna and Megan, on the porch. Their noses were only a few inches apart, and their bodies seemed in-tune with one another. From this distance, they didn't seem to need him for anything other than survival.

"I guess there's no reason I can't try," Clay said.

"There's a few out back," Lane said, her eyes sparkling with excitement. "They're trapped in the corral. No better way to practice."

Feeling almost outside of his body, Clay followed the scientists around the side of the farmhouse, to a rusted-out horse corral. Surrounded by the deteriorating borders of the stockade were four crazed, their limbs flailing and their tongues leeching out from their mouths. Aimless and disoriented, they were bumping around, unable to find a way out.

Two had been men; another a woman. And the fourth, well. Clay couldn't be sure, as it was so skeletal.

"How do I start?" Clay asked, smacking his hands together.

"Just try to direct your mind's energy toward them, maybe," Lane suggested. "Honestly, this is all guesswork at this point." She tapped the gun strapped to her right leg, adding, "If anything goes wrong, we'll take them out. Don't worry about making a mistake."

Clay took a deep breath and concentrated on the single crazed to the left. He pushed his emotions— his anger, his resentment, his everything—toward it. His fists were tight against his thighs, and his throat buzzed. He pushed harder.

With an audible wet crunch, its head exploded, splattering the corral with brains. Surprise robbed Clay of his concentration and he began to cough. Unable to react in any other way at this point, Lane laughed and put her hand on his shoulder.

"Maybe ease off on the anger a little this time,"

she said. "Maybe think more positive thoughts?"

"You sound like a girl scout leader," Clay said with a wry smile.

"Just do it," she said. "And try not to destroy them this time. We need them."

Clay squinted and tried again. In the silence that followed, he decided to try directing instead of destroying. He focused his thoughts on arms. And in jerky, uncoordinated motions, crazed all raised their arms as if in surrender. Clay held them like that for a moment before allowing them to collapse. As he let go, he realized he'd been holding his breath.

"Wow!" Lane exclaimed. "You held them for like a whole minute. Try again? Something bigger this time?"

Over the course of the next thirty minutes, he forced his mind into overdrive, experimenting with the legs and arms of the crazed, then controlling more precise movement. He found that he could control their fingers; he could tilt their heads. By the end of it, he began to spin them around in a macabre dance—something that had Lane holding her sides from laughter.

It had been a long time since Clay made someone laugh. He liked the feeling. Impulsively, he named them. "Larry, Curly, and Moe. Just like your silly candy stores," he told Lane. And then, tried a Three Stooges' show, making them dance and spin and fall on the ground. Lane laughed until she cried.

"You've almost got it, Clay," she gasped. "I reckon you're pretty close."

"I need more time to practice," Clay said, finally releasing the crazed. They began to roar their frustration at their lack of control. "Just a bit more time."

59.

Sherman, Quintin, and Rex returned to the farmhouse about an hour later, their pickup stocked with still more food. Piles of crackers, cans of soup and other necessities. The three men unloaded, passing supplies to Agnes, Alayna, and Megan, who organized them into piles.

On the other side, Maia and Brandon spoke in hushed whispers. Every once in a while, Brandon touched Maia's upper shoulder in an almost intimate (but maybe just friendly? he hoped) way.

Everyone seemed too comfortable there at the farm, and Malcolm was speeding away.

"No fuel," Rex grunted to Clay.

"Shit," Clay said. He was genuinely unsure if they had enough to get them to the base. Eyeing the sun, he reasoned that they still had plenty of daylight to get up there. "Well, there's no point sticking around here," he said.

"Except to rest up," Megan replied. "You all must be exhausted. I can't imagine—"

"Right now, we've got surprise on our side," Clay insisted. As he thought about it, about the hours they'd wasted at the farmhouse, he realized it had been a poorly conceived plan. Malcolm was racing ahead, maniacal and wild, thinking only of the ways he and the general could rule what was left of the world.

"Clay's right," Alayna said. "We can't sit back on this. Malcolm's out of his mind, and that works in his favor."

"He'll probably drive almost all the way to the military base before stopping to plan his own attack," Clay said, nodding firmly.

"I mean, we don't know how big the military base is," Quintin interrupted. "It could be a futile mission all around for us."

Clay shrugged, unsure of how to respond. "Sure. Fuck it. You're right," he said. "But regardless of all that, we won't know the truth until we get up there. And hemming and hawing at this farmhouse isn't going to do anything for us."

"How far do you think we are from the base?" Rex asked, spitting on the dried-out and cracked soil of the driveway.

"A few hundred miles," Quintin said.

"And fuel? We can find that on the way," Rex said, his eyes sizzling with the kind of manic energy Clay felt brewing inside himself. "Fuck it, we'll make it happen, Clay. Even if that bus of yours *is* a piece of shit gas guzzler, I guess it's all we've got."

Sherman stepped in front of Rex and glowered. Everyone froze. Looking down at Rex from his considerable height advantage he growled, "You want to talk shit about my church's bus again?"

The sentence was such a surprise, such a shock, that both Megan and Alayna laughed. Even Clay felt a smile escape. Rex clapped his hand on Sherman's shoulder, shaking his head.

"At the end of all of this, Sherman, I hope you stick around. I think I like you," he said.

60.

S un. Beating down on my back. I lick at my chin, feeling for leftovers from my last kill. The blood of that woman, oozing down my face, my neck. I drew it in, ripped at her flesh, hungry almost immediately for more. MORE.

But as I try to lurch myself toward the STENCH OF FLESH, I cannot move. I push all my energy toward my arms, my legs. *GO. EAT,* I tell myself. The way I always have, I always have. But nothing moves. I try to turn my head to see more, but even my neck is paralyzed.

On either side of me, there's more of me. Equals, like me. I see that we're all erect, standing straight up and down—our limbs rigid, and our tongues so suddenly returned our mouths.

Aaaaah!

HUNGER rips and tears into my brain, I can do nothing. I cannot even wail.

We are in a row, staring forward. And then, my right leg moves. Then my left. I'm moving forward. And incredibly, the men on either side of me move too. We seem to move mechanically. LEFT. RIGHT. LEFT. RIGHT. I cannot stop it. It's just happening—

Again, I try to see. Just to know! But my body is no longer my own. Just this ravenous, crazed mind

. . .

Suddenly, we turn about-face, finding ourselves in front of a FIELD of FLESHY MEN. I smell their blood, pumping in their veins. I KNOW what they taste like. I yearn to rush toward them, my arms outstretched. I know they couldn't outrun me, if only I had control. If only I could FIGHT . . .

But no. This invisible force pushes my feet to the ground, and I remain erect, straight up and down, surrounded by others just like me. What are we? Are we puppets? Whose machine is this?

Will I ever eat again?

61.

"I hear them," Clay muttered to himself, leaning back in the passenger seat of the bus. They were coming up on a cluster of parked vehicles—all scattered pell-mell across the pavement. He held his head, feeling the crazeds' thoughts crash through his mind.

"Well, this is as far as we can go," Sherman said, tapping the fuel indicator. "If we don't siphon out some gas, we'll be fucked in the next thirty miles. Crazed or no crazed, we've got to get off this bus."

Clay knew he was right. Reaching for his walkie-talkie, he connected with Rex behind them. "You see this cluster?" he asked.

"Yep," Rex's voice crackled.

"We've got to siphon," Clay said. "We won't make it if we don't."

"Roger that."

At the edge of the cluster, Sherman cut the engine. Clay turned to the exhausted, crumpled faces of the people in his bus. "We're going to have a few of you help siphon, but the rest you stay on the bus."

Maia gave him a look, one that spoke of "wanting to help." But Clay kept going, slicing his palm through the air. This wasn't going to be where Maia died—at the edge of some cruddy field, in the middle of nowhere. No way in hell.

"Maia, Marcia, Lane, Leland . . . Hank, if you want one, I'll give you a pass here," he said.

But Hank sprung to his feet, rifle in hand. "I'm standing guard," he said, bolting down the aisle.

To Clay's surprise, Lane was only a few steps behind. She pressed her palm against his chest, almost shoving him. "You fool," she said. "If you run into the crazed, I can't trust you to handle them yourself. You need someone to talk you down. Try to control them."

Lane put her hand on her rifle, showing she was prepared for whatever came along. Knowing this was practice he might need, Clay nodded, then gestured at the vehicles.

"Let's be quick," he said, his voice hushed. "Quick and as quiet as we can. You know they can smell us and hear us. The sooner we're back on the bus, the better."

With a last glance at Maia, peering through the dingy windshield, Clay ducked between the cars, with Lane in tow. They spread out like spiderwebs, curling around the cars beneath the burning sun. They worked in pairs, one standing guard while the other siphoned gas. No one spoke much. Alayna and Megan held hands atop the bus, surveying the fields on either side.

"They're coming," Clay whispered to Lane, feeling the aggressive thoughts stirring. "I know they're coming. They smell us."

He wasn't sure how he knew it, but he did. He jostled the last of the gas into his can and returned it to the bus, watching the horizon. He knew they would appear in just seconds.

"You have to control your mind, if you're going to

control them," Lane told him. Her knuckles were white, showing her own fear, but her voice was firm. "Concentrate. Remember how you trained your thoughts."

Clay walked toward the edge of cars, staring at a thicket of pines. Sure enough, a dozen or more of the crazed sprang from the shadows, their arms thrashing. He heard their guttural cries, could literally feel their pain, their need for flesh. His own tongue almost tasted it: this craving.

But, there was something else. The innate desire to feel something. To be something more than a monster.

There was something almost human about them. An otherness.

He couldn't explain it.

Agnes raised her gun first, firing one shot, then another. The second one tore into the skull of one of the front-running crazed. Lane followed suit, crying out to Clay. "DO SOMETHING. YOU KNOW YOU CAN!"

Clay's crew ran back toward the bus, their eyes showing white. They couldn't move quickly enough. The crazed were far too swift, like gazelle across the plains.

Clenching his fists, Clay forced himself to concentrate. He stared at the skeletal arms and legs, at the way they moved, and his face scrunched with concentration. Initially, he pushed too hard. Once again, a head exploded, splattering blood only inches from Brandon's feet. Holding back slightly, trying to balance it, Clay began to push against the crazed. Suddenly, their bodies leaned backward, away from him.

They slowed, became mechanical. Like robots,

with Clay holding the controller.

Clay pushed a little harder, walking toward them—like a shepherd to his sheep. As he neared them, that growing feeling—that they had THOUGHTS, that they were still IN THERE, in some capacity—seemed more and more evident. At fifteen feet away, he could see something glimmering in their eyes.

Something painful. Something beyond the hunger.

"CLAY! STOP SCREWING AROUND AND GET IN HERE!"

It was Lane, yanking him back to reality. He lost his concentration. The crazed were dopey for a moment before recognizing their surroundings. Clay back stepped up onto the bus and closed the door tightly behind him. The remaining crazed charged the bus, rocking it back and forth.

Rex's voice came from the walkie-talkie. "Clay, whatever the hell you did out there—you saved us," he said. "Damn. Maybe you have more control than you thought."

62.

As Sherman drove, Clay collapsed in the seat immediately behind him, exhausted. His hands continued to shake. He leaned his head back, wanting to catch just a moment of sleep before they arrived at Earlton.

But within seconds, Megan appeared beside him. Her eyes were haughty, removed. Crossing her arms over her chest, she leaned closer to him, almost breathing down his neck. Clay waited, knowing that anything she said, anything she tried with him, he could master. She was still just a stick-thin woman from Carterville, a snake of a woman who'd left Alayna behind.

Clay couldn't trust her.

"What is it, Megan?" he asked.

"I know about Alayna," she said, her voice low. Clay could hardly hear it over the bus engine.

"Oh?" Clay asked, giving her a small shrug.

"I know she's—she's pregnant," Megan said. "She didn't keep it from me long, you know. Told me straight out what happened. And now she's telling me she has the nanites inside her. Just like you."

Clay nodded. Megan's face crumpled slightly, showing her fear, her sadness. She fell into the seat beside him, staring straight ahead as she continued her speech.

"First of all, I can't believe the two of you. How could you possibly—"

"Don't do that," Clay said. "There's a lot of fingers that could be pointed around here, and a lot of those fingers would be pointed directly at you."

Megan didn't speak for a moment. Again, her chin quivered, showing her apprehension. Smashing her fist against her thigh, she said, "I just don't want Alayna to wind up like you. With all those—things—in her system? I mean, she's going to go crazy, too. Isn't she? She told me how you destroyed that church, Clay. You can't control yourself. And in Alayna's state, she has far more to care about than just herself. She has to keep herself alive—and sane—for the sake of the baby."

"Lane's explained that it's a bit different with Alayna," Clay said, surprised at Megan's apparent compassion. He saw the love in her eyes. "Because Alayna's pregnant, it's possible that her body is protecting the baby instead of allowing the nanites to take over. I guess we have to trust that, for now."

Lane got up, hearing her name. She brought Jacobs with her. "Clay!" she exclaimed, interrupting the moment. "Hey! Jacobs and I were just discussing something. Something pretty incredible. He was running through the numbers and thinks that maybe, just maybe, if we got you and Alayna into a fully-functioning lab, we could reverse the effects of the nanites."

Clay gaped. "What the hell are you talking about?" he asked. The bus bumped over a deep pothole, shaking them.

"It's not for certain, of course. And finding a functional lab will be a pretty difficult task. But if we can get you and Alayna into one in the next few weeks, I think we can actually leech the nanites out of your cells, on a DNA-level, and contain them. It has to do with the molecular structure of the nanites themselves."

Lane continued to prattle on, her hands whirling around her face as she dove into the science behind the extraction. But all Clay felt was hesitation, and disappointment. The power he'd used out on the field: the incredible capacity he had to direct hands and legs and elbows, an entire army of mostly-dead people—had been absolutely incredible. He'd never felt more superhuman.

But Megan was alert, listening. She gripped Lane's wrist, staring into her eyes. "You absolutely have to do this, for Alayna's sake, and the baby," she said.

"We'll need better tools to pull it off," Lane said, slipping a pair of glasses she rarely wore over her nose and grinning a wide, almost cartoonish smile. "But if we can get back to Helen—"

"Hey, gang?" Sherman called, making Clay's heart pump wildly in his chest. "Looks like we're coming up on the base. It's showtime."

63.

"You see that, Rex?" Clay muttered into the walkie-talkie, leaning forward in the passenger seat as the bus began to slow.

"I see it, all right," Rex answered. "Just a few shit-looking buildings that should have been knocked down a long time ago. I forgot that Earlton was so small. Ain't no cultural mecca, is it?"

"No. Cultural mecca, it's not," Clay said, finding himself chuckling. "Looks more or less deserted from here. But I guess we know better than to judge a book by its cover."

Earlton was no more than a collection of a few slanted brick buildings and some fast food stops, each with their bright logos stretching into the sky. Clay positioned his walkie-talkie on his hip and squinted, trying to take in the horizon line. "Something up there," he said to Sherman. "Some kind of perimeter. Let's keep driving."

They neared a barbed wire fence, nearly two-stories high, without an obvious energy field. There was what looked like a dilapidated guard shack down the fence line, its windows boarded over. The bus sputtered to a stop, allowing Clay to hear the murmured complaints behind him. "What the hell kind of place is this?" Brandon asked Maia. "I thought we were coming to a military base?"

"Seems like they left this place long ago," Agnes whispered doubtfully. "I don't think we're going to have much luck here. If Malcolm's coming here next, he'll just tear through us and then drive on somewhere else."

Clay felt the growing discontent. But, a guard leaped from the guardhouse, armed with a massive automatic rifle. The weapon was pointed directly at the bus, fully capable of pulverizing anyone inside.

Clay raised his hands, trying to show they came in peace. The guard shouted into a megaphone.

"MOVE ON, NOW," he boomed, "YOU HAVE NO BUSINESS HERE."

Clay glanced at Sherman, whose hands gripped the steering wheel tightly, showing the first moment of fear he'd seen from the burly man. Clay took their bus "megaphone," which Sherman had told him he'd used for the church years before and said, "I'VE COME TO SEE COLONEL WALLACE."

The guard didn't react. From the back of the bus, Lois said, "It's GENERAL Wallace, now."

Clay felt his eyes roll. Lifting the megaphone, he said, "SORRY. THAT'S GENERAL WALLACE WE'RE HERE TO SEE." There was still no reaction. "LET THE GENERAL KNOW THAT IT'S SHERIFF CLAY DOBBS FROM CARTERVILLE. I'M PRETTY SURE HE'LL REMEMBER ME. HE KNOWS WE HAVE A FEW THINGS TO CHAT ABOUT."

After a long, uneasy pause, the guard lifted a walkie-talkie and spoke into it. What he said, Clay could only imagine. Perhaps it was a request to murder them all.

Feeling a wave of impending doom, Clay lifted his walkie-talkie and began to speak to Rex. "Rex. I'd like for you to pull back, if you can. Maybe stay on the outside, just in case we need backup."

He should have thought of that before. He was playing too many of his cards at once. Rex began to ease backward, trying to distance himself from the base. But before he got far, a military Jeep pulled up behind him, and blared its horn, forcing Rex to stop. They had nowhere to go.

"MOVE FORWARD," someone blared from the Jeep.

And, on cue, the gates of the compound separated, like the gates of hell. They rolled forward, crunching against the pavement, until the space was wide enough for the bus, the pickup, and the Jeep to pass.

"Shit. Well, here goes nothing," Sherman said, dropping his foot on the gas pedal.

Clay had no answer to that.

64.

A fter Sherman guided the bus through the gate, another Jeep cut in front of them—its driver sticking his hand out the window and waving them forward. The compound was modest, probably a quarter mile across and deep, with a scattering of tents and crooked buildings along the southern edge. The soldiers looked scrawny and weak, strung out— their cheeks hollow and their eyes dark, like rats in a city. Clay only counted thirty or forty soldiers though, each one smaller and less intimidating than the last.

"They couldn't hack it against Malcolm's crew," Sherman muttered to Clay, saying what they were both thinking. "No way in hell. If Malcolm came in here looking for an alliance, he'd probably just murder them all in a single swoop."

Three Jeeps waited at the far edge of the grizzled-looking field where Sherman guided the bus to a halt. Rex rolled up beside them, the last Jeep parked beside him. They waited in silence, Clay's eyes swept the area for some sign of life.

In front of them was a large warehouse, painted a dark grey, its windows sealed. Large metal doors slid to the side, revealing four more armed soldiers, alongside a larger, bulkier form. This was the general: a face that had been burned into Clay's mind since those first few days in Carterville. His fists clenched, and a now-familiar rush of anger swirled up within him.

"That's him, isn't it?" Sherman asked.

"Uh huh," Clay grunted.

One of the soldiers shouted into a megaphone, "Clay Dobbs. The General requires your presence, unarmed."

The general placed his fists on either side of his waist—seemingly drawing himself taller. He exuded ego like a massive wave. Trying to match his ego with anger, Clay shoved open the bus door and stepped into the afternoon air. He strode toward the general, his movements exact, confident. As he did, he felt the way the crazed felt toward what they were most hungry for: FLESH. FLESH. BLOOD. EAT.

But when he was about five feet away, one of the military men stepped between them, pointing his weapon at Clay's chest. Clay stopped short, lifting his hands skyward. Still, his eyes held the general's, seeing a smile stretched over the man's lips.

"Well, well," the general said, his voice deeper than Clay remembered it. "If it isn't the man of the hour. Sheriff Clay Dobbs." He said the word "sheriff" sarcastically, as if it was a made-up title in a world he'd constructed. "To be frank, I thought I'd never have to deal with you again. I thought you'd been squeezed out long ago. Better that than me having to flick you away, like some sort of fly."

Clay crossed his hands over his chest, impressed by the sheer magnitude of the general's God complex. "You really think you own the world, don't you?"

"Own it?" the general asked. "Clay, there is no world but this one. This one right here, between these barriers. Do you know how I know that?" He gave Clay an ominous smile, then barked at his soldiers, "Get everyone off the bus! Disarm them. Take everything they have."

The soldiers boarded the bus, yanking Megan, Lane, Alayna, even Maia out roughly and pushing them into a line. Clay told himself, over and over, that it wasn't yet time to lose his cool. Maia blinked at him from the line, her bottom lip quivering. He reminded himself that she was his number one responsibility. If nothing else, he would make sure she lived. He'd die making sure of it.

Clay turned back toward the general, lifting an eyebrow.

"I suppose you don't want to know why I came all the way here? Just to shoot the shit, you probably think?" Clay said.

The general guffawed. The sound was unnatural, like metal scratching against metal. Clay's stomach twisted.

"Someone's coming after you, General," Clay said. "Someone with numbers much higher than yours, and—as far as I can tell—more weapons. You'll have no chance against them when they get here. They'll take everything you've got. And the leader, Malcolm? He's probably crazier than you. Although I can't say that for sure."

The general assessed Clay for a long moment, his grin growing wider, more sure. He laughed merrily, seeming to mock the way normal, happy people laughed. With their body, their soul.

But within seconds, he was upright once more, snapping his fingers. The larger of the two bi-pass doors opened behind him, revealing a troop of maybe a hundred soldiers. They were shadowed, gaunt, almost skeletal. And as they marched forward in precise unison, Clay's heart sank.

Each 'soldier' was a former human. Each was a crazed. And they seemed to be at the total and complete mercy of the general, who remained staring at Clay with a kind of horrible, mind-bending arrogance.

65.

The soldiers marched: left, right. Left, right. The greyish tone of their bodies was incredibly apparent in the light, as they emerged from the shadows of the warehouse. Their eyes were volatile, wild, filled with all the emotions Clay felt. Stirring madly. Making his insides scream.

KILL HIM, the voices cried. EAT HIM. MURDER HIM.

The words were so deafening that Clay couldn't ignore them. They felt personal. He could understand the unique voice and personality of each of the walking corpses before him, and he was sickened by all that was lost in to the world. Faced with the man who'd made this all happen—the general himself— Clay felt rage. A murderous kind of rage.

But even as he his mind swam through his incredible, intense fit of anger, Clay noticed that he could "feel" the pull of the device the general was using as well. His feet twitched beneath him as the crazeds' feet landed. His elbows twitched with theirs. More than once, he felt himself pulled forward, his physical body yearning to join their ranks.

LEFT. RIGHT. EAT. FLESH. TEAR. BONE. LEFT. RIGHT.

As sweat began to pour down his cheeks and

forehead, he felt a hand on his bicep, holding him back. He looked back into the eyes of Lane. She gave him a knowing nod, muttering, "The device. It can control you, too. Can't it?"

Clay hadn't the time to answer. The general began to brag. "This isn't all of them, Clay. I have several hundred more. And as soon as we round up more of them—rather easy in this new environment—I'll have the best army the world has ever seen. An army unrivaled by anything in Ancient China. The Greeks? They would have been slaughtered by the likes of my men. God knows, these soldiers? They're fighting machines. They yearn for nothing else but flesh. Even now, standing there, they're licking their lips. They want to rip into each and every one of you. But I'm holding them back."

"How kind of you," Clay snapped.

The general stopped the march, giving Clay time to regroup and regain control. After a deep breath, Clay pushed himself forward, stopping just feet from the general's face.

"But these aren't your soldiers," Clay said.

"What the hell are you talking about?" the general asked, his eyes flickering dangerously.

"They aren't yours. They still belong to themselves," Clay said. He'd never verbalized this opinion before, but he somehow knew their truth. "You have to see it in their eyes. There are humans inside those monsters. Beneath that urge to eat our mothers, fathers, brothers, sisters. Our accountants and our farmers and our truck drivers . . . the people who fell victim to this hellish science fiction trap. The one you set in motion, General."

"Enough!" the general said, clearly disgruntled.

"Oh, you didn't want to be reminded of what you

did to humanity?" Clay asked, his eyes blazing. "Because I think you should think about it. I think you should think about it every second of every day."

Then Lois was beside Clay, staring into the ranks of the crazed soldiers. She stuttered, "You—you've done it." Her face blanched. "You really did it. Your plan. It was all you. The reason for the secret labs ..."

"Of course, Lois," the general smirked. "Look at you, putting the puzzle pieces together," He gestured toward Lane, Marcia, and Leland, with another gleeful, and somehow ominous look. "And now that my top scientists have found their way back to me, I can move things to the next level. We have so much in production. So much! We just need more expertise to perfect these devices."

Lane drew back, suddenly terrified. In Clay's mind, a million tiny images flashed by—their time on the open road, of Lane protecting Alex, of Lane helping him learn to control the crazed, of Lane fighting beside them, each and every second, just to stay alive.

He'd be damned if he let the general destroy his group like this. He'd be damned if he let the general win: taking her bright and able mind and using it for such evil. Too much had happened.

As he stood there, his face turned a blotchy, tomato red. His fists clenched, his knuckles whitened. He could see nothing but bright white streaks. And just as it had before . . .

He felt his thoughts tighten and then leap away. The heads of three crazed soldiers suddenly popped, brains spewing across the cracked pavement. Lois shrieked and covered her mouth, in an attempt to stop her own vomit. Clay felt both tears and sweat on his cheeks. As another of the heads burst, like some kind defective fourth of July firework, Clay fell to his knees, gasping.

The general watched all this, stroking his chin. The four crazed that Clay had destroyed fell to either side of their lines, their limbs splayed.

"Interesting. Very interesting," he mused.

Clay tried to calm his unsteady mind. He didn't want to murder another one of them. He didn't want to smell another spray of brain matter, or spilled guts. Gasping, he shifted his eyes toward the general, who was staring at him.

"Men. Gather everyone. Take the scientists to the lab and put everyone else in the brig."

The human soldiers separated and began to divide them up. Clay felt utterly helpless, and his exhaustion made his arms feel like spaghetti.

"But Sheriff?" the general continued, his eyes glittering. "Don't get too comfortable. Sounds like we've got quite a bit to talk about. Quite a bit, indeed."

66.

Three of the soldiers herded them toward the side of the warehouse. Clay forced himself to move, watching helplessly as one of the soldiers took Maia's upper arm, leading her and Brandon somewhere else. With a lurch of fear, Clay cried out, "Where the hell are you taking them?"

The general raised an eyebrow, clearly loving the way he could control Clay—like a puppeteer and a puppet. He cackled. "Contrary to what you might believe, I'm no monster, Clay. They're children, for humanity's sake. I wouldn't throw them into the brig. That would be just cruel."

The irony of his words gave Clay pause. He had no ready response. His eyes followed Maia as far as they could. Another soldier was guiding Lane, Leland, and Marcia toward the lab, jabbing Lane in the back with his rifle. She stumbled at each thrust. Without even seeing her face, Clay sensed that she was crying quietly. Her allegiance to their troop was apparent. But now she was a tool in the general's game.

A hundred yards away from the large warehouse there was another. Two of the soldiers pushed the door open, revealing a wide-open expanse with a concrete stairwell off to one side, leading down and out of sight. Clay felt like a cow being herded to slaughter as the soldiers chivvied them to the staircase, and then down into the darkness below. Their movement remained constrained, preventing Clay from establishing any semblance of an escape.

The room was nearly equal in size to the space above, save the voluminous ceiling. On the far side, Clay could see the brig. It was nothing extraordinary, but it *was* enough to house dozens of prisoners easily. When they were closer, he could see several different cells. Their bars were sturdy, thick, and each cell closed at a corner, locked with what appeared to be a large skeleton key.

Megan slid up beside Clay. "I can't believe you got us in this fucking mess, Clay," she muttered. "Although knowing you, you lackluster sheriff for all those years . . ."

Clay kept his lips pressed together. He tried to remember exactly what he'd thought would happen upon their arrival. But now, exhausted from the destruction of the crazed, and being separated, again, from Maia, he could muster no response. He felt the rifle prod his shoulders, pushing him into the first of several cells. He dropped on a bench in the corner, bringing his hands to his forehead.

"Fuck," he yelled, as the other members of his crew were filed into cells of their own. They huddled together at the far end of each cell, eyes darting around like frightened animals. Rex, like Megan, was staring at Clay with hooded eyes, blaming him. And all the while, Clay felt the urgency of Malcolm's clan coming: their guns prepped and their minds energized, charged by Malcolm's charismatic rage.

They would be faced by an army of the general's crazed: all burning with the desire to tear into their flesh. And somewhere in the middle—between the bullets and the rotting flesh, would be Clay's team. Certain to be destroyed in the chaos.

And it was all his fault.

67.

Maybe an hour later, Clay remained perched at the edge of his cell, unmoving, unspeaking. He could hear several of the others around him, clearly despondent. Agnes seemed worried about Brandon and was whispering to Hank, "Do you think if I reason with the general, he'll bring Brandon over here? I mean, I've taken such a liking to him. I feel like a mother figure or something. I want to make sure he's being . . ."

Clay tuned the chatter out, which gave him a moment's reprieve. This feeling that his people were human first. That they were worried about one another, rather than simply angry at his decisions. But another wave of fear reminded him that his daughter was alone as well. She was still so terribly thin, weak—having to take frequent naps. The minute the attack began . . .

He needed to get close to her.

Smashing his fists on his thighs, he jumped up and began to pace his cell, alerting everyone to his anxiety. They said nothing, allowing the silence to hang heavy. After several minutes, Clay heard a crack at the door into the brig. The door swung open, and three armed soldiers came in. One pushed the key into Clay's door.

"You're letting us out now, huh?" Megan asked sarcastically.

"Just him," the soldier said. "And I think 'out' is the wrong term, here. Trust me. You don't want to go where he's going."

Clay forced himself not to look at his crew. He didn't want to see the fear in their eyes—or, worse, forgiveness.

The soldiers escorted him back up the stairs, and across the grey tundra just outside the warehouse. The grass was grizzled like an old man's hair, burnt up beneath the sun. It crunched under his feet and he wondered if anything would ever grow again.

"Pick up your feet," one of the soldiers ordered.

Angry, Clay snapped, "Only if you tell me what you've done with my daughter."

The soldiers didn't answer, and Clay could do nothing but follow, past the first warehouse toward a smaller facility, and then down another set of white-painted stairs. This basement had a single door, with a latch like a submarine's, sealed tight. The lead soldier un-cranked it, revealing a gleaming white laboratory. Bulbous brains, twisted and grey, floated in jars around the large room. And deep in the back, Clay could make out Lane's bobbing, brown ponytail.

Immediately, he felt a jolt of happiness. At least the three of them were still all right. Apparently, they were necessary for the General's plan.

To the right, elevator doors slid open and the general and two guards stepped out. The general gave clay a look that invited Clay to say something he'd regret.

He took the bait. "Goddammit, General. Whatever you want to do to me, make sure that

Maia's protected. That's all I ask."

The general snapped his fingers. Marcia, Lane, and Leland arrived at his side, all three red-cheeked. Lane's eyes were bloodshot, as if her crying had continued the entire hour they'd been apart. Marcia's normal temperamental attitude had been glossed over by fear. Her eyes were downcast.

"And tell me, Clay. How would you have me 'protect' your girl? You would have me let her go, is that it? Let her roam around outside, unable to defend herself? The poor girl probably doesn't even know how to shoot a gun. I bet you're regretting that, now, aren't you?" the general asked, leering at Clay. "Poor, weak, little girl. All hungry and tired. Guess you'll have to take your chances on my generosity, won't you? Guess it's your only option?"

Clay knew the general was right. Regardless, his fists raised. Two of the guards reached for his arms, pulling him back. Clay's mind stirred, making him dizzy. "What's your grand plan, anyway, General? Once you get your big army going, what's the next step? Just gonna sit here in your ivory tower?"

The general clicked his tongue. "Well, isn't this something. The bigwig sheriff doesn't have a clue what I'm getting up to, does he? Hah. Well, frankly, Clay, I'm disappointed. I would have thought you assumed I'd already been speaking with the other world leaders. They're ready to buy devices as quickly as we can make them. Ready to control their own armies of the dead. This is the future, Clay. This isn't just business. It's the way the world spins now."

Clay seethed. He strained trying to get free from the soldiers. "Is this how you get off? Playing war games with crazed monsters? Is this your power trip? The undead?"

The general reached behind his back, drawing one of the devices. He pointed it at Clay's heart. Before Clay could scream his protest, the general cranked it up.

Clay felt it instantly. Electricity, up and down his arms and legs, trying to drag him closer toward the general. He mustered up his energy, clenched his fists, and fought it. His eyeballs bulged from his sockets as he pushed against it, trying to stay in place. Even the General's soldiers had released their grip from his arms, watching his struggle. It was just Clay versus the device.

And somehow, it was working.

"Goddammit," the general muttered, upping the setting. The moment he did that, Clay felt himself drop to his knees. The world around him spun wildly. He attempted to steady himself, to pull himself upright. But the general continued to rail the device's energy at upon him.

Then, Clay saw only darkness.

68.

C lay tossed and rolled on the ground, every inch of him in pain. A scream escaped his throat, but he could hardly hear it over the thoughts of the crazed just outside. Somehow, his scream was only adding to their chorus, their inward agony.

While he writhed, the general motioned two of his guards to take him. They did, yanking him from the floor and tossing him on a chair. Clay saw nothing but bright spots when the general shut down the device down. But before he could recover, the soldiers had shackled him to the chair, clamping his biceps and forearms. He strained, feeling his skin break. Small droplets of blood appeared.

"You bastard!" Clay gasped. "Let me go. You can't just treat people like—"

The general snapped his fingers. "Marcia. I told you what to do, and you better goddamn do it."

Crying openly, Marcia inserted a needle into Clay's forearm. Clay watched, petrified, as she pressed the plunger in then pulled needle from his skin. Nearly instantly, his legs grew lax. Two soldiers pushed a large metal cage into the room. Inside, a crazed thrashed against the wire mesh, ramming its skull against the sides, its blood-soaked hair whipping around. It bared its teeth, biting its own lips and digging into the scabs. Clay stared at the strange being, trying to read the once-man's thoughts. Trying to "feel" what was going on behind his eyes.

But the general interrupted his concentration. "Do something," he ordered. "Like you did before. Pop his head off, anything. I want to see."

"No," Clay said with finality. "Absolutely not."

"Ha." The general leaned closer to him. "What could I do to get it going for you, Clay? What would make you obedient?" His eyes danced. "What if— hmm. What if I bring that pretty daughter of yours in here and let the monster loose? Would that help you, Clay? Would that encourage you to do what I want?"

Clay set his jaw. His eyes turned to Lane, on the far side of the room. She gave him a small nod. Her eyes seemed to say, "Just give him enough."

But controlling this new skill wasn't up to Clay. Not now, not yet. He squeezed his eyes almost shut, focusing intently. The crazed's arms grew lax and fell on either side of its skeletal frame. Its face stopped contorting, and it stared directly at Clay, becoming just a vessel.

"There he is," the general said. "Just like that."

Clay knew he had the control to do something more with the crazed. To lift his arms and legs; to even turn his body this way and that. But instead of showing off, he caused minor movements. He tilted the crazed's head to the left, then to the right, which seemed to impress the general only slightly.

"Dammit, Sheriff. You can do better than that. Maybe I really should bring that little girl of yours in here. I can just imagine how this monster would attack her. Wrapping his arms around her, ripping into her neck . . . Can't you picture it, Clay? All her pretty bright blood spilling from her porcelain neck?" He enjoyed Clay's anger rising. "It'll be just like when your wife died, won't it, Clay? Just like when Valerie lay ripped and bleeding, gnawed on by one of them. One of those monsters you keep saying are 'still human.' Ha. How hilarious."

Clay felt his heart nearly burst with anger. Turning his eyes back toward the crazed, his emotions caused the monster to explode—not just its skull, but everything. Blood and gore sprayed through the gaps in the cage, splattering against the sterile linoleum floor. Bones shattered: the larger ones impaling the mesh. Marcia turned away.

The general applauded. "That's more like it," he said. "How beautiful. You might be the most useful of all on this base at this very moment—even more so than these pretentious scientists." He smirked at Marcia, who was still trying not to vomit. He mocked her distress—as if the very idea of death was a joking matter.

Clay yearned to tear him apart.

"I think you'll be happy to know that your life will continue here," the general said. "If I find a use for something, you see, I like to keep it around. Even these monsters."

Fuck you, Clay thought. He clenched his fists beneath the restraints. No longer the Clay who'd allowed Malcolm to live; this Clay wanted to paint the walls with the general's brains.

A soldier's radio squawked.

"SERGEANT. There's something at the gate. We're going to need you out front. Over."

The sergeant reached for it, shrugging slightly. "We're a bit busy at the moment. Over."

"I don't think you're hearing me," the soldier

yelled. "You're going to need to get here right away. Bring the general, if you can convince that asshole to—"

Immediately, the soldier snapped it off, turning to the general. He flushed, furious and glared at Clay, almost begging him to make a single comment. To make one single, derisive comment.

But Clay wouldn't give it to him.

The general turned away. "I guess we better get up to see your little friend, eh, soldier?" he said, his voice gruff. "We can deal with Sheriff Clay Dobbs later." He jerked his head toward the guards at the door. "Take him to his cell. We'll continue with playtime later."

They uncuffed him from the metal chair. Clay forced himself to stand. Marcia and Lane pleaded him with their eyes. Lane, especially, seemed to be willing him to save them all.

But Clay knew in his heart that the days of saving everyone were gone. He'd lost so many. And now, separated from his daughter, he felt a rage he couldn't control. He was no longer sheriff. He wanted to tear the general's skull from his body.

And he wanted to feed it to the crazed.

69.

As the soldiers dragged Clay back to the brig, his head rolled from side to side from the drugs Marcia had injected into him. The world around him was blurry, almost foggy. He forced himself to blink several times and tried to straighten out his legs. Trying to walk upright. But before he could find his footing, the soldiers had pushed him into his cell. His cheek bounced against the floor. The soldiers clanged the door shut behind him.

Alayna reached through the bars separating their cells and touched Clay's shoulder. She soothed his tense muscles and spoke. "Clay? Clay, are you all right?" she asked, her voice frantic. "What the hell did they do to you, Jesus . . ."

Megan leaned against the bars, her arms folded across her chest. Her voice haughty, she said, "Looks like they really took a piece out of him. My oh my, I hope he recovers."

Alayna glared up at her, mouthing something, Clay couldn't make out what.

Lois knelt next to Alayna. "What happened up there, Clay?" she asked. "I told everyone they'd take you. They'd take you and they'd . . . test you. I know how the general thinks, and he thinks he can use you as some kind of—of weapon."

Clay looked from Lois' haggard face to Alayna's beauty, to Megan's disdain. He'd been their guide. He'd led them into the horrors of this prison, and he could see it in their eyes: they saw no real escape. This could very well mean their deaths.

Then it began. Gunfire. Explosions. Screams, echoing throughout the complex. Agnes shook the bars of their cells. She screamed, showing her first signs of fear.

"No! No! He's here—" she wailed.

It was what they were all thinking. Malcolm and his caravan of thirty-odd vehicles were surely bearing down on them, their guns in every window killing everything in their path. Malcolm was surely yelling into his walkie-talkie, delivering orders that meant destruction. Clay felt his heart shrouded with darkness.

Placing his palms flat on the floor, he tried to push himself up, but he was still too weak, too tired. He glanced up at Quintin, near the corner of the cell. The bulky man stared down at him with disdain. It very much seemed that the man was blaming him.

Clay felt his bearings coming back, little by little. His eyes turned back toward Alayna, who remained at his side. Her eyes glittered with fearful tears as she gazed up at the door of the brig as a wayward soldier stood—their guard—his rifle strapped across his chest. He looked no more confident than the rest of them.

"I'm sorry," Clay said, speaking to all of them. He was almost surprised at how strong his voice was, given how weak his muscles remained.

"I just . . . I feel so helpless," he said. "I can't do a single thing from this cell. And I want to be out there, ripping both the general and Malcolm to shreds."

"Don't be ridiculous," Megan scoffed. "We're all trapped in here. And it's not as if you could do anything if you were out there alone. You're only one man."

That spurred him enough to get to his feet. He shuffled forward, staring between the bars to his cell. The soldier continued to glance away and out of sight, his cheeks falling rapidly. His mouth was almost cartoonish, down-turned. Clay could almost see the devastation in his eyes.

"Hey. You," Clay said to the guard. Care to tell us what's going on out there?"

The guard tensed.

Clay gripped the bars of the jail cell, regaining even more strength. He peered out at the soldier, trying to read him. "I can see it written all over your face, soldier. Things aren't all rosy out there, are they? Come on. Tell me."

The guard glanced at Clay and then turned toward the commotion outside. He was trembling but gave them no information.

"Come on, man," Clay said. "We're all screwed, right? But wouldn't it make sense to have all able hands helping to defend this place? I mean, we've been up against these guys before. We might be able to lend—"

The guard lifted his hand, cutting Clay off, but visibly shaking. After a long, horrible pause, he whispered. "Sure. That would be fine. But—" He gulped. "I don't have the keys."

"Shit," Clay muttered.

The guard stumbled toward them, looking almost childlike. He eased along the cells, near where Quintin remained standing aloof against the cell wall, his arms crossed. The guard stared at Clay, fearful, watching him.

"You know these guys?" he asked. "You've dealt with them?"

Before anyone could reply, Quintin brought his hands from between the bars and grabbed the guard. He shook the boy, making him drop his weapon. The guard banged against the cell, clanking, while Quintin growled at him, "Let us the hell out of here!"

Outside, the attack continued. Gunfire peppered the door. Clay slid forward and put a hand on Quintin's arm.

"Hey. Hey," he said. "Stop it. He can't let us out."

Quintin stared up at Clay, incredulous. "You'd have me let him go?" he asked.

Clay nodded. "He doesn't have the keys. You've already knocked him around enough. He can't do anything for us."

Quintin let go and the guard scuttled away. As he was clear of the cells, a loud explosion rocked the foundation, making their ears ring.

70.

T he guard dropped to his knees and picked up his weapon. In the wake of the explosion, he scurried down the hallway, in the direction of the blast. He disappeared into the smoke and gunfire erupted. Clay was struck by the idea that Malcolm would come to them if the guard was cut down.

They listened, in agony, as the guard fought an intruder. It was clear within seconds that the guard had lost his rifle. The prisoners heard what could only be a fistfight. Clay held his breath. Megan wrapped her arms around Alayna, sliding her hands over Alayna's belly. The tension was high—charged with the belief that they certainly wouldn't make it out alive this time.

Silence fell. Clay listened intently trying to see down the corridor. After several moments, he heard a boot against the cement floor. Then another. The footsteps echoed against the walls. Clay's entire group sidled up against the edge of the cell and joined hands. Waiting.

A man appeared in the smoke. Clay recognized him instantly. His heart leaped in his chest, pounding against his ribcage.

"Adam?" he gasped.

Daniels gave him a cocky smile, lifting the

guard's gun over his head.

"Didn't think I was alive, huh?" Daniels said, his eyes gleaming. He reached the cell, taking in each and every one of them. "Didn't think Lieutenant Adam Daniels would make it?"

Clay cackled, smacking his hands on the bars to make them shake. "Jesus Christ, I didn't see any way you could have gotten out of that mess. Are you kidding me? This must be some kind of—"

But someone else appeared behind Daniels, in the smoke. Long muscular legs ending in combat boots. A pert figure in a dark green tank top with wide, bright blue eyes regarded him with interest. Clay's jaw dropped. She gave him a mocking smile.

"Go on. Tell me how shocked you are," Sam said, her smile now almost ominous. "Trust me. I couldn't wait to see you get into some kind of horrible scrape, Clay. Look at you. Behind bars. Into more trouble, all because you couldn't leave well enough alone."

Clay couldn't help the smile on his own face. He shook his head slowly, incredulous. "And look at you, there showing a heart of gold. Saving my ass, again."

"Well she sure as hell saved mine," Daniels said, gazing at Sam with adoration.

"Yeah, what happened? I thought, the grenade—" Clay began.

"Well, I used the grenade to destroy the ladder to the bell tower, just to keep the crazed away," Daniels said. "I wasn't completely ready to give up hope, you know. But I was watching, waiting for the crazed to leave me alone, and wouldn't you know it? They didn't."

"Turns out they were hungry for Adam here," Sam said, chuckling. "But I came by soon enough. I'd been following Malcolm up north and I heard some of your walkie-talkie chatter on my way up. Drove past the church and figured somebody up there needed saving."

Behind Clay, he heard Agnes weeping tears of joy. Hank held onto her shoulders, pressing his lips against her forehead.

"She's my savior," Daniels said, his voice shaking. "I would have been dead if not for her."

Clay allowed a long moment's pause before saying, "Well, get us the hell out of here, then! And tell me, what's going on out there? It sounds like a war zone."

71.

S am moved swiftly through the outer office, hunting for the keys. She kicked open the cabinet drawers, slid her fingers over the pads of paper, the knives, and other weapons. She called out to Clay as she searched.

"It's what you thought," she said. "Malcolm attacked the base head-on, I'm afraid. And it's not a pretty sight. He's got far more weapons than your arrogant general. Although it does seem that your general has something no one else possesses."

Sam turned toward him. Her eyebrows high, she whispered, "But I suppose you've already seen his crazed army, haven't you? I imagine it's the first thing he would have showed you. The arrogant prick."

Daniels hunted in another corner, chuckling. After tearing through another cabinet, he drew out a jangling bunch of keys. His eyes twinkled as he held them high. "Ah. Just where I thought they were," he crowed.

Agnes clapped. The others flew to the cell doors, waiting impatiently as Daniels sauntered toward them, swinging the keys.

"Yeah, what's that about, Clay?" Daniels asked, flipping through the keyring to find the best fit. "This army of the dead—"

"He's got that device, remember?" Clay said. "It can control them. He wants to monopolize the crazed, and even sell the device to world leaders and make a profit. It's—it's deplorable. He doesn't understand that those crazed out there, well. They're still human."

Sam exchanged a look with Daniels. It seemed they had a language of their own, one created on their way to rescue everyone. Clay could sense their disbelief.

"Anyway, it doesn't matter what I know about these people, or what I don't," he said. "It just matters that we get out of here." Daniels slipped a key into the lock. "How did you get in here, anyway?"

Daniels shrugged and yanked the door. Quick like rabbits, Agnes, Hank, Lois, Alayna, and Megan burst into the hallway outside. Sherman, Rex, and Quintin marched behind them, in no apparent hurry, eyeing Daniels and Sam. Sam's eyebrows rose at their performance. This was their reunion, Clay knew. But they weren't the type to show emotion. Especially not if it was real.

"Well, I was stationed here a few years ago," Daniels said. "I infiltrated and exfiltrated this place numerous times for various—shall we say—amorous reasons." He grinned playfully, showing deep dimples.

Megan rolled her eyes toward Alayna, who giggled good-naturedly. Outside, the battle raged on: bombs blasting, and soldiers screaming: voices echoing against the buildings. It illustrated this world so perfectly it sent shivers down Clay's spine. They had to get moving.

"So, what's our plan?" he demanded, searching

Daniels' face. "We'll get out the same way you guys got in?"

Sam's eyebrow twitched, almost in a threatening way. She leaned toward Clay, her face angry and resentful.

"That all depends," she said. "That all depends on if we want to run. Run away. Or if we should end all of this: like we should have, long ago."

Clay turned his attention to the rest of the crew. They stood in a staggered line against the cement wall, staring intently back at him. Their arms were crossed firmly against their chests, and their eyes were firm, filled with a single emotion: one of revenge.

"I say we kill the asshole," Hank said, smashing his fist against his palm. "Take him out. Make him pay for what he did to Walt."

The others nodded their agreement, staring at Clay. Sam cleared her throat.

"What do you say, Clay?" she asked, challenging him.

Clay's head swam. He knew, there was a single—horrible—problem that could derail any possible plan.

"Okay, okay. I'm in," he began. "But what are we going to do about the general's army of the undead? How can we possibly defeat both Malcolm and—them?"

Sam clucked her tongue. "You didn't think I'd come here without a plan, did you?" she asked. "When we parted ways back in Dearing, I went back to the container yard where Malcolm and I used to work. I found a number of trailers, absolutely stuffed with weapons. So that was a check, you know. But only a little bit later, I found a few more survivors. All of them as able-bodied as anyone who's survived this long. They could handle the weapons I gave them, without question. And now? I've got sixty armed and ready men here with us at this very moment."

Daniels nodded firmly. Clay's expression was incredulous. He leaned back, suddenly realizing that this plan—it could work.

"But we might not even need them," Sam said, her eyes glittering. "Because in here? We have an advantage that you probably didn't even consider. We're inside the Trojan horse, in here. Especially with Adams knowledge of the place."

Daniels cut between Sam and Clay, speaking excitedly. "In fact, I know where the armory is, as well as the barracks. I'd wager that I could convince some of them to switch to our side of the fight. Almost a guarantee."

72.

D aniels raised his rifle and called, "If you'll just follow me, there's a staircase down this way. It'll take us to the underbelly of the entire base. From there, we can get to everything. But watch your step. I can't handle another broken body around here, you hear?"

Clay fell into pace next to Daniels, while Sam followed at the back with Quintin and Sherman. Sam and Daniels had enough weapons for Sherman, Quintin, and Clay, but Megan and Rex both had to settle for knives from Daniels' boot knife straps. Megan brandished hers, holding Alayna's hand, whispering to her. Clay could almost make out the words. "Don't worry. I'll protect you."

Daniels guided them to the staircase, down one long flight, and then another. It felt like they were being swallowed by the Earth. As they descended, the noise from the battle above diminished, leaving them in silence.

"Is this the same as it was when you were stationed here?" Clay asked, glancing around at the cement walls and floors.

"We had a bit more light back then," Daniels said, reaching for the wall. He slid his hand against it, searching for a switch. "I still remember the way, though. The buildings are interconnected. We can circle the entire base without seeing daylight. It just takes a bit longer."

"I just don't think we know what we'll run into down here," Agnes said nervously. "I mean, since the general took over, who knows what he's using this for."

Sam scoffed, "It's clear he doesn't use it for anything. Otherwise, there'd be, I don't know . . . more light?"

Daniels increased his speed, hurrying them down the dark corridor. He nearly slammed his head against a wall at the turn and grunted. The rest of them were breathing hard, trying to keep up. Clay continued to glance back, counting them—reassured that Sam was still at the rear.

Daniels skidded to a halt, and Clay nearly ran into him. When he stopped, he realized they'd come to an intersection of five different tunnels. Each tunnel was like a black hole of probability. Clay wondered how on Earth Daniels could possibly remember which path led where.

"What now? Rex asked.

Daniels tipped his feet first down one path, then another. He shifted his weight from side to side, looking childish. And then realizing he was losing their confidence he started himself down his first choice. They hurried after him, no one saying a thing, but everyone alarmed by his hesitation.

Finally, they saw a light at the end of the tunnel. It felt like more than a metaphor. They began to speed up, Alayna muttering, "About time. This has to be a way out . . ."

But as they drew closer, Clay began to feel dizzy. His brain filled with the voices again. They cried out in confusion and pain. FLESH. FEED ME. GOD, I'M SO HUNGRY. I HAVE SO MUCH PAIN . . .

Clay staggered, gripping THE SIDES OF HIS HEAD. As he slowed, THEY entered into A cavern-like arena, with a strange, ghoulish-green light overhead. The voices continued, bouncing around his skull. Alayna covered mouth, and Megan gasped. Around them were dozens of cages, each occupied by screeching and wide-eyed members of the crazed army. Their tongues lolled from their mouths; blood oozed from their eyes. And they ached with hunger—their minds filling Clay's, telling him, over and over again—

FEED US. GOD, I WANT THE FLESH.

Clay fell to his knees. Another wave of dizziness surged through him, making his forehead burn. He couldn't fight through their thoughts. As the others gathered around, he lost consciousness.

73.

"Jesus Christ," Daniels muttered, taking several steps toward the caged crazed.

Clay blinked back to life moments later and staggered from his crouch. Daniels paced around the cages, disbelief on his face. The crazed continued to slam against the bars. Slowly, Clay recognized something a bit different about them. Each of them wore similar clothing. Military garb.

"All of them . . ." Daniels gasped, "are wearing fatigues. Goddamn."

"They're part of the general's undead army, now," Clay said. The hundred-or-so soldiers, all scrambled over one another—their arms stretching out from behind the bars.

Daniels was speechless. Clay was about to ask if he was okay when he spun back toward the tunnel. He pointed. "If this is the old barracks, then I know where the armory is. It's not far. Come on."

Clay and Sam exchanged a glance, as Daniels led the group back into the tunnels. He ran almost too quickly, trying perhaps to outrun the memory of what they'd just seen. Clay stayed with him, forcing the others to play catch-up. As they moved, the sound of the crazed's voices in Clay's head got fainter, and he was able to think clearly once more.

He breathed a sigh of relief.

Five minutes later, Daniels skirted around a final corner and into the armory. They arrived breathless. Daniels rummaged through the many containers, throwing open cabinets and revealing row upon row of rifles, handguns, and grenades.

But after scouring through everything, Daniels wasn't happy. "It's mostly depleted," he said, opening a completely empty container and kicking at it. "Shit."

"There's enough for us here," Clay said, trying to up the morale. He scanned their faces, seeing the exhaustion. "There's enough for us to destroy them all."

Daniels wasn't listening. He crossed the armory to a smaller cabinet and yanked it open to reveal several earwigs. He began to pass them out, instructing them, "Put these in your ears. We'll have hands-free communication. Better to pay attention and keep your hands on your rifles at all times, you understand? No more of this walkie-talkie bullshit."

Clay slipped his in, watching the others do the same. Alayna, Megan, and Rex chose weapons. Rex looked at them with a tenderness most reserved for children. He holstered a handgun, and then held a rifle across his chest, tapping it with his forefinger. The exhaustion was gone.

"All right, team," Sam said. "I think we should separate into three groups. Two of us, maybe hang back. This could be a safe space. A place to come back to; a place they don't know we know about. Understand?"

Nods of understanding bounced around the room, while they adjusted their weapons in their hands. Clay divided them up, feeling like he was preparing to slide a knife into the "beast." He put himself with Sherman and Sam, recognizing they'd be the strongest team—a team to tackle the bigger fighters, up top. Then, there was Daniels, Quintin, and Agnes, with Alayna, Megan, and Rex in the final grouping.

"Hank and Lois, you two hang back," Clay instructed. He couldn't imagine that Lois could run quickly, at her age. And Hank seemed to be a bit too wild to avenge Walt's death.

Daniels found maps of the underground tunnel network. "Yes, yes, yes," he muttered. "This is perfect . . ." He started to trace out three separate routes to the command center.

"This is where the general has to be. It's the safest place in the entire compound." He made an X at the command center. "This is where we have to go if we want to take him down."

"And what about Maia?" Clay demanded, assessing the map of the compound. "Where would she be? Where would he take her?"

"And Brandon!" Agnes piped up.

"Right. Where are they?" Clay asked. "I can't—I can't lose her again . . ."

Daniels rapped his knuckle against the command center once more. "Naw, I reckon she's right there, too. In the general's quarters, right above the command center."

"You really think so?" Clay asked.

"I'm sure," Daniels said. He began to roll up the maps, his motions quick. "Now, let's roll. We're losing time."

74.

C lay, Sam, and Sherman retraced their steps through the darkness, their boots echoing on the cement. There was only the occasional bark from Sam, who managed to watch the map and tell them their turns: left, right, then another right, as they raced toward the command center. Clay's heart pounded rhythmically inside his ribcage, his muscles were firm—strong from the weeks of the nanites coursing through his system. He was more "them" than himself, now, he thought.

"Another left up here. Twenty feet!" Sam called.

"Here!" Sam muttered, making her voice quieter. "We've got to go up these steps. And we'll be just outside the command center."

They stopped, blinking up into a small staircase. Imagining Maia at the top, Clay led the way, taking two and then three steps at a time, until he reached a hulking door. It had a single, metal knob in the center, which Clay twisted to the left, cracking the door open. A burst of fresh air rushed over them, along with the sounds of the battle raging outside. From here, he could feel the thoughts of the crazed outside, in their "mechanical" army bodies. FEED. FLESH. HELP. HELP. The words were clearer and clearer, despite the horrible noise: gunfire, explosions, the cries and screams of the men on the field, drawing their last breaths.

It was war.

"Clay. Don't," Sam whispered into his ear. Her voice was softer than he'd ever heard it. As if she comprehended the weight of this moment.

Clay shoved open the metal door, allowing them to see the command center door just across the corridor. Clay activated his communications. He muttered, "Daniels. This is Clay. Do you read me?"

He cut his head to the right, suddenly realizing there was something very wrong. Daniels sounded panicky. "We're under fire, Clay," he howled. "We should be able to handle them—damn, have you seen Agnes with a rifle? But we won't make it to the command center, no sir," he continued. "The others, they'll find you. Rex? Megan? Alayna?"

"That's a no for us, Clay," Alayna replied, making Clay feel momentarily grim.

"Don't tell me you're under fire, too?" Clay asked, feeling the panic inch into his own psyche.

"No. It's not that. I think the maps are a bit outdated," Alayna replied. "Because we followed it exactly and ended up back at the armory with Lois and Hank, here."

"Fuck!" Clay cried, feeling fear rise within him. "We're losing time. I can't wait for both teams to get over here. The battle's getting closer, and Maia—I have to get to her—"

Sam touched Clay's arm, looking at him with hard eyes. Clay turned off his communications.

"We can't wait. You're right," Sam told him. "I say, we charge in there. We fucking kill him before Malcolm does. That way, we won't have to handle both of them at once."

As if in slow motion, Clay felt himself nod. Something in his brain clicked into place, telling him that this was it. The end, or the beginning. The next few minutes would settle it forever.

"All right," Clay agreed. "Here goes nothing."

75.

C lay rammed into the door, breaking the latch clean off. He tipped his head to the side, indicating that Sam and Sherman should enter first. They barreled into a shadowy corridor at the edge of the command center. Clay followed, his rifle ready, his ears attuned for any possible noise. Down the dark hallway, A beam of light cut the gloom. They raced toward it— like stragglers toward heaven. And as they neared, they began to hear the general barking orders.

"What the hell do you mean, they're coming up fast? I thought you said the minute we had control over these dead assholes—" the general shouted.

Clay crept toward one side of the open doorway, watching as the light was cast across his forearm, glistening against his rifle. Sam ducked to the other side. They waited, their eyes locked on each other.

"I mean, what good was all the effort? The whole project, if these bleeding monsters can't destroy the very thing they've been engineered to destroy—other humans? This should have been an incredibly big recruiting day for us, men. Each and every human out there? Should have been a new soldier by the end of this. And yet—"

Clay gave Sam a sharp nod. It was time. Without

speaking, they burst into the room, dropping to a crouching position on either side of the doorway. A long oak table gave them some cover. The general was pacing beside a wall of monitors. His goons burst up from their chairs, reaching for their weapons. Clay and Sam sprayed bullets at their ankles from beneath the table.

Sherman burst into the room, attempting to drop down to his knees as well. But the soldiers were too quick, putting a bullet into his chest. He fell back like a tree being cut down. He dropped his rifle, shoving it toward Clay's feet.

But Clay and Sam didn't react. They were machines now: knowing only that if they made a single misstep, their lives were over. Clay crept around, coming up on the right side of the table and peppering bullets one of the soldiers. The general ducked and cowered, while nearly a dozen of his men continued to return fire.

Within seconds, only four of the general's soldiers remained standing, and two of them had dropped their rifles to their sides. One howled, sounding forlorn. But seconds after his cry, Sam lifted her rifle and put a bullet in his skull.

Clay was oddly impressed with Sam's lack of empathy. With her chill.

Clay and Sam burst up from either side of the table, aiming at the three remaining men. Clay felt murderous, wild—his blood bursting against his eardrums. As they advanced, the soldiers retreated, their own rifles at their sides. Clay's fingers twitched, yearning to finish off every last one of them.

From the hallway that they'd entered through mere moments before, a powerful explosion filled the room with roiling smoke and debris, making Sam and Clay leap out of the way. One of the general's soldiers cried out. Through the smoke, Clay could make out the large, dark shapes of six men.

"Shit," Sam muttered, edging her elbow into Clay's side. "Shit, shit shit—"

As the smoke cleared, Clay recognized Malcolm, with five of his men. Malcolm was staring intently at Clay and Sam with a kind of revere. An almost childlike joy.

"Well!" he said, clucking his tongue. "I never thought I'd get the pleasure of killing you, Sam. And Clay—well. What a pleasure to be able to kill you twice!"

76.

T hree of Malcolm's men closed in on them. Clay scanned the room for options. All the while, he could feel Malcolm's eyes boring into him. Assessing him. He was smirking.

"Sam, Sam, Sam," Malcolm said. He loomed over her, nearly a foot taller than she was. His nose was mere inches from hers. But Sam didn't cower or show fear, she smirked back at him.

"Fuck off, Malcolm," Sam said and raised her rifle.

Malcolm reached over and pushed the barrel down, shaking his head. "I don't think I need to tell you your manners need some work, do I, Samantha?" he said.

Malcolm's entourage had total control now. One of them circled the room, putting the end of his gun into the back of the general. He eased up from his crouching position, his hands quaking in the air. He stared at Malcolm, aghast.

As the general stood, shaking like a child, Alex and a few other of Malcolm's men swept in. Alex glanced at Clay and cackled to himself. He crossed the room and disappeared up a set of steps. Several of Malcolm's men followed.

Clay felt sure he knew where Alex was going.

Maia.

"Come now, Sam," Malcolm said, almost whispering. His voice was loving and tender, making it all the more maniacal. "Tell me. How'd you get little Clay out of that jam, back there? How did you get all the way here? You can tell me. I'm your old pal. Isn't it mature of us to try to stay friends after the relationship falls apart? Isn't it?"

"Don't tell him anything, Sam," Clay said.

Robotically, Malcolm turned to Clay, assessed him, dismissed him and moved on to the general, who quivered—the gun still lodged into his back.

"General! Greetings," Malcolm exclaimed. "I can't imagine a worse rival, really. Look at you. So frightened by just a little poke in the back!"

Shamed, the general stood straighter, bringing his shoulders back. He glared at Malcolm, his shaking subsiding. "What kind of shoddy army do you have behind you? It's clear you've got no real plan beyond this. As if *you* could have the creativity for it. For taking over the world—"

"I'm going to stop you right there, General," Malcolm said. His hand remained on Sam's gun—clearly not trusting her. "General, whatever you think you had planned with those monsters out there . . . well, whatever it was is now canceled. Great idea, though. Until it all fell apart."

Wallace glanced at the three remaining soldiers, all of whom had their hands raised. "I don't know what on earth you're talking about. My army will tear you apart. They've been trained for this. And I have them at my will—"

"Oh yeah?" Malcolm said. He reached into his backpack and drew out a rifle-sized mechanical device.

It was the very device he'd stolen the day before. Clay's stomach clenched. He imagined all of them: the army of the crazed, blasted—dead and lax, soulless, now—across the field. Malcolm looked endlessly impressed with himself.

"What the hell is that?" Wallace asked, tilting his head. "What the hell—"

"I stole it from our mutual friend Clay here," Malcolm said. "How funny that it would come in so handy. It really is the luck of the draw, isn't it? This apocalypse?" He chuckled. "Although, I like to think I have a bit more smarts than others. And certainly, a big enough army to support me. Although you call them shoddy—they're pretty fucking powerful, General. And they're out there, slaughtering your army as we speak."

One of the general's soldiers broke toward the staircase, trying to grab a weapon that had fallen earlier. As he dove, performing a kind of horrible "Hail Mary," Malcolm pulled Sam's gun from her arms and dropped him with a bullet through the temple.

He collapsed to the floor, blood pouring from his head. The entire room gaped at the casual violence. Clay's nose filled with the smell of blood.

Malcolm turned his attention back to General Wallace. "I'm sorry. What was it we were talking about?" he asked.

There was a commotion on the steps. Brandon and Maia appeared, with Alex behind them—his gun against their backs. Maia's eyes were red-tinged and fearful. Brandon's arms shook with rage. They were unarmed, completely at Alex's mercy.

"Son!" Malcolm called, gleeful. "My, I didn't think you had it in you. You've brought my girl back to me!"

He turned his eyes toward Clay. "Really, you never know what to expect from a child. Will they be like you? Or will they disappoint you? Or—I suppose in this case, will you live to see them die?"

77.

"She didn't expect it, Dad," Alex said, continuing to stab Brandon and Maia in the back with his rifle. "She nearly shit her pants when she saw me, I swear. Terrified her—"

"That's well and good, son," Malcolm said, nodding slowly. "I can't say I've ever been prouder of you. Putting this little bitch in her place, no matter her age—"

As he spoke, three figures burst in through a far door, weapons blazing. Clay dropped to his knees, bringing his head down. Nearly half of Malcolm's men fell. Clay stared into the now-dead eyes of one of them for a long moment, watching as the light escaped.

Malcolm dropped to the floor next to Sam and Clay. Alex had run toward the staircase, pushing Brandon and Maia in front of him as the assault continued. Clay realized he recognized the voice howling over the gunfire.

"GET DOWN! PROTECT YOURSELVES!" the voice cried.

It was Daniels. He, Quintin, and Agnes were tearing through the room, Agnes' hair whipping behind her. She jabbed her rifle at the heart of one of Malcolm's men, squeezing the trigger. He fell back, crashing into a wall.

Malcolm heard Daniels as well. With a quick motion, he snagged Clay's collar, along with Sam's gun, and dragged them both up. He brought the gun against Clay's skull, and said gleefully, "All right, that's quite enough. Whoever you are, I'll put a bullet through the Sheriff's if you don't stop right now."

Without a second thought, Daniels, Agnes, and Quintin dropped their guns and raised their hands. Agnes' face was blotchy with shock, as if each murder surprised her more than the last. Beside her, Quintin grunted, eyeing Sherman—now dead and growing cold. The few of Malcolm's surviving men started collecting the fallen guns.

"As I was saying," Malcolm said. Still holding Clay's collar, he turned toward Alex, his eyes excited. "I was saying that my boy here, my boy—he captured this little lovely Maia."

Clay's cheeks burned. He noticed Alex was standing proudly next to Maia. Brandon was pushed off to the side, his face scrunched with concentration. He was straining against the ropes that held his hands behind his back.

Brandon lunged at Alex, trying to push him over the guardrail and down the steps. Alex teetered on the railing for a long second before bouncing back, bringing his knee against Brandon's nose. Brandon fell back against the stairs, head rolling to the side. Maia let out a screech, watching as Brandon lost consciousness. It all happened so quickly, like flashes of light.

Then Alex was stood over Brandon, gloating. He pounded his fist against his chest "Did you see that, Dad?" he cried out. "Did you see how he bounced?"

Malcolm cackled, releasing Clay. He nodded

toward his son, his face glowing with fatherly pride. The entire room was deathly silent, except for their mirth. But as their chuckles echoed all around, Clay looked upon his perfect offspring—Maia, her porcelain skin, her curly hair, her thin, weak arms. Her lips trembled as she gazed down at Brandon— looking lost, unsure. Meek.

Then Maia lifted her hands to the chain around her neck. The very golden chain that Alex had gifted her from that rest stop, what now felt like a million years ago. She ripped the pendant from her neck and jabbed the end of it into Alex's jugular—the soft part of his neck, so tender to the touch. As she pushed harder, blood began to erupt, painting Maia's skin before cascading to the floor. Alex's face went from gleeful to terrified. His skin was the color of clouds. He lurched forward onto his knees beside Brandon. He had no control and tumbled forward, leaving a trickling waterfall of blood running down the steps.

"WHAT THE FUCK? WHAT THE FUCK DID YOU DO!" Malcolm cried. He sprinted toward Alex's body. But before he could reach him, Sam broke free from the soldier that held her and punched Malcolm directly in the face, slamming him against the wall.

Malcolm's face hit the wall, but he bounced back quickly. He drew his pistol and pointed it directly at Sam's head. He stabbed the pistol at her over and over again as he spoke. "You. Dumb. Bitch. You fucking horrible bitch. You thought you could get me? With a single punch? You dumb—dumb—"

Clay leaped on him like a jungle animal, pulling him to the ground. Malcolm's gun flew from his hand, firing wild. The bullet missed Sam's skull by less than an inch on its way to General Wallace's chest. Immediately, Wallace went down, blood darkening his olive-drab shirt.

The gun clattered to the floor, spinning toward Sam's feet. Before anyone could stop her—before a single syllable could be spoken—she reached down, caught it mid-spin, and brought it to bear on Malcolm's skull.

"Don't cry, baby," she whispered.

And pulled the trigger.

78.

T he room was silent. The noise from the gunshot continued to ring in Clay's ears. He stared down at Malcolm's skull, at the way it had carved apart from the impact of the bullet. Sam stood above him, huffing, her hands shaking. Her nostrils were flared, yet her eyes were set. She'd done the one thing she'd set out to do. She'd killed him.

"Fuck," Agnes whispered, saying what they were all thinking. General Wallace, Malcolm, and Alex were all dead on the floor—while about a dozen other men were scattered across the room, minutes past saving.

Sam swung her gun, pointing it at each of the remaining hostiles in turn. Rex, Alayna, and Megan barreled into the room, their guns pointed at Malcolm's men. Megan coughed exactly once, showing only a moment's shock at the carnage. Rex cut across the room, covering three of Malcolm's men near the staircase exit. He stopped when he saw Alex, pale and sprawled near the steps. "Huh," he said, spitting on the ground. "Huh, indeed."

Malcolm's goons and the two remaining soldiers dropped their weapons and raised their hands. Maia ran to Clay, wrapping her arms around him. Clay hugged her close, allowing himself to breathe again.

"I won't let that happen again," he told her. "That will never, ever happen again."

Brandon coughed from the stairs. His eyes opened, and he stared at Alex's bloody corpse.

Clay broke the hug with his daughter, wondering at Sam. She seemed to be growing more and more human. She reached up and pulled the tie from her ponytail, allowing her blonde hair to tumble around her shoulders. Contrary to everything he knew about Sam, she'd begun to cry. Outside, the battle seemed to be tapering off, as if the soldiers no longer knew what they were fighting for.

"We need to get out there. Put an end to this," Sam said.

"And who put you in charge?" Clay asked her with a smile.

Sam's eyes went to Clay's, assessing him. In that moment, Clay felt sure she would either smack him across the face or laugh out loud. To release the tension, Daniels stomped up, wrapping his arms around both Sam and Clay—leaning his head into the space between them.

"Jesus, guys. Can we have just a moment without fighting? Just a moment—" Daniels laughed. He touched cheeks, trying to hide his own tears. "Jesus Christ."

"All right," Clay said. He could feel everyone's exhaustion, but they had one more thing to do.

"Before anyone's in charge, we need to neutralize the rest of Malcolm's people, and convince the General's soldiers to stand down," he said.

Daniels stood upright, his face suddenly stoic. He took one of the automatic weapons that had fallen to the ground and gave Clay a firm nod. "I'll take Agnes and Quintin with me. We'll take the General's soldiers . . ." He paused, giving weight to the moment. "I know their language. I think I can convince them that it's over."

"Great. We'll handle Malcolm's crew," Sam said. "Without their leader, I think they'll see just how empty this is." She smacked her hand on her thigh, looking almost incredulous. "I think they'll see just how silly it is that we're all fighting one another, when really, we should be building. That's all we have left to do. We have to create a new world."

79.

Daniels strutted down the long command room, wearing a sleek new outfit—one fit for a General—his muscles straining against the fabric. He held his hat in the crook of his right arm. With his chin held high, he addressed Clay, Lois, Sam, and Lane. After a shower and a shave, it wasn't at all apparent that he'd spent the previous twenty-four hours up and moving—convincing Wallace's army to stand down and address him as acting general.

"They've been given new orders," Daniels said. "They're to bury their dead, along with Malcolm's, and they're going to clean this place up. They're gathering the rest of the crazed into the barracks down below, for research purposes."

"Wonderful, Daniels," Lois said, bringing her palms together. Her hair had been styled, swept back behind her ears. Her face was void of makeup, clean and shiny. She gave them each a weak, but confident smile. She looked like she'd aged ten years. "We thank you for your concise and wonderful service. It's so good that the men see something of themselves in you. Will it be a difficult transition?"

"From what I've learned, morale was incredibly low under the general's command. I plan to fix that, of course." He leaned in. "It seems that the general was actually starving them for long periods of time, just to ensure that they would rely on him for everything, and after a while, they were too fearful to try to leave. They knew they would turn into one of *them* within hours."

"Shit," Sam whispered. She wore her blonde hair down, and it curled at her shoulders. Clay couldn't help but marvel at how feminine she looked. She wore clean clothes she'd found in one of the barracks, along with dark makeup, which she said she'd found in the General's quarters. "Apparently he had women around. Who knows where they are now," she'd explained.

Clay couldn't help but wonder what had happened to them. Had the general thrown them to the crazed as some kind of experiment?

It was best not to think of the horrors of the past, now, he thought.

"Thank you for keeping the crazed alive for now," Lane said, interrupting Clay's train of thought. She pointed at a series of charts, which she, Leland, and Marcia had drawn up over the previous twenty-four hours. "As you can see, we're going to proceed with project 'Reverse the Nanites.' But as you've probably guessed, it's not going to be easy. Clay's a perfect example, as is Alayna. I mean, their nanites have mutated beyond our control. And we're not sure how many more of those exposures exist. It'll have to be taken on a condition by condition basis. Regardless . . ." She paused, slipping her hands across her cheeks—she sighed at the daunting task before her. Before all of them. "Regardless, it's a long road ahead. But we're making a game plan. We're in contact with other facilities around the world, and we've stopped anything that General Wallace had spun into motion. We're—we're going to be all right."

"So, the crazed are definitely all around the world? Every country?" Sam asked, her voice soft.

"Yes. Unfortunately, so," Lane said. "Our goal is to figure out if we can reverse the nanites and bring them back from the edge of humanity. And if we can't, well." She bowed her head, unable to speak the words that they were all thinking: if there was no solution, they would have to fight the crazed forever. Until every single last one of them was dead.

Clay could feel their thoughts, pulsing behind their eyes.

"And what about Alayna?" Clay asked, his voice cracking slightly. "You said the pregnancy might not be affected—"

"I'm still addressing the Alayna situation," Lane said, a small smile on her lips. "Your child will be safe, Clay. And, as far as I can see, Megan's taken over. Protecting Alayna. Reassuring her. All these months, I thought Alayna was the strongest woman I'd ever met in my life. But now, I realize we were all putting on a show, weren't we? A show of strength. She should be allowed to rest, now. And Megan, well. She's helping her do that."

Clay allowed this to sink in for a moment. After the battle, his face still spattered with other people's blood, he'd fallen to his knees in the grass, gazing around him. Initially, he tried to take stock of who was still alive. He knew that Brandon and Maia had stayed inside the command center, that they were obeying their orders to "remain safe." He spotted a bludgeoned Agnes, who'd been taken down by one of Malcolm's men. He took off his shirt and gently covered her face and body, feeling that familiar ache. He'd lost so many on the road to the end. How many more was he prepared to say goodbye to?

"Anyway, what Alayna's doing is what we all should be doing," Lane said, snapping her pencil against her palm. A small tear started down her cheek. "Alayna's repopulating the planet. I know it's going to take us a while to feel safe again, to feel like ourselves. To even feel up for—for something like new life and new love. But I hope we all give it a chance. We have to."

Lane stepped away from her maps and charts, settling into her chair and letting out a soft sob. Lois got up and stood with Daniels. "I suppose I'll say what we're all thinking," she said, sounding, for perhaps the first time, like the mayor Clay had left behind in Carterville. "It's not going to be easy over the next few months and years. Humanity's managed to destroy much of itself. But we have the gumption and the drive within all of us to fight back. And to build a better future. A future not so keen on building warriors just for the sake of war. A future centered on hope."

80.

Two months later, Clay found himself on the front porch of a two-story house in downtown Helen, watching the sun peek in and out of autumn clouds. The weather was beginning to get cold, and he rubbed his hands together before pouring two cups of coffee. Splashing a bit of milk into one of them, he passed it to Alayna, in her rocking chair. She gave him a smile, patting her pregnant belly. She seemed to glow.

"You always remember how I take my coffee, Clay," Alayna said. She whispered. "Don't tell Megan that I'm drinking this. She wants to play everything by the rules, and that means no caffeine. But I read in a baby book upstairs that a cup every once in a while won't hurt a thing. So, I will take this single bit of luxury, thank you."

"Your secret's safe with me," Clay said. He took a sip and put his hand over Alayna's. He'd felt the baby move for the first time a month or so ago, and the contact—with another being, another life—had thrilled him. "There he is," he said when he felt the familiar kicking once more. "He knows I'm here."

"Why are you so sure it's a boy?" Alayna asked, teasing him.

Clay shrugged. "I suppose it's true that the

strongest people I know in this new world are women. But I don't really care either way."

Maia appeared at the steps of the old house, wearing a thick sweater over a loose dress. She waved at Alayna, giving her a bright smile.

"Hey there!" Alayna called. "Come up here and give me a hug. You don't reserve all of them for Brandon, do you?"

As Maia swept up the steps, her face went red with embarrassment. She muttered into Alayna's ear, "Don't talk about Brandon in front of Dad!"

"Oh, come on. Your dad's not THAT big of an idiot," Alayna said.

Maia snickered. Reaching into her backpack, she took out a small crocheted hat—in bright pink. She stretched it out slightly, passing it to Alayna. "I stole some hours between shifts at the cafe to make this for you," she said. "I'm finally going to have a sibling! I'm praying for a girl."

Maia winked at Clay, knowing full well his opinion on the sex. Clay chuckled. A creak inside the house sent his eyes toward the door, where Megan appeared. Her face was still severe, almost pinched, when she saw Clay. As if she was still jealous of all the time Clay and Alayna had spent together after she'd had abandoned them. But in a fit of drunkenness several weeks before, Megan had broken down and whispered to him, "It's just that I still feel so guilty for what I did. All those months, up on Rex's roof—what was I doing? How could I have abandoned the love of my life that way?"

Clay had long renounced his "feelings" for Alayna, recognizing that they were nothing more than attachment to the life he'd had in Carterville. The way his mind burned, after finding out that

Valerie had died, had shown him that his love for Alayna was nothing more than a passing fancy. Skin on skin when he thought he was going to die.

"Coffee, huh?" Megan asked, putting her hands on her hips. She clucked her tongue at Alayna but forced a smile. "You know you shouldn't be drinking that."

Alayna rolled her eyes. "I guess I'm in for a lecture," she said to Clay and Maia. "Protect me from her when the baby comes, won't you?" She leaned toward Maia, her eyes bright. "At least I get to be the fun Mom, right?"

"Hey. I'm not totally uptight," Megan protested. She slid her hand on Alayna's shoulder lovingly, a gesture that showed their bond was more than the bickering.

"Well, I have to head to work," Maia said, taking a step toward the yellowing grass below. Her eyes flickered toward Clay, who'd grown accustomed to walking her from Alayna's to the downtown cafe in the afternoons, where she'd taken a job under Hank's management.

"I've always wanted to own my own coffee shop," Hank had said when they'd arrived back in Helen. They had been stricken at the empty town (one that was incredibly safe to inhabit, but one that needed a bit of life pumped into it). And so, they'd begun to resurrect community elements. Lois had begun having small church services on Sundays, for those who wanted to attend, and Hank had opened the cafe. Clay had taken up residence as both sheriff and as local movie theater proprietor—rigging up a small theater in a barn he'd taken over, just five minutes' walk from downtown.

The cafe was the real heartbeat of Helen, drawing

stragglers in on their journeys elsewhere (and often convincing them to stick around). People communed over cake and coffee, switching to beer and wine in the evening. Maia had learned much in her conversations with these men and women, their lives now and what they hoped for the future. "Helen is safe," she always told them, Clay knew. "Helen is where we're starting the next generation. It's where we're rebuilding. Why not help us?"

"Oh, honey," Clay sighed, drawing Maia in for a side-hug as they walked from Alayna's house. "Things just keep changing, don't they?"

"For the better, I think," Maia said. "We've grown in population by fifty since last week, Hank was telling me. And even Samantha hasn't left yet. Brandon was sure she'd hit the road the minute we got into Helen. That she was meant for other things. But she—well. You've been spending a lot of time with her, haven't you?" She smirked.

Clay had. Something about the drama, the anger that had existed between him and Sam had brought them close. She often popped by with a six-pack on her way to her house, just over the field from Clay's, and they would stay up late, talking about their past lives. About the world they wanted to build. Clay had been surprised to discover that Sam had any optimism in her at all—knowing only the cold, hardened and pessimistic Sam from before. But now she was letting her hair grow long, hanging in curls on her shoulders. She wore dresses, sometimes. And once, Clay had caught her talking with Alayna about the baby in excited whispers.

"Sam is—well. She's a good person to have around," Clay heard himself say. His heart bumped in his chest, showing he had a few more opinions about that than he really wanted to let on.

"Dad, it's Samantha," Maia said, giving him a sneaky look. "She told me she's always preferred Samantha. Even Quintin has started calling her that. And you know, he's like her brother."

"Right. Well, I suppose I should make the switch—"

"You really should. Because Samantha is part of her new life."

They got to the café and Clay peered in, seeing Lois and Lane at a table together, sipping coffee and discussing something stretched out on the table between them. He knew they weren't getting closer to a cure, but Lane, Jacobs, and Marcia were hunting for one, every single day. To their right, Rex was alone, reading a book (turned out he was particularly keen on paperback romances) and sunk a fork into a piece of pie. Hank manned the register, underneath a large framed photo of Walt he found when Jacobs got them back on the internet. He adjusted the frame, the memory of his best friend coloring the moment.

"Dad, do you think you can be part of this new life?" Maia asked him. "Build something new? Maybe even . . . fall in love?"

Clay turned his eyes toward the fields, at the edge of the town. He thought back to Ralph, who'd breathed his last breath just a block away. He remembered those lost days at the hotel, the ones camping in the mountains, the many, seemingly endless days on the road. And he shook his head, incredulous that something, God or another higher power, had kept him alive through all of it.

He was allowed another chance.

"I'll miss your mom forever, you know that?" Clay

asked his daughter, his heart finally light.

"Me too," Maia whispered."

"But in the last few months, I've realized that I'm ready to build something else," Clay told her, surprising even himself. "A life with you. A life being an uncle to Alayna and Megan's baby. A life maybe . . . maybe with Samantha." He shrugged. "But at the end of the day, it's a life. And I'm grateful to have it."

Maia kissed Clay on the cheek, darted into the cafe and wrapped an apron around her waist. As she tied it, Clay turned his attention back to the field— and saw three of the crazed scurry past, just outside the town. They'd learned where the barriers were— and if they crossed them, they'd be killed.

Now they were like deer. A part of the natural world. One Clay's crew would have to live alongside, perhaps forever. The Earth had tilted. And Clay had shifted along with it, like any survivor must.

ABOUT THE AUTHOR

Paul B Kohler is the Amazon Bestselling Author of Linear Shift author, as well as the highly-acclaimed novel, The Hunted Assassin. His remarkable novel series, The Borrowed Souls is also gaining traction with its readers. Aside from his longer works, a number of his short stories have been included in various anthologies. His latest short, Rememorations, has been included in The Immortality Chronicles - a Top 5 SF Anthology and Hot New Releases. Rememorations was also nominated for Best American Science Fiction.

When not practicing architecture, Paul works on his writing. He lives in Littleton, Colorado.

To learn more about him and his books, visit www.PaulKohler.net

Made in the USA
Columbia, SC
30 January 2024

31060701R00181